CONVERSATIONS
WITH THE
HIGH PRIEST OF
COOSA

The University of North Carolina Press   Chapel Hill & London

CHARLES HUDSON

Conversations with the
HIGH PRIEST
of COOSA

© 2003 by Charles M. Hudson

All rights reserved

Set in Monotype Garamond

by Tseng Information Systems, Inc.

Manufactured in the United States of America

The paper in this book meets the guidelines for
permanence and durability of the Committee on
Production Guidelines for Book Longevity of the
Council on Library Resources.

Library of Congress

Cataloging-in-Publication Data

Hudson, Charles M.

Conversations with the high priest of Coosa /
Charles Hudson.

  p. cm.

ISBN 0-8078-2753-3 (alk. paper)—

ISBN 0-8078-5421-2 (pbk.: alk. paper)

1. Domingo de la Anunciación, Father, 1510 or 11–
1591—Fiction. 2. Luna y Arellano, Tristán de,
1510–1630—Fiction. 3. Spaniards—Southern
States—Fiction. 4. Mississippian culture—Fiction.
5. Southern States—Fiction. 6. Coosa Indians—
Fiction. 7. Explorers—Fiction. I. Title.

PS3608.U5425 C66 2003

813'.6—dc21   2002011995

cloth 07 06 05 04 03 5 4 3 2 1

paper 07 06 05 04 03 5 4 3 2 1

For my students, who taught me

Contents

Introduction *xi*

Acknowledgments *xix*

A Letter *1*

1 The Coming of the *Nokfilaki* *7*

2 The Contest between the Four-footeds and the Flyers *14*

3 More Animal Stories *20*

4 Rabbit *30*

5 Master of Breath and the Great Ones *38*

6 Sun, Corn Woman, Lucky Hunter, and the Twosome *52*

7 Horned Serpent, the Clans, and the Origin of Bears *72*

8 The Vengeance of Animals, the Friendship of Plants,
   and the Anger of the Sun *86*

9 Divination, Sorcery, and Witches *97*

10 Sun Chief and Sun Woman *120*

11 Tastanáke and the Ball Game *134*

12 Everyday Life Is Their Book *145*

13 *Posketa* *152*

14 The Last Conversation *176*

A Note on the Spelling of Creek Words *189*

Sources *191*

Illustration Credits *215*

Index *219*

Illustrations

Route of the Luna Expedition to Coosa *3*

Raven *8*

Turkey *16*

Peregrine falcon *17*

Terrapin *23*

Wolf *24*

Hummingbird *26*

Great blue heron *27*

Kingfisher *29*

Rabbit *31*

Otter *32*

Bear *35*

Ásse *39*

Shell cup *40*

Rim-incised pot *41*

Ivory-billed woodpeckers *42*

Water spider *56*

Wild Thing and his brother *58*

Deer *60*

Blue jay *62*

Carolina parakeet *63*

Chunkey stone *65*

Cougar *67*

Hornworm and hummingbird-hawk moths *73*

Páássa (button snakeroot) *74*

Meekko hoyanéécha (willow) *74*

Heche lopóchkee (tobacco) *74*

Heche pakpakee (lobelia) *74*

War club pipe *75*

Chipmunks *89*

Cardinal *95*

Divining with beads *100*

Red sumac *107*

Tufted titmouse *114*

Chickadee *115*

Great horned owl *117*

Water hemlock *118*

Etowah site *126*

Horned serpent (Citico gorget) *129*

Looped square gorget *156*

Tastanáke warrior *161*

The Etowah statues *169*

Lady of Guadalupe *182*

Sapeya crystal *183*

Introduction

This book is intended for anyone who has viewed museum displays of artifacts made by the late prehistoric Southeastern Indians or, even better, stood atop one of their earthen mounds and asked the questions: What manner of people made these things? How did they conceive of the world in which they lived? How did they explain events in their everyday lives?

Archaeologists and historians can suggest answers to some of these questions, but they cannot tell us definitively about the philosophical or religious thought processes of these people. This book begins where the reach of archaeology and history ends. Blending extant information with carefully considered fiction, *Conversations with the High Priest of Coosa* endeavors to represent the world of the Indians of the late prehistoric Southeast as they believed it existed. Defining a work such as this one is a challenge. Some may think of it as a historical novel, and I certainly hope that, at some level, many readers will enjoy it as they would a more traditional work of fiction. My preference—borne out of many years of research and teaching in the field of anthropology—is to call this work a fictionalized ethnography, for although it is most definitely a fictional work in a number of important respects, I have endeavored to make it as true to cultural and social facts as it is in my power to do.

My aim in this book is to reconstruct the belief system, or world view, of a late prehistoric southeastern people for which there exists hardly any primary documentary evidence. This belief system shaped the mentality of the people of the Coosa chiefdom, a once powerful polity whose existence became so lost to history that its homeland in northwestern Georgia and the Tennessee Valley has only been satisfactorily located in the past twenty years. This Coosa chiefdom existed alongside other similar chiefdoms in a social world—called Mississippian by archaeologists—that dominated most of the American South between the eleventh and sixteenth centuries. But that world collapsed more than three hundred years ago, and today the polity of Coosa and its neighboring chiefdoms, and the larger world in which they existed, are nowhere to be seen.

To say that Coosa and its world disintegrated is not to say that Coosa people are extinct. Although many Coosas died in the sixteenth and seventeenth centuries (most particularly because of Old World diseases), some of them survived, and their descendants have been scattered. Many of them live now in the state of Oklahoma as Creeks, Koasati, Seminoles, and so on, and it is possible that bits and pieces of the cultural traditions and beliefs of the Coosa are retained by some of these descendants. Yet after so much time, to ask one of these distant living descendants about details of the old Coosa belief system would be about the same as asking a contemporary German about the belief system of the ancient Germanic tribes who did battle with Roman legions.

There are, however, a few existing sources that can shed some factual light on these time-shrouded questions about the Coosa world. Historians, archaeologists, and others have given particular attention to the records of three Spanish expeditions that penetrated Coosa in the 1500s. In 1540 the Hernando de Soto expedition traveled through the length of Coosa, from north to south. From the documents of the Soto expedition, scholars learned that Coosa was a paramount chiefdom. That is, the chief of Coosa commanded a simple chiefdom, some twelve and a half miles in diameter, living along a stretch of the Coosawattee River in what is now northwestern Georgia. But this same chief of Coosa was also a paramount chief, wielding power or influence over several other simple chiefdoms to the north, up to about present-day Knoxville, Tennessee, and south to about present-day Childersburg, Alabama. The Soto chroniclers recorded scraps of information about the physical layout and social structure of Coosa, but they wrote essentially nothing about the inner world of Coosa beliefs, knowledge, and traditions.

The next group of Spaniards to reach Coosa was a detachment of men from the Tristán de Luna expedition. Luna attempted to found a colony at Pensacola Bay in 1559, but his colonists soon ran short of food, and most of them moved northward to the town of Nanipacana on the Alabama River. When they failed to procure the needed food at Nanipacana, they sent a detachment of men farther north to revisit Coosa, which the Soto chroniclers had described in such glowing terms. They arrived in Coosa in August 1560 and remained there for over a month before returning to Nanipacana. From there they fell back to Pensacola Bay, where the expedition further disintegrated and the people experienced great privation before abandoning the colony.

From documents from the Luna expedition, scholars have been able to derive better information about the geographical and social context of Coosa than they could from earlier records from the Soto expedition. Domingo de la Anunciación, a priest who went with the detachment of men, wrote letters from Coosa and also contributed to a much later account of what happened there. He described physical features of the main Coosa town and even some of the customs of the people. While he was there, he had with him as translator a woman whom Soto's men had enslaved twenty years earlier and had taken to Mexico. From Anunciación's writings, it is clear that through the offices of this translator he had an informed grasp of what transpired there, but sadly his writings reveal next to nothing about the inner world of Coosa thought and belief. This deficiency is particularly disappointing because, of all the sixteenth-century Spaniards who visited Coosa, Anunciación had the education and sensibility—and the necessary competent translator—to tap into the mysteries of that world.

The third expedition to Coosa was led by Captain Juan Pardo, who took a small contingent of men northward from the newly established colony of Santa Elena on Parris Island, South Carolina. In 1567 he went up the Catawba River to the vicinity of Asheville, North Carolina, and then across the mountains to Chiaha, a chiefdom in the Tennessee Valley that was affiliated with the paramount chief of Coosa. The documents of the Pardo expedition yield insights into the political structure of the chiefdoms of South Carolina and eastern Tennessee, plus a few invaluable words of the languages spoken in eastern Tennessee, but they reveal virtually nothing about the Coosa belief system.

With the historical record revealing so little, scholars have turned to other forms of evidence in their effort to understand Coosa—particularly the archaeological record. Archaeological research on Coosa began with the inquiries of amateurs in the middle of the nineteenth century and began to be conducted professionally in the early decades of the twentieth century. It was only at midcentury, however, that truly modern research began. By the 1980s and 1990s archaeologists had accumulated enough information from excavations and surveys in Coosa country to be able to say quite a lot about the material life of the people who once lived there. Archaeologists can now describe their houses and public buildings, their means of procuring food, the layout of their villages, and many other aspects of Coosa life. Most notably, they have constructed a map of the locations of the constituent towns of Coosa, as well as the towns of other chiefdoms in the paramountcy. Interested readers can find an admirably concise account of both the archaeological and historical information on Coosa in Marvin T. Smith's *Coosa: The Rise and Fall of a Southeastern Mississippian Chiefdom* (Gainesville: University Press of Florida, 2000).

I was a member of the consortium of scholars who in the 1980s and 1990s reconstructed the routes of exploration of Soto, Luna, and Pardo, and who located Coosa on the landscape and worked out some of its social and political characteristics. I well remember the excitement we felt as piece after piece of information fell into place to make up the picture of Coosa we have now. And yet, after all those pieces were in place, our reconstructed Coosa was only a skeletal representation of what was once a vibrant society. Perhaps because I had been trained as a social anthropologist, I longed to hear the people of Coosa talking about their world as they experienced it. I longed to hear a Coosa expound on the hidden causes of things.

If only we had a description of Coosa philosophy comparable to that produced by the French social anthropologist, Marcel Griaule, who studied the Dogon of west Africa in the 1930s and 1940s. Griaule made repeated and prolonged visits to the Dogon for fifteen years until he began asking questions an ordinary Dogon person could not answer. His questions exceeded the bounds of their "simple knowledge." At this point, he was directed to Ogotemmêli, an old blind man who had thought long and hard about the world as it existed for the Dogons. Ogotemmêli agreed to be interviewed by Griaule, and in a series of remarkable conversations over a period of thirty-three days, he revealed to him the inner nature of the Dogon world. Griaule recounted this experience in his book *Conversations with Ogotemmêli,* one of the jewels of twentieth-century French social anthropology.

Recalling the experience of Griaule, I asked myself: What if Domingo de la Anunciación had encountered a Coosa wise man who had enough understanding of Europeans to engage with him in conversations about the Coosa world? Like Ogotemmêli did with Griaule, such a Coosa wise man would no doubt have perceived Anunciación—

ignorant as he was of Coosa beliefs and knowledge—as a mere child, and logically he would have first told him stories suitable for a child. Then, logically, he would have proceeded to tell him about other, more complicated matters. But unfortunately, such a meeting of minds never took place. Anunciación never sought out a Coosa version of Ogotemmêli, and a factual account of the Coosa world from the inside out can never be had.

There was, then, only one possibility left. I decided that I would do for Coosa in fiction what Griaule had done for the Dogon in nonfiction. Domingo de la Anunciación would serve as a fictionalized European inquirer, with a fictionalized version of his female Coosa translator—whom I have named Teresa—by his side. I could easily invent a Coosa wise man the equal of Ogotemmêli. I determined to discipline and inform my fiction with as much indirect factual evidence as I could muster; I wanted the Coosa world I portrayed to be as close to the real thing as this limited form would allow. Yet, to what ethnographic source could I turn for religious and mythological content that would be most analogous to the real Coosa world view? I could have drawn upon the recorded oral traditions of well-documented preliterate peoples of similar political structure in Southeast Asia, Polynesia, or the southwestern United States. This solution, however, would hardly have been acceptable given the significant differences between those peoples and the people of Coosa.

An alternative strategy, and the one I took, was to use extant but fragmentary oral materials from the various Native American peoples of the seventeenth- to twentieth-century Southeast, employing threads of fiction to stitch these pieces together into something like a coherent system of belief. Though fragmentary, this southeastern ethnographic material is more than merely analogical. Some of the sources I have used came from biological (and, presumably, cultural) descendants of the Coosa chiefdom. Other sources came from people who were descendants of some of the other chiefdoms living in the Mississippian world of which Coosa was a part.

The sharing of ideas and symbols throughout this Mississippian world is supported on at least two counts. First, John Swanton, the Smithsonian anthropologist who was the preeminent collector and transcriber of oral literature from native peoples of the American Southeast, noted that many of the stories he collected were shared by seemingly disparate people in the early twentieth century, when he did his fieldwork. One might dismiss this claim by arguing that such sharing of stories was a late occurrence, a twentieth-century phenomenon among Indians who were by that time mostly or completely assimilated into American society. But there is a second body of evidence that a southeastern world of meaning existed during the Mississippian period, namely, a set of very specific Mississippian symbols and items of ritual paraphernalia that were shared all across the southeastern United States. The Southeastern Ceremonial Complex, first identified by Antonio Waring and Preston Holder in 1945, is a group of artifacts, symbols, and motifs far too specific in their shared traits to have been independently invented. If people at sites as widely separated as Mt. Royal, Florida, and Spiro, Oklahoma, shared such specific symbols, it stands to reason that they also shared many ideas and understandings.

It is also notable that some of these Southeastern Ceremonial Complex symbols are consistent with creatures of the imagination in the oral traditions and rituals of widely separated southeastern peoples. For example, as late as the early twentieth century both Creeks and Cherokees told stories about a monstrous serpent with deer horns on its head. Such a horned serpent—sometimes with wings—is one of the motifs of the Southeastern Ceremonial Complex, and there are other, more abstract, symbols that are consistent with later southeastern social practices and rituals. For example, the Southeastern Ceremonial Complex looped square—a square with loops at each of the four corners—is a dance pattern that endured into the twentieth century.

Yet another body of evidence argues for the legitimacy of using oral traditions from the seventeenth through the early twentieth century as evidence of beliefs that plausibly were held in Coosa in the sixteenth century. John Gregory Keyes, in a study of the mythology of Native Americans in the Southeast throughout this extended period of time, found substantial continuity in the motifs that made up the stories. What changed over the centuries were the social meaning and function of the myths. The very earliest recorded stories from the Southeast legitimize the hierarchical standing of ruling elites; they set forth a ranked order of supernatural beings who prefigure the hierarchy in the chiefdom itself, and they serve as charters for rituals and ceremonials. All of this is missing in later stories, but the constituent motifs show impressive stability through time.

It should be noted that I am not using later historical materials as a means for arguing for the existence of earlier historical actualities, a practice early ethnohistorians called "upstreaming." I claim much less—namely, that in this case it is reasonable to use fragmentary cultural materials from a later era as a basis for writing disciplined fiction set in an earlier time.

The people of sixteenth-century Coosa spoke several languages of the Muskogean language family. Therefore, whenever possible I have drawn on stories and legends from Muskogean-speaking groups, particularly Creek, but also Alabama, Koasati, Seminole, and, to a lesser degree, Choctaw, Chickasaw, and Apalachee. But when there are gaps in Muskogean materials—and there are quite a few—I have drawn liberally from the customs and traditions of Cherokees, Natchez, Tunica, and others.

Because the materials collected by James Mooney, Franz Olbrechts, and Jack and Anna Kilpatrick on the Cherokees are far more copious and internally consistent than for any other southeastern group, I have in several places drawn on Cherokee culture and ritual practice in an effort to address important aspects of Coosa life for which there is no obvious corresponding Muskogean information. There is, for example, no Muskogean equivalent of the Cherokee story of Lucky Hunter or Corn Woman, the origin of bears and the bear-man, the origin of disease and medicine, the anger of the Sun, or the witch Spearfinger. I have adapted these Cherokee stories to my purpose, and in places I have added a Muskogean cultural veneer to them.

The existing record of Muskogean-speakers is also inconsistent regarding color and directional symbolism. Swanton collected no fewer than seven different variants of Muskogean color symbolism, and none of them possesses the symbolic integrity of the Cherokee system. Therefore, in an effort to maintain the integrity of my reconstruction of Coosa symbolism, I have had little choice but to fit out Coosas with the more consistent system of the Cherokee, which was likely similar to that of Muskogean-speakers. In a few instances I have modified Muskogean myths to agree with Cherokee color and directional symbolism.

In an effort to create a seamless depiction of a Coosa wise man revealing the innermost religious and philosophical conceptions of an extinct world, I have adopted the convention of setting apart the old man's stories from his disquisitions with white space. In endnotes, indexed to particular words or phrases, I indicate the sources of the stories he tells. Some of his stories are quoted almost verbatim from stories recorded from Southeastern Indian informants, though in all cases I have silently excised obvious anachronisms and borrowings, and I have altered wording to make the texts of these legends and stories stylistically consistent with my own text. Some of his stories I have cobbled together using pieces of several recorded sources, sometimes interlarding text of my own devising. Finally, some of his stories are my own creations based upon bits of information gleaned from archaeology, history, and social anthropology. At the beginning of the endnotes, I characterize the authorship of the stories in terms of percentages of (1) direct quotation, (2) paraphrase, (3) original adaptation of existing myths, and (4) original material.

I want to say a little more about an important character in these stories—Domingo de la Anunciación. Although he is fictionalized here, Anunciación was a real person, and where his beliefs and opinions are displayed in the book, I have worked to maintain a perspective consistent with that of a sixteenth-century Spanish priest. I depict Anunciación as having been altogether secure in his Christian faith and comfortable in his mission of persuading non-Christians of the error of their ways. He lived two centuries before European intellectuals began coming to grips with the idea of cultural relativism. By contemporary standards he is what we would call ethnocentric—quite as much so, I would imagine, as his Coosa interlocutor. Because much of the book is written from Anunciación's point of view, however, it is worth noting that his beliefs and opinions about Coosa are not my own.

Finally, I hope that some who read this book will be impelled to go further and read the archaeological, historical, and ethnographic sources on which it is based. I believe that even though this is a work of fiction, those who read it will be equipped to read the primary sources with enhanced understanding.

Acknowledgments

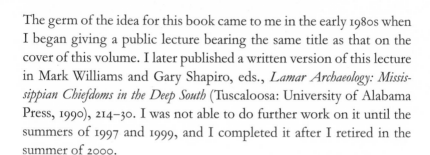

The germ of the idea for this book came to me in the early 1980s when I began giving a public lecture bearing the same title as that on the cover of this volume. I later published a written version of this lecture in Mark Williams and Gary Shapiro, eds., *Lamar Archaeology: Mississippian Chiefdoms in the Deep South* (Tuscaloosa: University of Alabama Press, 1990), 214–30. I was not able to do further work on it until the summers of 1997 and 1999, and I completed it after I retired in the summer of 2000.

Because this book had such a long gestation, I am unable to remember and properly acknowledge all who have given me benefit of their criticism. For reading and criticizing the entire manuscript, I acknowledge the anonymous readers for the University of North Carolina Press. I owe a considerable debt to my archaeological colleagues David Hally, Richard Polhemus, Marvin Smith, and Mark Williams. I am likewise indebted to my colleagues in literature: John C. Guilds, Jim Kilgo, and Hugh Ruppersburg. I am grateful to John Worth and Barnet Pavao-Zuckerman for advice on particular matters. Peggy Galis and Christina Snyder read the manuscript and shared their thoughts with me. I was stimulated as well by the spirited criticism and discussion of the graduate students in my seminar on Southeastern Indians in fiction in the spring of 2000: Eric Bowne, Brian Campbell, David Cozzo, Kelly Orr, and Verónica Pérez Rodríguez. I owe a special debt to Karen Booker for reading the entire manuscript, for devising an easy-to-use orthography for spelling Creek words, and for regularizing my own haphazard spellings. For helping with the illustrations I am grateful to Jefferson Chapman, Susan Curtis, Frank Hamrick, Marvin and Julie Smith, and Mark Williams.

This book has benefited from a close critical reading by Lisa Scheffer, who has herself undertaken to depict the sixteenth-century Southeast in fiction. Most of all, I am grateful to my wife, Joyce, for reading the manuscript with a cold but loving novelist's eye.

While still in manuscript, this book found its first audience among the bibliophiles of the Folio Club of Athens, Georgia. Needless to say, I alone bear ultimate responsibility for what is written here.

CONVERSATIONS
WITH THE
HIGH PRIEST OF
COOSA

A Letter

To the Most Reverend Father Provincial, Fray Domingo de Santa María

Most Reverend Sir:

I am writing to tell you what I learned in Coosa. A man of your eminence, who has the responsibility for evangelizing so vast a land, can ill afford to spend time reading about such provincial matters. I can well understand that you might lay these pages aside unread. But even though my brothers and I have failed in our effort to bring the poor lost sheep of Coosa into the Christian fold, how long can it be before others, more fortunate than we, will undertake to build towns and cities in La Florida, and other friars will again come to save the souls of the heathen? It is for those coming after me that I particularly intend these pages.

We knew when we first reached the capital town of Coosa that it was not the rich and fertile province we had expected it to be. Coosa is densely wooded, and the Indians clear only enough land to plant corn and beans for the coming year. They also depend upon wild meat, and upon forest products such as nuts, roots, and shoots of cane. Their principal town is situated in some hills at a place where two small streams come together. In the middle of the town is a plaza with a tall pole near its center, rather like the stone *rollo* in some of our old Spanish towns. A large flat-topped earthen mound lies at the edge of the plaza, and on top of it is a house in which their chief lives. The town is encircled by a high palisade wall of vertical posts strong enough to repel an attack by other Indians, but it could never stop a Spanish military attack. The plaza is ringed all around with compact, square houses, with sunken floors and with the excavated dirt banked up around the outside walls to serve as insulation and as a dam to keep the rainwater out. Each house is capped with a pyramidal thatched roof, overhanging broadly on all sides, and with a small smoke hole in the apex of the roof. Large families have two or more houses clustered together around a small courtyard, and each house has near it a *barba-coa*, a rectangular storage house raised high on eight posts. The Indians lounge about in the shade beneath these *barbacoas*. Scattered along the banks of one of the streams for a distance of about two leagues are two large towns and five small ones, each with its plaza and central pole.

To forestall the possibility of conflict between our soldiers and the Indians, we encamped at a distance of an arquebus shot from the main town. The soldiers built small, makeshift *ramadas* in which we slept, and we took care to post sentinels to prevent a surprise attack.

During our stay, when our valiant fighting men went with the warriors of Coosa to chastise their errant tributaries, the Napochín, we saw that, even with the food we took from the Napochín, our governor Don Tristán de Luna would not be able to succeed in founding his colony. How discouraging it was to have come so far and suffered so much, only to fail in our attempt to make this a Christian land. But for all the time we remained in Coosa, Fray Domingo de Salazar and I did not cease to labor to bring the Indians out of the darkness in which they live.

When I first reached Coosa, I wrote letters comparing the people unfavorably with the people of Nanipacana, whose towns lay in a cluster between this province and the Port of Ochuse on the Gulf of Mexico. The temples at Coosa are small, rustic, and not much attended by the people. Moreover, I later found that the high priest of Coosa, whom they call the Raven and who is their most respected keeper of knowledge and traditions, dressed not in the heathen finery of the chief and his principal men, but in the poor clothing of one who does not care about appearances. I had frequently seen an old man who would often appear when there was a public event. He clung to the edges of the crowd and stood in the shadows. He watched everything that happened, saying nothing. On his bony shoulders he wore a tattered white deerskin mantle. In his hair he sometimes wore a tuft of black feathers. He was a grave, solemn old man, and yet as he walked about with his dignified step, he would hum songs softly to himself.

Had I been more observant, I would have noticed that the people of Coosa were careful to pay him deference. It was not the honor people accorded him, however, but an action of his that made us take special notice of him. Soon after we arrived, he startled our translator, Teresa de Coosa, by addressing her in Spanish. Then he asked her in the Coosa

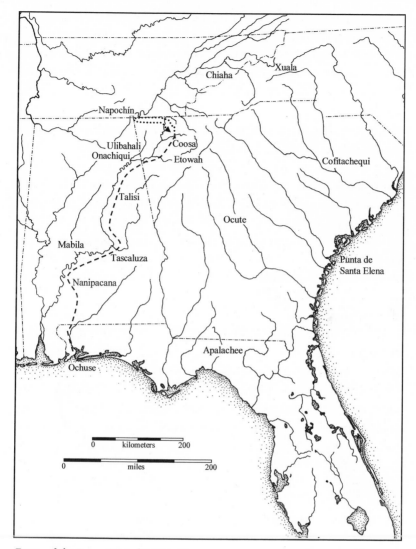

Route of the Luna Expedition to Coosa

language what had happened to the Sun Woman whom Soto's men had taken from Coosa at the same time they enslaved Teresa, who was then a young girl. Teresa told him that the woman had fallen for a time into the hands of a cruel master, who in beating her had put out one of her eyes. Though she was now half blind, Don Tristán de Luna had thought that this woman, because of her high standing in her native land, would be an asset to his venture. But before the expedition departed from Mexico, she ran away and hid herself. She did not want to return to her birthplace. Teresa said that on hearing this, tears welled up in the old man's eyes, and he turned his back and walked away.

How did the old man learn to speak Spanish? When I sought out the Raven, I learned that twenty years ago he befriended two men who had come into his land with Hernando de Soto and remained there. One was a black slave named Robles, a Christian, who fell ill while Soto was in Coosa and could not travel when the expedition moved on. The other man was Feryada, a Levantine, who stayed behind by choice—a deserter. It was from these two that the old man learned a few words of Spanish and had learned something about our country and our ways. Indeed, we found that the chief of Coosa, even though he had reason to hate Spaniards for what he and his people had suffered at the hands of Soto, nonetheless commanded the Raven to learn from Robles and Feryada as much as he could about our ways. Perhaps he thought it would aid him in taking revenge on Spain should the opportunity arise. But that information proved to be of no benefit to him. He died before we returned.

The Raven told me that Robles and Feryada themselves died eight or ten years ago. They died naturally, the old man said, but who can be sure of their fate? The priest long pondered what he had learned from them, and in doing so he got some grasp of how we Christians think. He also learned from Robles and Feryada that we look down on Coosas as being poor ignorant savages. But he persuaded himself that we would not hold this opinion if we could only come to know and understand what the Coosas understand about the world, just as he had learned something of how we think.

Unlike the chief, the Raven lived to see our return. He came to see this as an opportunity to persuade us Christians of the nobility of the Coosa mind. To that end, he told me that if I would agree to certain conditions, he would reveal to me the beauty, as he put it, of the Coosa world. He insisted that we could only converse after the sun had set. By rights, he said, he should not converse with me until after the first frost, for to do otherwise would anger the snakes. However, frost was not so far away, and I am, after all, not a Coosa, but he cautioned me to be careful as I went about through the land, lest I suffer snakebite. In their ignorance the savages believe that the tribe of snakes are offended by those who do not honor them when they are about in the land during their summer season.

This was not the only obstacle. When he realized that Teresa de Coosa, a woman, would have to be present at all times in order to translate our words to each other, he at first reversed himself, saying that he could not talk to me after all. The Indians are quite as intent on keeping the sexes separate as were the ancient Israelites. I told him that he need not fear his secrets being compromised: Teresa is now a Christian, not an Indian; the people of Coosa shun her, and her own kinsmen do so most cruelly. I told him that when we departed from Coosa, Teresa would surely depart with us. Finally, the Raven agreed, though reluctantly, and our conversations began. Teresa translated, and I wrote down what I could as he talked. After each conversation, I would read through my notes, and Teresa, as best she was able, corrected and amplified what I had written.

This is a true record of what I, Domingo de la Anunciación, your most unworthy servant in Christ, have heard and understood.

Coosa, October 15, 1560

The Raven would only converse with us at night. During the day, he said, children are always peering through the cracks in his walls, listening for what might pass between himself and his visitors. Women, too, are bad about prying into the affairs of men. Later I learned that Coosas are suspicious of anything that moves about in the darkness, whether animal or human, and since the last thing Coosas want is for suspicion to fall upon them, they do not travel about much at night, and that is the best time for privacy.

His house lay on the side of the plaza nearest the mound and the chief's residence. As we stooped and entered the low doorway, stepping down to the sunken floor, we saw the old man sitting on a bed built against the opposite wall. It took some time for our eyes to adjust to the light from the tiny fire in the hearth in the center of the earth floor. The pyramidal ceiling of the house was supported by four stout posts, each set midway between the corners and the center of the floor. Beds were built around the walls at a height convenient for sitting. Small clay-plastered partitions built at the ends of the beds provided a little privacy. Closely woven split-cane mats lined the walls. The entire surface of the pyramidal ceiling, from where the central support posts joined the roof beams up to the apex, was plastered with clay mixed with grass for insulation and also to protect the roof from sparks that might drift up in smoke. The house smelled of the smoke of countless fires, strange foods, and dressed deerskins, and of the dried herbs hung from the roof beams and around the walls.

The Raven arose and stirred the fire, collecting coals and unburnt pieces of wood into the center of the shallow clay hearth in the center of the floor, and after a moment the fire began to brighten the room. Teresa and I were startled by a coarse *pruk, pruk* from a dark corner of the room. I could not see what made the sound. But then as the fire blazed up, I saw that it was a raven the old man had tamed and was keeping as a pet. It looked like one of the crows that raid Coosa

Raven

cornfields, but ravens are nearly twice the size of crows; they make a different sound, and normally they stay up in the mountains, away from Coosa villages and fields.

As the old man showed us where we were to sit—I on the bed beside him and Teresa on a stout basket beside one of the support posts—he pointed to the bird and said: "His name is Pruk." When Teresa translated the Raven's words, she pronounced the bird's name as he had spoken it, which was very close to the sound made by the bird himself.

After Teresa and I seated ourselves, the Raven began talking to us in a deliberate way, choosing his words carefully and speaking them in measured sentences. As Teresa translated, I wrote as rapidly as I could.

"What a time of suffering, disorder, and confusion we Coosas have had since you people first came to our land. No Coosa will forget that spring, one short lifetime ago, when we first heard from a man of Ocute that a band of strange men were traveling about. They were so peculiar they at first seemed not to be men at all—but they were men, and they bled when they were cut. Though they were not numerous, they were as confident as a falcon among doves. They had bested the Apalachees, and they walked through Ocute unopposed.

"The man of Ocute said that these people possessed wonderful weapons, unbelievable weapons—incredibly long knives. These knives were sharper than a sliver of hard cane or a splinter of fat-lighter pine. And most astonishing of all, these long weapons could not be broken. The man of Ocute said that these people came from the sea, and that their skin, where the sun did not strike it, was as white as sea foam. That is why we call them *Nokfilaki,* people of the ocean foam.

"Upon our first hearing of these strangers, some Coosas said that we need not be alarmed; we had only to bide our time. They said that soon the *Nokfilaki* would be among the wolves of Cofitachequi. The woman chief of Cofitachequi would kill them and drink their very blood. But before long we heard that the *Nokfilaki* had walked through Cofitachequi as easily as one walks through a morning mist. And worse, they had taken hostage a woman of the female chief's clan.

"Then word came from a runner from the Chiaha, our allies up the valley to the north. The *Nokfilaki* had come to that land, and now they were on the move again, heading toward Coosa. They were enslaving people in the towns through which they passed—the young boys to work for them and the women to use as they pleased. They had wantonly destroyed some cornfields at Chiaha, and they seemed to be growing more belligerent and dangerous with every passing day.

"Many people of Coosa were now frightened. Others, and most especially our young men, clamored to kill the *Nokfilaki.* They wished to cut their bodies into pieces and hang them in trees for the birds to eat. Others said it would be better to capture the *Nokfilaki* and put them to work at menial tasks, like gathering firewood and carrying water.

"But the Sun Chief of Coosa was calm. No Coosas had seen these intruders; no one had seen how they waged war; no one had seen one of their long knives that could not be broken; no one had seen the huge beasts on which they were said to sit and be carried about in the land.

"The Sun Chief called a council of chiefs from all parts of Coosa. The chiefs assembled and quickly agreed that it would be better if they all combined their forces and acted together to resist the *Nok-filaki.* But it was the Sun Chief who first suggested that it would be better still if they could unite with their old enemy to the south—Chief Tascaluza—and thus make themselves an even more formidable force. Many Coosa warriors, who had bitter scores to settle with Tascaluza, would not hear of it. The Sun Chief answered them in this way: How will those of you who are killed by the *Nokfilaki* take vengeance on the people of Tascaluza? In the end, the assembled chiefs reached a consensus, and the irate warriors fell silent. Runners were sent to Tascaluza, and to the surprise of some, the word quickly came back that Chief Tascaluza would cooperate.

"The *Nokfilaki* came to Coosa, and as was our custom when powerful chiefs meet, we carried the Sun Chief out on a litter to meet with the chief of the *Nokfilaki*. We made a great show, with the Sun Chief's retainers singing and playing on flutes, but the *Nokfilaki* could not hide their contempt for us, nor did they much try. They were far more terrible than we had feared. Not only did they possess miraculous weapons, but they wore on their bodies clothing so hard no arrow could penetrate. They seemed to be like so many snapping turtles, evil in temper and secure against all weapons. And not only did they ride upon the backs of those great beasts we had never seen before, which jumped about, snorting and farting, but the *Nokfilaki* also had at their command large dogs, dressed in the same impenetrable clothing that they themselves wore, that would attack and kill anything or anybody. They were man-eaters on leashes.

"Their chief was Soto, a man whom some of the *Nokfilaki* feared and hated almost as much as we did. He was a dry man, humorless, and always searching the faces of his men for hints of insubordination. He demanded that the Sun Chief hand over slaves and women, and with this the people of Coosa began to flee into the woods to find refuge. But the *Nokfilaki* sallied out and rounded up many of them, doing injury to some. Soto took hostage the Sun Chief, some women—including Teresa and the chief's sister—and some of the chief's principal men, and he said that he would throw them to the dogs to be killed and eaten if any of us attempted to interfere or resist.

"We could not understand what Soto wanted. Did he wish to be a paramount chief over Coosa? If so, why did he keep traveling from place to place? He showed us a yellow metal band he wore on one of his fingers, a metal that resembled our sacred metal—Thunder's metal—but when we showed him some of our sacred metal, he was contemptuous. Soto said it was not the same as his. Ours is of a redder color and is softer. Soto kept demanding to know where was the greatest chief in the land. He wanted to find a chief greater than Sun Chief and a land more splendid than Coosa. He was as greedy as a cougar, who after killing a deer, will kill a second, far more than he can possibly eat, and he will lie between them to prevent any other from eating. We told him that a greater land lay ahead, and we gave him guides to lead him to the land of Tascaluza, where a trap was being laid for him.

"Chief Tascaluza launched his surprise attack on the *Nokfilaki* at Mabila, one of his subject towns. Days later, when we first learned what had happened there, we could not believe it. Even though we had surprise and a much larger number of fighting men on our side, the *Nokfilaki* drenched the ground with the blood of the warriors of Tascaluza and Coosa. Even though we set upon them the finest of our young men, trained from childhood in the warrior's art, the *Nokfilaki* cut them down like dry cornstalks. Tascaluza's chiefdom was ruined, bespoiled by the angry *Nokfilaki,* and Coosa suffered grievous losses. The life we knew before the *Nokfilaki* was altered on that day. The world is different now.

"When the *Nokfilaki* departed from Coosa, two of their number remained behind. One was Robles, who, just as they were about to leave, was kicked by one of the beasts on which they rode and suffered a terrible break in his leg. The *Nokfilaki* were unwilling to carry him through the long time of healing that lay ahead, and so they left him in Coosa. For many weeks he could not walk. Eventually his leg healed, but the broken leg was shorter than the other, and he walked with a limp. Robles was no good for war, but he would work at whatever needed to be done, and he was a cheerful man.

"Robles had not been born in the land of the *Nokfilaki*. He was born in a village, among farmers and hunters like ourselves, and he had been captured when he was a young boy and taken as a slave to the land of the *Nokfilaki*. His hair was as tightly curled as grape tendrils, and his skin was very dark. The children of Coosa liked this man very much, and they called him Burnt-by-the-Sun. He began learning our language quickly, and as he did he also learned our customs. He said that they were not so different from the customs of the village where he was born.

"Feryada, the second *Nokfila* to remain with us, did so against Chief Soto's wishes. When the *Nokfilaki* departed from Coosa, Feryada lagged behind the others until he had fallen out of sight, and then he

returned to Coosa. A day or two later, Indian runners came from Ulibahali saying that Chief Soto was angry at Feryada for trying to stay
behind and that he must return to the *Nokfilaki* at once. He was assured that Chief Soto would forgive him if he would come back. But
Feryada laughed at this, indicating by signs that Soto would throw
him to the dogs. He remained here, and he had some very hard things
to say about Soto and the *Nokfilaki*. Moreover, in time I realized that
though Feryada seemed at first to be a Christian like the other *Nokfilaki,* he was in truth not a Christian. When the runner came from
Soto to Coosa, Feryada drew a Christian cross in the dirt, spat upon
it, and scuffed it with his feet. He indicated by signs that his god was
not Christ, but a spirit called Allah.

"Feryada, however, was never content in Coosa. Later he wished
that he were back in his own homeland. He even wished that he were
back with the *Nokfilaki*. He learned our language only slowly, and he
was not as interested in Coosa ways as Robles was.

"I had many talks with Robles and Feryada. Not even Robles
learned the language of Coosa perfectly, but in time we understood
each other well enough. The questions I asked about the land from
which the *Nokfilaki* had come often exasperated them. They said that
I asked them the meaning of things that any child should know. Their
saying this amused me because they asked the same childish questions
of me.

"It was Robles who first told me that the *Nokfilaki* can speak by
making marks on thin white cloth [he meant paper], which they can
send by a runner to another *Nokfila,* who can then look at the marks
and speak the same words of the man who made the marks. And what
is even more astonishing, a *Nokfila* can look at these marks four life-
times later, and he can repeat the words exactly. With such marks on
thin white cloth, as you yourself are making now, beloved knowledge
can be kept forever.

"We Coosas only possess the knowledge that can be held in memory. Only a few of us are able to learn it well. And yet we try to increase
our knowledge. That is why we were willing to give food and shelter
to Robles and Feryada for so many years, forgiving them their blun-
ders as they learned to behave and act as true men. We wished to learn
from them, though much of what they said was so extraordinary we
doubted that it was true.

"They told us that in the land of the *Nokfilaki,* people live in vast villages, and they are as numerous as ants. They are so numerous, some of them only grind grain into meal; others only weave cloth; others only make weapons; others only build houses — and nothing else. How could a man not know the ways of animals and how to hunt them? How could a man not know how to grow corn? Or how to build a house? We could not believe such stories."

The Raven stopped his talk at this point, saying he had told me enough for one night. He took little comfort when I tried to explain that what Robles and Feryada had told him was true. The man who makes meal is a miller; the one who makes cloth is a weaver; the one who makes weapons is a blacksmith; and the one who builds houses is a carpenter. The Raven said that if this were true, it was a pitiful way for men to live. They would only be half-men, he said.

He said that the next time we conversed, he would tell me some stories. We would start in shallow water, as he put it. These first stories would be some that are known to every Coosa, man or woman, adult or child. Later we would go into deeper water.

After I returned to my *ramada* for the night, I sat by the fire reflecting on what the Raven had said. What he said about Hernando de Soto agrees with what the people of Nanipacana told us when we moved there from the port of Ochuse, the place where our governor Don Tristán de Luna landed and we unloaded our ships. The people of Nanipacana said that theirs had formerly been a great province, but they had been devastated by an army of people like ourselves who had been there earlier. It was plain to see that many houses in Nanipacana were vacant, ruined. Clearly the people of Nanipacana had been party to the conspiracy of Tascaluza.

My final thoughts on this eventful day were on Robles and Feryada. How would it have been for these two to live out their lives cut off from Christian brotherhood? Did the struggles of the Coosas become their struggles? Or were they only scorned and despised by the pagans, made strangers to human kindness for the rest of their days?

2 *The Contest between the Four-footeds and the Flyers*

The next evening Teresa and I returned to the Raven's house. Our commander, Mateo del Sauz, had forbidden Christians from entering the Coosa town after sundown, but he approved an exception in my case when I explained the purpose of my nightly visits. Fully expecting to breathe the corrupting air of the Devil's own philosophy, Teresa and I prayed for God's mercy before setting out on our visit.

As would be his habit, the old man greeted us and stirred the coals of his fire. His great black bird hopped down from his perch and strode over to the old man, looking up at his master with a cocked eye. The old man threw down a handful of boiled hominy, and the bird ate his fill and flew back to his perch, where he ruffled and preened his feathers.

"He begs for food," the old man said. "And when his begging fails, he steals it. I think he is happier as a thief than as a beggar."

When this spectacle was over, the old man directed us to take the seats we had taken before, and then he sat down on his bed. His practice was to either lean back against the wall or sit forward, resting his chin in his cupped hands. After a time of silence, he would begin to talk, and as he talked the fire gradually died down. I have recorded here exactly what the old man said as nearly as I could understand it, without regard to its merit in the eyes and ears of God, for which I beseech God's understanding and forgiveness. My only intention is to put into the hands of the friars who come after me a tool by which they might lead these savages out of their benighted condition into the light and love of our Savior Jesus Christ.

After the customary time of silence, the Raven began by saying that he would tell us a story of events in Ancient Days. This, he said, was the time when the earth was still moist. Many creatures existed on earth at this time, but their characters were not completely fixed. Any creature might behave in any way whatever. The events that occurred in those days shaped the character of the earth's creatures forever after.

This is the story the Raven told.

A CONTEST BETWEEN THE
FOUR-FOOTEDS AND THE FLYERS

"The creatures decided to have a contest, and they divided up into two great teams: the four-footeds on one team and the flyers on the other. They found a tall dead pine tree to serve as a goal.

"On the appointed day the two teams took to the field. The four-footeds, with Bear as captain, were painted and dressed in their finest. They ran across the field, some slow and some fast, some ponderous and some fleet. The flyers, not to be outdone, were also in their finest, but with their many-colored feathers, they needed no paint or fine clothing. All came out to play except the night birds — the owls and whippoorwills — and the ravens, who keep aloof in the high mountains. With Eagle as captain, they came flying across the field. Some, like Chickadee and Tufted Titmouse, fluttered about in confusion; others, like Crow and Kingfisher, swooped mightily; and they all swirled round and round the pine tree. It was enough to make you dizzy.

"The contest began when a ball was tossed up into the air. Alligator lashed his tail about, frightening all the creatures, and he snapped up the ball in his ferocious teeth and began running toward the goal, his great body flouncing from side to side.

"The birds tried to strip the ball from Alligator. Blue Jay, crying murder, tried and failed; Ivory-billed Woodpecker, who was a flying war club, pecked mightily on Alligator's head, but failed to dislodge the ball; Mockingbird, the cleverest of the flyers, cursed and heaped scorn on Alligator in seven bird languages, but Alligator paid no attention, and he lumbered closer to the pine tree goal. As one flyer after another tried and failed to come up with the ball, Alligator's wife ran alongside the field shouting at the top of her lungs: 'Look at the old toothy one go! None will stop him now!'

"But Alligator's wife forgot about Eagle, who had soared higher and higher into the sky until he was such a speck that only another flyer could have seen him. When Eagle folded his wings and dropped down from the sky, screeching his war cry, all the other birds pulled

Turkey

back. Eagle struck Alligator's nose so hard that it broke. Alligator's teeth parted, and at this moment Turkey ran over on his skinny legs, and with his long neck he reached in and grabbed the ball in his beak. As Turkey ran to the goalpost, his spurred legs were a blur. Then he flew up on his powerful wings and scored a goal.

"As the first victor in this game, Turkey wears to this day a scalp-lock on his breast, and strings of fingernails around his ankles, and Alligator has a sunken place on his snout where Eagle smashed into it.

"Now the score was one to nothing in favor of the flyers, but the four-footeds were still confident of their superiority. Bear, who was strongest, ran to the edge of the field, ripped open a fallen, rotted

Peregrine falcon

tree, and picked up its trunk in his paws and threw it a great distance. Terrapin—a giant terrapin, not the small one of today—whose hard shell was proof against all weapons, raised up on his legs and crashed down, saying that this is the way he would treat any flyer that crossed his path. And Deer, the fleetest of all the four-footeds, began leaping over the backs of his teammates, impudently waving his white tail in the air.

"While the four-footeds were showing off, two little creatures hardly larger than mice came over and asked to join the four-footed team. Both of them had four feet, and they had teeth, but they were so small and harmless looking, the four-footeds laughed at them. Deer looked away haughtily, browsing on a succulent bough. Bear, while looking at the two little creatures intently, reared up and then plunged downward, stomping his huge paw on a maypop fruit the size of a turkey egg, which burst, and then he stomped a second one.

"Bear's threat was not lost on the two little creatures, who scurried away and climbed up the tall tree where Eagle perched.

"'We want to play with the flyers,' they said.

"'Well, you are bigger than Chickadee and Tufted Titmouse,' Eagle said. 'The trouble is, you have no wings. But maybe we flyers can fix you up.'

"Eagle and Peregrine Falcon talked it over, and they cut two pieces of excess leather from the head of their drum. They took these two strips of leather, fixed splints to them, and attached them to the sides of one of the creatures. 'You shall be called Bat,' they said.

"Then Eagle and Peregrine Falcon grabbed up the other little creature, who was a tiny squirrel, and with their powerful beaks they stretched the skin between his fore and hind legs on both sides. 'You shall be called Flying Squirrel,' they said.

"Someone tossed the ball up into the air, and Bear reared up on his hind legs, waiting to catch the ball in his huge jaws. But Flying Squirrel leapt from the tree where Eagle had perched and glided down and snatched the ball away from Bear. As he sailed across the field, gliding closer and closer to the earth, Deer pursued him closely. Flying Squirrel tossed his head, flipping the ball up to Purple Martin, who caught it and darted this way and that, doubling back upon himself. Try as he might, Purple Martin could not reach the goal because Cougar was guarding the post, leaping into the air and swatting with his fearsome paws.

"Finally, Purple Martin looped round and round and tossed the ball to Bat, who began flying even tighter and more confusing twists and turns than Purple Martin had done. Cougar kept leaping and swatting, but even when he swung at Bat's blind side, his paws hit nothing but air. Bat soon scored another goal.

"Now the score was two to nothing. The four-footeds were so humiliated at being bested by such small creatures, they quit the field, each blaming the other for breaking training. It is partly because of his valor in the ball game that we do not kill Flying Squirrel, though this is also because he goes about at night. We also pay this courtesy to Bat for his great valor as a ball player, and even more so because he, too, goes about at night.

"Because of his superior play in the great ball game, Purple Martin was given a gourd in which to build his nest. You have seen the gourd houses we hang up around our gardens for purple martins. They pay us back by ridding our gardens of troublesome insects."

The Raven fell silent. I waited for more until I realized he was finished for the evening. He stretched, and then sat up straight and looked at me for a response. What was I to make of this preposterous story? Were the mysteries of Coosa to be found in such stories? It was a story like those told by illiterate peasants in Spain, but the Raven clearly regarded it as something more serious than that, almost as we regard the Holy Scriptures.

"You tell a story in which mammals and birds talk to each other," I said. "Do you believe that this is really true? That dumb beasts actually talk to each other as you and I are talking here?"

The Raven explained that this contest was played in Ancient Days, when things occurred that could not occur today. He said that it took place in the same time as did a story told to him by Robles, in which a serpent persuaded the Christian first woman Eve to eat an evil fruit. "Where is there such an artful serpent today," he asked, "and where is there a tree with fruit so powerful it can sully and pollute the whole world?

"Besides," the Raven said, "the four-footeds and the flyers still talk to each other, though not so well as in Ancient Days. All Coosa hunters have observed that when blue jays shout *jeeah, jeeah* excitedly, deer stop browsing and look about for the cause of the blue jays' distress, and often as not they raise their tails and go running for cover."

I tried to explain to him that the serpent in the Garden of Eden was the Devil in disguise. But the Raven could see no difference between happenings in the Garden of Eden and the fantastic events in his own story. I did not argue with him, for I did not want to lose his trust. Besides, I was somewhat heartened by the fact that he had traded stories with Robles and Feryada and had compared theirs with his own. Despite the trivial nature of these stories that he tells, I saw that there might be more substance to the man than I had at first believed.

As Teresa and I walked home to our quarters, I resolved that I would continue to listen intently and write everything down. I cautioned Teresa to translate his stories as accurately as she was able. I determined that the best course would be to appear to take such nonsense seriously, but to question the old man about evident absurdities and contradictions. In this way I hoped to understand how Coosas think about the world and to find ways in which we can call their beliefs into question. In so doing we will help them see the errors of their ways and lead them to the light of Christianity.

When we next went to his house, the old man was waiting for us. As we took our seats, Pruk flew down from his perch and began striding around, trying to get the old man's attention.

"I'm ignoring him," he said.

Pruk walked over and, with elaborate hesitation, pecked at the old man's foot. Then he leapt comically into the air as if he were avoiding a strike from a snake.

A while later, as Teresa and I were exchanging pleasantries with the Raven, we heard a clatter from the corner of the room. Pruk had sauntered over to a covered jar and pushed the lid off with his beak. He got out some grains of corn stored inside and gobbled them down as quickly as he could.

"You see," said the Raven, "for Pruk thievery is the best sauce."

He walked over and replaced the lid on the jar, weighting it down with a heavy rock, and then he shooed Pruk back to his perch.

"Tonight I will tell you some shallow stories," he said. "They are stories that float on the surface like autumn leaves on a river. Anyone, even children, can see and understand autumn leaves floating on a river.

"After the great ball game in Ancient Days, the creatures came to be separated into the two great divisions of creatures: four-footeds and flyers. But there were still many more distinctions to arise. The adventures the animals had in those days made them what they are today. Here is a story to show you what I mean."

RACCOON AND POSSUM

"When Possum met Raccoon she asked: 'How is it that you have such pretty rings on your tail?'

"'Easy,' Raccoon said. 'I wrapped strips of hickory bark around my tail and stuck it in the fire. As you can see, it came out beautifully.'

"Possum got herself several strips of hickory bark and wrapped them about her hairy tail. But when she stuck her tail in the fire, it blazed up, burning off all the hair and leaving her with a rat's tail.

"She was so mortified at how ugly her tail had become, she curled up into a ball and played dead. Her nose lay near a little pouch on her stomach, and as she breathed into it, little possums formed there, and it has been thus with possums ever since."

"Do you know possums and raccoons?" asked the Raven. "They are two small animals of our country. Robles and Feryada were fascinated with them. Both of these animals are active at night, but what is oddest about the possum is that when her babies are young, she carries them in a pouch on her belly. The raccoon is marked by its striped tail, which makes us think of the division between day and night, with light followed by dark, and then light again. What is notable about raccoons is that they seem to grieve at night, walking sleeplessly with dark circles around their eyes. People in their grief sometimes come down with the raccoon disease. Unable to sleep, they walk about restlessly at night. This disease can sometimes be cured with a medicine made of mistletoe, a plant that grows not with its feet in the soil, in the manner of all other plants, but high up, in the limbs of trees. People say that mistletoe has no feet on which to walk, and thus it can cure people from wandering.

"Now here is a story about quite a different four-footed. Terrapin is as slow as Mink is quick. He is a great favorite of Coosa children."

THE TERRAPIN'S BACK

"Possum and Terrapin went out together to hunt persimmons and found a tree full of ripe fruit. Possum climbed the tree and was throwing down the persimmons to Terrapin when a wolf appeared and began greedily snapping up the persimmons as they fell, so that Terrapin could not reach any of them. Possum waited for his chance and at last managed to throw down a large bone, which he had carried with him up into the tree. When the wolf jumped into the air and snapped it up, the bone stuck in his throat and choked him to death. 'He's just dead meat now,' said Terrapin down below. 'I'll take his stupid ears for hominy spoons.' And Terrapin cut off the wolf's ears and started home with them, leaving Possum grinning and eating persimmons high up in the tree.

"After a while Terrapin came to a house and was invited to have some *sááfke* gruel from the jar that is set always beside the door. He sat down beside the jar and dipped up the gruel using one of the wolf's ears for a spoon. The people noticed his heedless insult of wolves but said nothing. When Terrapin had eaten his fill he went on and soon came to another house and was offered more *sááfke*. Again he dipped up the *sááfke* with the wolf's ear, and after he had had enough he continued on his way.

"Soon the news went around that the Terrapin had killed the wolf and was using his ears for spoons. When the wolves heard of this insult they were very angry. They all got together and followed Terrapin's trail until they caught up with him and made him their prisoner. They held a council to determine what to do with him and decided to boil him. They brought out a large earthenware pot, but Terrapin only laughed at it, saying that if they were stupid enough to put him into that thing he would kick it all to pieces. So they decided instead to burn him in the fire, but Terrapin laughed and said he would pee on the flames and put them out. Finally they decided to throw him into the deepest hole in the river to drown him. Terrapin begged and begged them not to do that, but they paid no attention and dragged him over to the river and threw him in. He fell through the air a long way, then bounced off of a rock, plunged happily into the water, and swam away.

"When he hit the rock, it broke his shell in a dozen places. But he sang a medicine song.

> I have sewed myself together.
> *Matoo!*
> I have sewed myself together.
> *Matoo!*

All the pieces did come together, but the scars remain on his shell to this day."

"This is one of Terrapin's best stories," said the Raven. "We like to say about Terrapin that there is only one thing he does well. He is not fast, or agile, or handsome. He is no good at fighting with bow and arrow or war club. But with his patience and persistence and his hard shell, there is no one who can defend himself as well as Terrapin can. He is a master of defense.

Terrapin

"As for wolves, they are some of the cleverest and most sharp-sensed of the four-footeds. Unlike many other four-footeds, wolves live in towns of their own, and because they cooperate on the hunt like people do, they are dangerous and formidable. Still, they can be overcome through cunning."

GROUNDHOG'S TAIL

"Seven wolves once caught Groundhog and said, 'Now let's all go and have something good to eat.' But Groundhog said, 'When you find good food you must rejoice over it, as people do at the green-corn dance of the *posketa*. I know you mean to kill me, and I can't save myself, but if you want to dance, I'll sing for you. I have learned an entirely new dance. It goes like this: I'll lean up against each of seven trees, one after the other, and you will all dance out away from these trees and then as I give the signal — *now!* — turn and come back to the next tree. When the dance ends you may kill me and eat me for dinner.'

"The wolves were very hungry, but like people, wolves are fond of playing and having a good time, and they wanted to learn the new dance. They told Groundhog to go ahead with his dance. Wagging his long tail about — for he had a long tail in Ancient Days — Groundhog leaned up against a tree and began his song. All the wolves danced out away from the tree, until he shouted *now!*, and as he began singing again, they danced back to the tree. 'You're doing well,' said Ground-

Wolf

hog, and he went over to the next tree and started the second song. The wolves danced out and then turned at the signal and danced back again. 'That's, oh, so fine,' said Groundhog, and went over to another tree and started the third song. The wolves danced their best and Groundhog encouraged them, but at each song he went to another tree, and each tree was a little nearer to a hole he had dug under a stump. At the seventh song he said, 'This is the last dance. When I say *now!* you will turn and come after me, and the one who catches me may have me to eat.' So he began the seventh song and kept it up until the wolves had danced out away from the tree. Then Groundhog gave the signal — *now!* — and he made a leap for his hole. The wolves turned and began running after him, but he reached the hole first and dived in. Just as he got inside, the foremost wolf caught Groundhog's tail in his teeth and gave it such a pull that it broke off, and Groundhog's tail has been short ever since."

"That is one of the favorite stories of Coosa children," said the Raven. "It tells so much about groundhogs. To this day they never stray very far from the burrows they dig, and one must be a better than average archer to kill one. But it is well worth the trouble because groundhogs are tasty when stewed, and their skins are just the size and thickness for making drumheads.

"Each of the four-footeds has his story, and for many of them songs are sung and dances are danced in their honor. When we encounter these creatures in the hunt, the stories and songs come to mind. And when a hunter kills an animal—or when he tells about his exploit later—he will sometimes do a step or two of the dance that mimics the slain animal.

"Each of the flyers also has his story, and some few of the flyers have many different stories. Because the flyers won their contest with the four-footeds in ancient time, we know they are superior to them. Coosas are fond of flyers, and we use their feathers to embellish our bodies. We pay close attention to the speech of the flyers, who, because they safely inhabit the realm above us, are friendlier to people than the four-footeds are. Bobwhite Quail is especially friendly to people, as you will see in my next story."

HOW BOBWHITE QUAIL GOT HIS WHISTLE

"In the old days Terrapin had a fine whistle, but Bobwhite had none. Terrapin was constantly going about whistling and showing his whistle to the other animals. Soon Bobwhite became jealous, and one day when they met, Bobwhite asked Terrapin if he could try out his whistle. Terrapin was afraid to risk it at first, suspecting some trick, but Bobwhite said, 'I'll give it right back to you, and if my using it makes you uneasy, you can stay near me while I practice.' So Terrapin gave his whistle to Bobwhite, who walked around blowing on it in fine fashion. *Bobwhite. Bobwhite.* 'How do I sound?' asked Bobwhite.

"'Oh, you sound very good,' said Terrapin, walking alongside.

"'Now, how do you like the sound it makes from over here?' asked Bobwhite, running ahead and whistling a little louder. *Bobwhite. Bobwhite.*

"'That's fine,' answered Terrapin, hurrying to keep up, 'but don't run so fast.'

"'Now, how do you like this?' called Bobwhite, and with that he flapped his little wings, gave one long whistle, *Bobwhite,* and flew to the top of a tree, leaving poor Terrapin to look for him on the ground. Terrapin never got his whistle back, and he grew ashamed to be seen,

Hummingbird

and ever since he shuts himself up in his box when anyone comes near him."

"Everyone likes that story," said the Raven, "because everyone likes bobwhites. And they like us as well and make their homes near ours. They are fond of our old fallow cornfields, and also this season's cornfields. Their cheery song is a comfort and a sign that all is well. For when something is moving about, bobwhites do not whistle. They signal danger by suddenly flying up, flapping their wings so furiously they sound like large bees. They are good to eat, but they are so small and alert they are hard to kill.

"Not every bird is fleet and agile. The great blue heron is to the flyers what the terrapin is among the four-footeds."

THE RACE BETWEEN HUMMINGBIRD
AND GREAT BLUE HERON

"Hummingbird and Great Blue Heron were both in love with the most beautiful bird in the world. This most beautiful bird preferred Hummingbird, who was as handsome as Heron was awkward, but Heron was very persistent. Finally, Beautiful Bird told Heron that he must challenge Hummingbird to a race, and she would marry the winner. Hummingbird was so swift—almost like a flash of lightning—and Heron so slow and heavy, that she felt sure that Hummingbird would win.

"The two birds agreed to start from her house and fly a circuit around the edges of the world, and then back to the point where they

began. The one who came in first would marry Beautiful Bird. At the signal, Hummingbird was out of sight in an instant, leaving his rival to lumber along after him. He flew all day, and he was far ahead when evening came and he stopped to roost for the night. But Heron flew steadily all night long, passing Hummingbird on his perch soon after midnight, and he continued on until he came to a creek and stopped to rest at dawn. Hummingbird woke up when it became light, and he flew on again, thinking how easily he would win the race, until he reached the creek and saw Heron spearing breakfast minnows with his long beak. Hummingbird was very much surprised, and he wondered how this could have happened, but he flew swiftly by and soon left Heron out of sight again.

"Heron finished his breakfast and started on, and when darkness fell he kept going as before. This time it was hardly midnight when he passed Hummingbird asleep on a limb, and in the morning he had finished his breakfast before Hummingbird caught up with him. The next day he gained a little more, and on the fourth day he was spearing minnows for dinner when Hummingbird passed him. On the fifth and sixth days it was late in the afternoon before Hummingbird came up, and on the morning of the seventh day Heron was a whole night's travel ahead. He took his time at breakfast and then fixed himself up as nicely as he could at the creek. Early in the morning he arrived at the starting place where the most beautiful bird in the world lived. When Hummingbird arrived in the afternoon, he found he had lost the race, but the most beautiful bird declared she would never have such an ugly fellow as Heron for a husband, and so she stayed single, and none of her lineage is alive today."

The Raven smiled and shook his head. "I always feel sorry for Great Blue Heron when I tell that story. Do you know these birds? They are sometimes at war with each other. With their long legs and their gawky necks, it is comical to see them fight.

"It is late, and I cannot tell you stories about all the flyers, but I want to tell you a little story about Kingfisher. As you traveled upriver, you surely saw this bird perched on branches hanging out over the water. Kingfisher is vain and wears a white shell necklace tightly about his neck. But he is a special bird, a great favorite of priests and healers and of all who wish to discover the hidden causes of things."

HOW KINGFISHER GOT HIS BEAK

"Some old men say that in the beginning Kingfisher lived near water, but he did not have either webbed feet or a good beak and he could not make a living. The animals held a council over his plight and decided to leave his feet as they were but to make him a fish spear. So they made him a sharp awl and fastened it onto the front of his mouth. He flew to the top of a tree, sailed out and darted down into the water, and came up with a fish on his spear. And he has been the best fish-spearer ever since. But his feathers will not turn water like those of a duck, and he has to shake the water out of them when he comes up from a plunge."

"That is only one small story about Kingfisher. There are many more I could tell you if we had the time. Creatures that are at home in more than one realm are special. Kingfisher flies, and so he is of the above. But he can also dive into the watery realm, completely immerse him-

self into it, and he can find and catch a fish so small that only he can sense its presence. Then he flings himself up out of the water, shakes the water off his wings and body, flies with his fish to the limb of a tree, and shouts victory at the top of his tiny lungs. Unlike all other birds of Coosa, Kingfisher digs a burrow into the face of a steep bank and builds his nest there. When I wish to know the hidden causes of things, how I would like to be Kingfisher, who enters the <u>under world</u> so easily."

Teresa sensed my unease and was becoming restless. She knew I was losing patience with the old man. I complained to him that the stories he was telling were still no more than children's fables. When would he tell me stories for adults?

"First, learn the names of the leaves that float on the top of the water," he said, "and then we will look beneath the water for things both named and nameless."

above : sky : Birds
middle : land : Four footeds
underworld : water : Fish

The next time we entered the old man's house Pruk was sitting on his shoulder. If I did not know better, I would swear that the bird was talking into his ear. The creature seemed to glare down his great, black beak at us, ruffling his feathers slightly, and then he flew a circuit around the room and lit on his perch. Because he is such a large and ominous bird, Teresa and I ducked as he swooped close to our heads.

The old man was still perturbed over my impatience when our last conversation ended. "It is not that I am telling you the stories of children," he said. "It is that the creatures I have told you about are what they are, and they behave as one expects them to behave." He reached down and pulled out a short length of split cane from an old, frayed basket that lay beneath the bench on which he sat. "Most of the creatures of the world are straight," he said, holding up the piece of split cane by one end. Then he grasped the opposite end with his other hand and gave it a sharp twist. "But a few creatures—most particularly Rabbit—are twisted. They are full of surprises, as you will see in the stories I will tell you tonight."

HOW RABBIT STOLE OTTER'S COAT

"In Ancient Days the animals were of different sizes and wore coats of various colors and patterns. Some wore long fur and others wore short. Some had rings on their tails, and some had hairless tails. Some had brown coats; others had black or yellow coats. They were always arguing about who looked best, so at last they agreed to hold a contest to decide who wore the finest coat.

"They had heard a great deal about Otter, who lived so far up the creek that he seldom came down to visit the other animals. It was said that he had the finest coat of all, but no one knew exactly how it looked because it had been a long time since anyone had seen him. They did not even know exactly where he lived—only the general direction; but they knew he would come to the contest when the word got out.

Rabbit

"Now, Rabbit wanted to win the contest, but he knew he had no chance against Otter, so Rabbit began scheming to cheat Otter out of the prize. He asked a few sly questions until he learned what trail Otter would take. Then, without saying anything, Rabbit went on ahead, and after four days' travel he met Otter. He knew him at once by his beautiful coat of soft dark fur. Otter was glad to see him and asked him where he was going. 'Oh,' said Rabbit, 'the animals sent me to bring you to the council. Because you live so far away, they were afraid you might not know the road.' Otter thanked him, and they went on together.

"They traveled all day toward the council ground, and at night Rabbit selected their campsite, since Otter was a stranger to that part of the country. They cut down bushes for beds and prepared their camp. The next morning they started on again. In the afternoon Rabbit began to pick up pieces of bark and wood as they went along, tying them into a bundle. When Otter asked what this was for, Rabbit said it was firewood to help them stay warm and comfortable at night. After a while, when it was near sunset, they stopped and made their camp. When supper was over, Rabbit got a stick and whittled it down to a paddle. Intrigued, Otter asked what it was for.

"'I have good dreams when I sleep with a paddle under my head,' said Rabbit.

"After he finished the paddle, Rabbit began to cut away the bushes, clearing an open trail down to the river. Otter, more intrigued than ever, wanted to know what this was for.

Otter

"Said Rabbit, 'This place where we are camped is called The-Place-Where-It-Rains-Fire. Sometimes it rains fire here, and the sky looks a little that way tonight. You go to sleep and I'll sit up and watch, and if fire does begin to rain down, as soon as you hear me shout, you run and jump into the river. Better tuck your coat under that rock over there, so it won't get burnt.'

"Otter did as he was told, and the two of them curled up to go to sleep, but Rabbit kept awake. After a while the fire burned down to red coals. Rabbit called softly to Otter, but he was fast asleep and made no answer. In a little while Rabbit called again, but Otter never stirred. Then Rabbit piled hot coals onto the paddle and threw them up into the air, shouting, 'It's raining fire! It's raining fire!'

"The hot coals fell all around Otter as he awakened and jumped up. 'To the water!' cried Rabbit, and Otter ran and jumped into the river, and he has lived in the water ever since.

"Rabbit took Otter's coat and put it on, discarding his own, and he went on to the council. All the animals were there, and everyone was looking out for Otter. At last they saw him in the distance, and they said one to the other, 'Otter is coming!' and they sent one of the small animals to show him to the best seat. They were all glad to see him, and each went up in turn to welcome him and admire his coat.

But Otter kept his head down, holding one paw over his face. They wondered that he was so bashful, until Bear came up and pulled the paw away, and there was Rabbit's split muzzle. As Rabbit sprang up, Bear struck at him and pulled his tail off, but Rabbit was too quick and got away. He lost his coat, however, and the animals returned it to Otter, its rightful owner. And all Rabbit got for his trouble was a ridiculous short tail."

"So that is Rabbit," said the Raven. "He is the very soul of vanity. He is not content to be who he is, nor is he content with his appearance. He is jealous of others and of what others possess. Jealous people injure themselves, and they often injure those who are closest to them. Moreover, Rabbit seeks to achieve his ends not by skill and hard work, but through trickery. He wants to do everything the easy way, as this next story shows."

HOW BUCK DEER GOT HIS HORNS

"In Ancient Days Buck Deer had no horns. His head was smooth just like a doe's. He was a great runner, and Rabbit was a great jumper, and the animals were all curious to know which of the two could go farther in the same amount of time. They talked about it a good deal, and at last they arranged a match between the two and made a large pair of antlers for a prize to go to the winner. The two were to start together from one side of a thicket and run through it, then turn and come back, and the one who came back out of the thicket first was to be given the horns.

"On the appointed day, all the animals gathered, and the antlers were laid down on the ground at the thicket's edge to mark the starting point. While everybody was admiring the horns, Rabbit said: 'I don't know this part of the country. I want to take a look through the bushes where I am to run.' They thought that would be all right, so Rabbit went into the thicket. He was gone so long that at last the animals suspected he must be up to one of his tricks. They sent a chickadee to look for him, and in the middle of the thicket he found Rabbit gnawing down the bushes and pulling them away until he had a trail cleared nearly to the other side.

"The chickadee quietly flew back and told the other animals. When Rabbit came out at last, they accused him of cheating, but he denied it until they went into the thicket and found the cleared trail. They agreed that such a trickster had no right to enter the race at all, so they gave the antlers to Buck Deer, who was declared to be the best runner, and he has worn them ever since. They told Rabbit that since he was so fond of cutting down bushes, he might do that for a living thereafter, and so he does to this day."

"Have you ever hunted rabbits?" asked the Raven. "They still work hard at clearing small trails through the brush, and so the best way to hunt them is to find their trails, which they always prefer to use when they go about. All you have to do is take a length of twined fiber, make a noose, and position it on the trail, but be careful to thread a length of hard cane on the twine above the noose so the rabbit, once you snare him, cannot chew through the twine.

The old man shook his head and smiled ruefully. "Poor Rabbit. He is always getting himself snared in one way or another. In Ancient Days he was famous for getting his way. Though it often happened that his envy brought its own punishment."

RABBIT AND BEAR

"Bear invited Rabbit to dinner. When he arrived Bear called his wife and said: 'Cook up some beans for dinner. Rabbit loves beans.'

"'But there is no grease to cook with them,' said Bear's wife.

"'Oh,' said Bear, 'that's no problem. Bring me a knife.' She brought him a knife, and Bear took it and split between his toes, while Rabbit looked on in wonder. 'Hmmm. No grease between my toes,' said Bear. 'Well, I know where there is some.' So he cut a small gash in his side and out ran the grease. His wife caught it in a pot and cooked the beans, and they had such a fine dinner that Rabbit and Bear vowed they would always be good friends.

"So Rabbit invited Bear to take dinner with him the next day.

"'Where do you live?' asked Bear. Pointing to an old sedge-grass field, Rabbit replied, 'Way over yonder in a fine house.'

"Bear started the next morning and sought in vain for the fine house, but while wandering about in the sedge he almost stepped on his new friend, who was sleeping in his bed in a clump of sedge.

"'What's this!' cried Rabbit, waking with a start. 'What are you tramping over me for?'

"'Oh, I was trying to find your fine house, but it looks like this

Bear

sedge field is it.' Not at all embarrassed at having been caught in a
lie, Rabbit laughed and invited Bear to be seated, and said he would
order up their dinner now. He called to his wife and told her to cook
up some beans for them.

"'But there is no grease,' she said.

"'That's a small matter,' said Rabbit. 'Bring me a knife.' When his
wife came with a knife, Rabbit held up one of his forefeet and split
between his toes. 'What, no grease here? But I know where I can find
some,' and he gave the knife a thrust into his side. But blood gushed
out instead of fat, and he fell to the ground with a scream.

"Bear cried, 'You skinny little fool, your body is not like mine.' He
lifted his friend all covered with blood and put him on his bed. 'Send
for the doctor,' said Bear to Rabbit's wife, who was weeping bitterly.

"'Run for the doctor,' she said to one of their little children, who
ran at the top of his speed.

"Turkey Buzzard, a famous doctor, came in haste and patched Rabbit up, and in no time at all, he was his old self again."

"That is the way Rabbit is," said the Raven. "Always trying to get everything for himself. It is not that creatures other than Rabbit are never envious, or jealous, or greedy, or never wish to take clever shortcuts. But beings who are on a straight path suppress such feelings. Rabbit, however, can suppress nothing. That is why he is mad for copulation. Rabbit is girl crazy, and he will do anything to lie with a woman."

HOW RABBIT SEDUCED HIS WIFE'S SISTER

"Rabbit was lying down with his head on his wife's lap and she was gently rubbing it. Presently her beautiful sister, who lived with them, rose and said, 'I must go after water,' and she went out.

"Rabbit jumped up and said to his wife, 'I must go and take care of business.' He ran across the stream and hid in some low bushes.

"Then the girl came to the stream and began to get water. From his hiding place, Rabbit asked her in a disguised voice:

"'Is Rabbit at home?'

"'Yes,' she replied, looking in the direction of the voice, but not seeing Rabbit.

"'Tell Rabbit that all the people have agreed to undertake a big hunt, and they have sent me to tell him to be sure to come. He must travel ahead and select a camp and build a fire. No man is to take his wife with him, but every man must take his wife's sister.'

"The girl ran to the house, and Rabbit ran around a different way. When the girl came in, he was again lying with his head on his wife's lap, as if nothing had happened.

"The girl told them what she had heard, but she left out the part about every man taking his wife's sister. Rabbit waited a moment, and then he asked, 'Is that all?' She then told the rest of the story.

"Rabbit's wife said, 'Well, I will stay at home. You must go, my sister, on the hunt. Both of you must go.' Then Rabbit's wife made all things ready for them, and Rabbit and the girl went to the appointed place, reaching it just before the sun went down.

"Rabbit built a fire and swept the ground. He pretended to be perplexed that the other hunters had not come.

"'I am so disappointed,' said he, and running to a log, he jumped up on it and held up his paw to shade his eyes, looking in all directions to see if the hunters could be seen.

"The sun went down, and Rabbit complained bitterly that the hunters had not come. As it grew dark he said, 'Let us go to sleep. You make your bed on that side of the fire, and I will make mine on this side.'

"The place he had selected for the girl had an anthill on it, and when she lay down she could not sleep. She tossed and scratched, tossed and scratched. Then Rabbit began his wooing, and without much trouble he succeeded in seducing his wife's sister."

"In that story he got away with his trick," said the Raven. "We cannot help but smile at him. Rabbit is not an admirable creature, but he is never boring, and perhaps that is why we never tire of hearing stories of his exploits. Coosas will sit all night listening to stories about the outrageous deeds of Rabbit, but that does not mean that they wish to be like him. Far from it. When Coosas play the ball game against another team, they will take the hamstrings of rabbits, cook them into a putrid stew, and then they will sprinkle the stew on the path that the opposing team is to take. This will render the other team timid and skittish. If anyone on a team is infected with the soul of Rabbit, the other players on the team cannot depend on him. Rabbit might be a funny fellow, but you don't want him playing ball on your team."

"But why," I asked, "did all the other four-footeds turn out well and Rabbit turn out so badly? Why is Rabbit, as you say, twisted?"

"Rabbit is an error of *Hesaaketamesee,* the Master of Breath," the old man replied. "In the earliest of Ancient Days, creation got off to a bad start."

I pressed the old man to elaborate, but he said that he was tired, and that it would take a long story to answer my question. So Teresa and I took our leave.

As we walked back to the part of the town in which the Christians were living, I asked Teresa about this new character, the Master of Breath.

"The Master of Breath is God," she said simply.

Hesaaketamesse — God

5 *Master of Breath and the Great Ones*

I was anxious for this conversation to begin. Was I at long last going to learn something about Coosa philosophy that would go beyond what the Raven called leaves on the water? Teresa and I settled into our customary places, but the old man would not be hurried. He insisted on brewing up a beverage out of a small variety of holly leaves that he had parched in a pot over a fire. "This is *ásse,* our beloved white drink," he said, though this made no sense to me because the beverage was very dark in color. Before he would begin, he insisted that I drink a draught of the stuff from a conch shell cup filled almost to the brim. Its taste was somewhat bitter but not unpleasant. The Raven also drank down a large cup of it, but he offered none to Teresa. He continued to regard her, as before, as someone who was present and yet not present. A few minutes after he drank his cup of *ásse,* I was disturbed when the old man stepped outside of his house and vomited, a revolting act to which there was more significance than I at first realized, and about which I will write more at a later time. The old man seemed to expect me to do as he had done, but even though I feared the beverage might be an emetic, I had no inclination to vomit.

I was taken aback when he then spoke sharply to Teresa, questioning her closely about some matter. From what I could gather, he at first doubted the truthfulness of her response and pressed her to answer further. When I asked her to tell me what had passed between them, she became evasive. I insisted that she answer, and at last she replied: "He wants to know if I am *eepóóska*—a menstruating woman."

I was appalled that the old man would ask such an improper question of a woman. I was also baffled. Why should her menstrual condition have any bearing on whether our conversation should proceed? For such was the implication of his questioning her. But, rather than inquire about it and allow him to embark on one of his digressions, which invariably followed a path so winding it would tempt a saint to blasphemy, I pressed him to tell me about the Master of Breath.

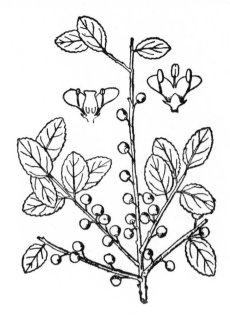

The old man leaned back against the wall and closed his eyes, as was his habit when he was choosing his words most carefully.

HOW THIS WORLD BEGAN

"In earliest Ancient Days, there was only the watery under world below and the upper world above, and *Hesaaketamesee*—the Master of Breath—lived in both. But most particularly the Master of Breath lived in water, the stuff on which all life depends. Moist is life, and dry is death. The upper world is like an inverted bowl that one lays upon the ground, except it has a number of levels. [The Raven illustrated this by picking up a small stick of wood and drawing a design in the dirt floor: a circle made of two concentric lines.] The upper world is

the abode of all the original great four-footeds and flyers. They are creatures such as Deer, Eagle, Peregrine Falcon, Possum, Terrapin, and many others. They have the same form as their descendants today, except that they are much larger and more perfectly formed. Rabbit,

Shell cup

Bear, and several other creatures were not at first among their number.

"All in the upper world is clear, blindingly clear. There is no uncertainty in the upper world. Words are uttered in the upper world, but they are words so stark and pure they hurt your ears. A word uttered in the upper world is as strong as a tree crashing down in the heart of an ancient forest. They are words like:

> Red is the blood.
> White is the spittle.
> Red is not white.
> White is not red.
> Red is the left hand and
>   white is the right hand.
> When red left clasps white right,
>   that is life.
> When red left and white right unclasp,
>   that is death.

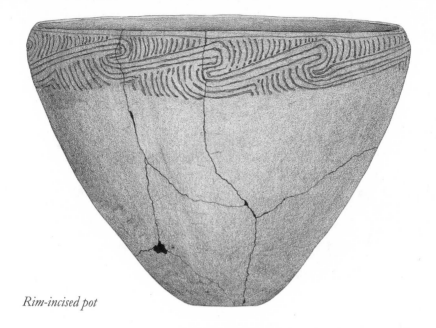

Rim-incised pot

Such words are the old, straight, beloved speech, and they can never be doubted. To the ears of ordinary people such words are like thunder-claps.

"The under world lies beneath the water, a place of chaos and confusion. The creatures of the under world are not like the creatures of this world, the earth. Their features are confused. In the under world snakes have wings, fish have antlers, cougars have fins. Creatures in the under world do not walk one step after another, but move with the curvy crawl of a snake." [He picked up the stick, and beneath the concentric circles he drew a curved line. I had previously seen this curved line incised on Coosa bowls and jars, just beneath the rims.]

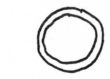

"The creatures of the under world speak, but it is all mumbles and hisses. One catches only a word here and there, and these are often ambiguous. Only a few people can make sense of the language of the under world; it is the language of things hidden and of things yet to be.

"So in the beginning there were only these two levels, the upper world above and the watery under world below. Before long, the creatures of the upper world began wondering what lay beneath the water. They were bored. There was no delight in being in the upper world because there are no surprises there. They asked for a volunteer to dive beneath the water to see what could be found. They first asked four ivory-billed woodpeckers who were clinging to some clouds, with the tips of their tails sticking down into the water. But the woodpeckers refused, and their tails bear water markings to this day. One animal after another was asked, but each said he would not go because he was not at home in the water. Even animals that were at home in the water—beaver and otter—refused to go and search for a firm place. Finally, Crawfish offered to go down. He descended to the water and swam in every direction, finding no place where he could rest. Then he dived down to the bottom, and after a little while he came up with some soft mud in his pincers. When this tiny bit of mud reached the surface, it began to grow. It grew and it grew, faster and faster, until it made the island on which we all live today.

"At first no one could see this newly made land. Everything was in darkness. Firefly flew around trying to illuminate the world, but his light was too faint. So the Master of Breath took some mud and made it into a male sphere and he spun him around very rapidly until he began to glow like a clay pot that is being fired. Master of Breath flung him out into space, but he only glowed faintly white and did not give out nearly enough light. So Master of Breath took up some more mud and fashioned it into a larger female sphere, and he put a fierce spin on her so that she glowed ever so brightly red, like hickory wood coals in a hearth. 'You shall be Sister Sun,' he said, 'and that other one will be Brother Moon.' After he had made Brother Moon and Sister Sun, Master of Breath had little bits of mud sticking to his hands. Irritated, he flung them up into the sky to form the stars. That is how it all began.

"There is much to say about Sun and Moon. Sun sucks up water from the earth—on hot days you can see fogs, vapors, and clouds. It is the Moon who gives it back as rain, hail, and snow. Red Sun illuminates the day, and White Moon illuminates the night. This arrangement works very well, though on occasion a great toad in the upper world tries to swallow them. When that happens, you can see his toad's mouth move across the luminary, and the world begins to darken. This makes people anxious, and they run out of their houses and make a great deal of noise to frighten off the toad.

"The Sun is mistress of the upper world." [As if to illustrate what he said, he took his stick and drew a small circle-and-cross within the circles he had drawn earlier.]

"Even though Sun and Moon are sister and brother, they are not close," said the Raven. "My next story explains why."

WHY SUN AND MOON ARE NOT TOGETHER IN THE SKY

"Sun resides in the east and Moon, her brother, resides in the west. In Ancient Days, Sun had a lover who came each month in the dark of night to lie with her. He would always leave before dawn, and even though she talked to him all night, she never got to see his face and she could never learn who he was. She was curious to know, and at last she devised a plan to find out. As they were sitting together in the dark of the house where she lived, she placed her hand in the ashes of the fireplace, and then she rubbed her lover's face, saying 'Your face is so cold. Come closer, and I will make you warm.'

"The next night, when Moon rose up in the sky, Sun saw to her horror that his face was smudged with ashes. Then she knew that he was her mystery lover. Thus discovered, Moon was so ashamed of himself that he began keeping as far away from Sun as he could, staying on the other side of the sky.

"As for Sun, she was furious at what Brother Moon had done. Whenever she thought about it, she would become so angry that she would bleed from her body. Whenever she was in this condition, she and her brother were particularly careful to avoid each other because any conflict between them would have caused a calamity for the world."

"What a way to start the world!" said the Raven. "It was a grievous offense, even in Ancient Days, for brother and sister to lie together. Still today Moon always keeps his distance from Sun, and when she comes up in the east while he is still going down in the west, he makes himself into a pale wisp so that he can hardly be seen."

He shook his head. "Sun and Moon are such powerful spirits, so hard to fathom. Coosas do not refer to them by their names but instead call them 'luminary of the day' and 'luminary of the night.' We also call them 'Grandmother' and 'Grandfather.' Anyone foolish enough to utter their real names without first taking precautions will suffer for it.

"Were we taking precautions when we drank the *ásse*?" I asked him.

"Yes," said the old man. "But I don't want to talk about that now. I want to tell you what came of Sun and Moon lying together so shamefully."

WHERE THUNDER CAME FROM

"The product of Sun's incestuous relationship with Moon was an infant who did not glow continuously, as did his mother and father. Instead, he gave off flashes of light. Separately, each of his parents doted on him. Sun dressed him in lightning, and Moon dressed him in the colors of the rainbow. They named him Thunder. He inherited some of Sun's anger, and he is an active fellow, always hurling his lightning arrows and war clubs down to earth. Whenever one of these strikes a tree, it shatters it, riving off bark and splinters, and the tree usually dies. The splinters from lightning-struck trees are powerful. People give such trees a wide berth, and if they happen to go too close to them they break out in sores."

"Thunder is an interesting fellow," said the Raven. "He combines fire and water in his being. Thunder adores the sacred metal [he meant copper], which is the metal of the sun because it shows her color, and it is also the metal of the moon because it shines like the surface of water. When, in some of our ceremonies, we gaze across the surface of a river and see the reflections of the rising sun, it has the same appearance as Thunder's metal.

"Now I will tell you how fourness came into the world."

MASTER OF BREATH AND THE FOUR DIRECTIONS

"At first the earth was moist, water-logged, and it seemed on the verge of sinking back beneath the water. So the Master of Breath took four cords—red, white, blue, and black—and attached them to the four edges of the island earth, in the directions of the four winds. He tied the red one to the east—*hasóóssa;* the black one to the west—*hasakláátka;* the blue to the north—*honiltha;* and the white to the south—*wahála.* Then he tied the other ends of the four cords to the sky vault. This is what keeps the earth from sinking beneath the water. [The old man picked up his stick and drew a looped square on the floor.]"

"The cords have to be renewed," said the old man, "for if they were to break, it is beneath the water we go! One of the purposes of our *posketa* ceremony, celebrated every year, is to renew these cords.

"I will tell you now about how the land came to be as we know it."

THE MOUNTAINS, THE SEVENTH HEIGHT, AND THE UNDER WORLD

"At first the earth was flat and very soft and wet. The animals in the upper world were anxious to get down, and they sent out different flyers to see if the land was dry enough. But none of them could find a place to alight, and each one came back again to the upper world. At last the animals were sure the earth had had time enough to dry, and they sent out Buzzard and told him to go and make it ready for them. This was great Turkey Buzzard, the grandfather of all the turkey buzzards we see now. He flew all over the earth, low down near the ground, but the land was still soft. He flew for so long that he grew very tired, and his wings began to flap and strike the ground. Wherever they struck the earth there was a valley, and where they turned up again there was a mountain. When the animals above saw this, they became afraid that if Buzzard did not cease his flapping, the whole world would be mountains, so they called him back. This country around us is where his wings hit, and the land of Coosa remains full of mountains to this day.

"When the earth finally dried out and the animals came down, it was still too dark to see very much. So they set the Sun on a groove to go every day across the island from east to west, just overhead. But this made it too hot, and Crawfish—the Earth-Maker—had his shell scorched a bright red, so that his meat was spoiled, and Coosas do not eat it. They put the Sun another handbreadth higher in the above, but it was still too hot. They raised her up another time, and another, until she was seven handbreadths high, just under the sky arch. They saw that this was right, and they left it so. This is why priests and healers call the highest place 'the seventh height,' because it is seven handbreadths above the earth. Every day Sun goes along just beneath the sky arch, and at sundown she goes beneath the edge of the arch and returns at night over the upper side to the starting place.

"In addition to the world above and the world in which we live, there is another world under this one, and it is like ours in everything—animals, plants, people—save that the seasons are different. The streams that come down from the mountains are the trails by which we reach this under world, and the springs at their heads are the doorways by which we enter it. But in order to go into the under world one must fast and be purified by going to water and must have one of the under world people for a guide.

"We know that the seasons in the under world are the opposites of ours because when you put your hand in the water of a spring it is always warmer than the air in winter, but it is colder than the air in summer."

"The under world is what makes everything so interesting," said the Raven. "It is full of surprises. Under world creatures have beds to sit and sleep on, just like we do, but theirs are made of snakes plaited together. And their footstools are actually large turtles. Sit on one of those and see what happens!

"When the plants and animals came down from the upper world to this world, they began to turn into the ordinary plants and animals that we know today."

NIGHT CREATURES AND EVERGREENS,
RABBIT AND HORNED SERPENT

"The Master of Breath told animals and plants to watch and keep awake for seven nights, just as young men now fast and keep awake when they pray to their medicine. The animals and plants tried to do this, and nearly all were awake through the first night, but the next night several dropped off to sleep, and the third night others were asleep, and then others, until, on the seventh night, of all the animals only Owl, Cougar, Bat, and Flying Squirrel were still awake. To these were given the power to see and to go about in the dark. Of the trees, only the cedar, the pine, the spruce, the holly, and the laurel were awake to the end, and to them it was given to be always green and to be greatest for medicines. To the other trees the Master of Breath said: 'Because you have not endured to the end you shall lose your hair every winter.'

"Master of Breath wanted some new creatures living on the earth. He copulated with Earth, who would have refused him had she not been so moist and tangled up with vines. It was a bad happening all the way around. What later issued from this coupling was not what the Master of Breath intended. When it was born, it was a wet thing, with its hair plastered against its sides, with long ears, a ridiculous tail, and a leering split muzzle. The creature looked up, and when he saw Master of Breath he tittered, cackled, and guffawed, falling to the ground, slapping his sides. It was Rabbit.

"Earth was still moist and heavy, still not dried out by Sun. Rabbit, lacking any shred of modesty, was sure that he knew how to populate the earth with new creatures. So he lay with Earth, his own mother. She was furious, but she was still too heavy with moisture to resist. In no time at all, the issue of this unfortunate union was Horned Serpent—a creature with the body of a rattlesnake, but with antlers and a cougar's head. One antler is the red of summer, the other one is the blue of winter. Horned Serpent is a huge, powerful creature who is at home everywhere, and therefore he is not truly at home anywhere. He can live beneath the water and beneath this world; he is also at home on earth; and amazingly, it is even said that he can sometimes spin round and round and fly into the above. Horned Serpent was born full of resentment because of his disreputable father. Horned Serpent and Thunder, both born of incest, have always been allies, and they are the masters of rain. Horned Serpent is so powerful he can change the course of rivers.

"Horned Serpent can make blue lightning and a sound like thunder, and he will rear up out of the water in a storm and let Thunder shoot his yellow lightning arrows at him. But they are only playing, and Thunder's arrows never find their mark. Sometimes in a storm Horned Serpent will rear up on the land, do great destruction in a powerful, spinning, roaring wind, and then pull his tail up into the clouds and disappear. He sheds his horns and they grow back in different colors. These horns that have been shed are powerful medicine. There is nothing stronger. Red horn is the best, and even some shavings from one of these enables one to powerfully attract both game and women.

"With creatures like Rabbit and Horned Serpent being born, the Master of Breath knew he had to do something about the wet earth. So he ordered his helpers — the four winds — to dry it out. First came the red wind of the east, the wind of spring; next the white wind of the south, the wind of summer; then the black wind of the west, the wind of fall; and finally the blue wind of the north, the wind of winter. With each blowing in its turn, they soon dried out the earth.

"Chaos comes from the likes of Rabbit and Horned Serpent, but the four winds bring us order and balance. They are always busy, blowing this way and that, and they are the messengers of the Master of Breath. We are ever mindful of them and try to keep them constantly adjusted. If one of them blows too hard, we invoke its adversary to blow in and oppose it. If all four were to blow at once, it would surely blow down everything on earth. At times we feed small pieces of venison to fire. One piece goes in the center, and then other small pieces are fed to the four directions. Then the rest of the meat is passed through the flames and given to the women to cook for the priests. This helps to appease the winds and keep them in balance.

"The best wind is the mild one from the south. Sometimes the west and south winds blow at the same time, and it brings in a great deal of rain. If the north wind is too much in power, it becomes very cold, as in the winter season. In the summer, the red, white, and black winds combine their forces to completely oppose the blue north wind. But then we need the cold wind again for the winter rest that brings the spring. All of the winds are good in their turn, so long as they stay in balance."

The Raven fell silent, and I was about to speak when we were startled by a muffled, mournful sound outside the house. The black bird stirred on his perch and said *pruk, pruk,* ruffling the feathers on his chest and upper legs, making himself appear to be larger than he was. The old man got up and stepped outside. He listened intently, and then he came back in. "It is only a great horned owl," he said as he stroked Pruk's feathers. "Ravens hate great horned owls."

Now, finally, I could ask him some questions. I hardly knew where to begin. "Why did creation go so badly?" I asked. "Why could not the Master of Breath create the world as he wished?"

"Ah," said the old man, "Feryada asked the same thing. It is different with Allah, he told me. According to Feryada, there is no god but Allah, and Allah is all-powerful. But Master of Breath is not like that. He is the greatest spirit, but not the only spirit. And Rabbit was not his only error."

The conversation agitated my spirit. These were such absurd beliefs. Huge, preexisting animal spirits in Heaven who are responsible for creating the earth! The sun and moon as spirits, not planets! A deity who is more lustful than he is supreme, who copulates with the earth, and who cannot seem to do anything right! And Coosas believe they have an answer for everything. How can the Gospel ever find a way into their world? Where are its weaknesses, its unguarded portals? I decided to challenge the old man.

"What does the Master of Breath look like?" I asked.

"No one has ever seen him," the old man said, "but the priests among us who listen at shoals where water breaks and rushes say they sometimes hear the Master of Breath in the water. And of course we can hear him in the wind. But no one has ever seen him. He has no body. He is breath."

"If the Master of Breath is so powerful," I asked, "why did he make so many errors? Why Rabbit, Horned Serpent, and Thunder?"

"Perfection belongs to the upper world," the old man said. "The upper world is as perfect as the under world is imperfect. What the Master of Breath seems to have wanted was a world between these two—the earth on which we live."

Then he put a question to me. "If your God is so all-powerful, why does Satan exist? Robles and Feryada often spoke of Satan when things went wrong for them."

Here, I thought, was a chance to penetrate his dark world with the light of God. I started to explain to him how evil entered the Garden of Eden.

"Oh," he said, "you mean with Adam and Eve. Robles and Feryada told me about them. The Sun also begat such a couple—First Man and First Woman, and I will tell you about them the next time we converse."

As we returned to our quarters, Teresa and I walked in silence for a long time. My head was swimming with all that the old man had told me. It shocked me that though he had already heard from Feryada and Robles the truth of God in our scriptures, this knowledge served only to reinforce his own distorted views. Did they tell him about the true beginning of the world, when the earth was without form and void, and there was darkness over the deep and the Spirit hovered over the waters, and God said, "Let there be light"? Would not the Raven say that this is exactly what he told me in that fantastic tale of his? Did Feryada and Robles tell him of Noah and the receding flood, and the raven and then the dove sent out to find dry land? It is the same tale, he would say. I know he would say that. So what hope do we have to bring the true light to these people if everything we tell them is folded into their own all-encompassing darkness? I was very discouraged.

When Teresa spoke, she too was low in spirit. She was exhausted, she said, and she felt oppressed by the rules the old man was enforcing upon her, rules that she as a Christian had renounced. I counseled her to be patient, reminding her that God depended upon her translating the old man's words for me. I assured her that God knows that the dark ways of her childhood world had been purged from her soul forever.

Had Teresa truly rid herself of her pagan ways? Back in Coosa, with all the familiar scenes of her youth before her eyes, was she not in her deepest heart torn between the angels of Christendom and the demons of Coosa?

When I went to fetch Teresa to go to the old man's house, she was pale and trembling and said that she was ill. But when I touched her forehead, it was cool, and she did not smell of illness. Without her, I could not communicate with the old man, and I insisted that she accompany me. He had at last gotten beyond telling children's stories. I was curious to know what the old man would say about the creation of the first man and woman. These were the errors that future Christian missionaries would have to surmount if they wished to bring the Coosas to Christ. Without Teresa I could learn nothing. She relented and came with me.

As the fire crackled in the hearth, the old man again served me a shell cup full of the *ásse* drink. As I held the cup to my lips and drank the bitter brew, he uttered the long, drawn-out syllables *Yah-hóó-la*. When I asked Teresa what these syllables meant, she shrugged her shoulders and gave me a blank look.

Again the old man studiously ignored Teresa while he and I drank the *ásse*. But when he saw how pale she was and how she faltered, he questioned her as he had done in the past—especially sharply, it seemed to me. When she answered him, she lowered her eyes and would not meet mine.

What she said in her soft voice satisfied him, and he began to speak.

FIRST MAN AND FIRST WOMAN

"Once in Ancient Days the Sun had a very bad time. As she began arising in the east, she saw her smudge-faced brother fading away in the west. Then, making her fiery journey across the sky, she looked down on the earth and saw Rabbit hopping about like a lunatic, leering up at her with his split-lipped grin. And she saw Horned Serpent roiling about, smashing foliage and hissing his foul breath up and down the sides of *eekana lthafone,* the Backbone of the Earth, the ridge of mountains just to the north of Coosa.

"The Sun became angrier and angrier at the disorder and broken rules on earth. She got herself into such a state that drops of her menstrual blood fell to earth, and it so happened that two drops fell on some foliage that Horned Serpent had crushed up into a tangle. As the two drops of the Sun's blood hit the tangle of foliage—those destined to be the most wondrous plants—they began to sizzle, and smoke, and then they began to wriggle. At last, two beings emerged from the tangle—First Woman and First Man. They came to life on a mountain where the stones were piled up by Horned Serpent's writhing.

"First Man and First Woman were hungry as could be. How would they be able to make a living? First Man journeyed to the western mountains to look for food, and there he found a cave whose entrance was covered with a large rock. He peeped inside and saw that it was teeming with all the best animals, the succulent ones. Then he made himself a bow out of a length of black locust wood, and he made some arrows out of cane. He pulled back the rock, and when a deer sprang out, he dropped the rock back in place to keep the others in. Then he quickly drew his bow and let loose an arrow, striking squarely into the deer's vitals. He took his kill back to First Woman, and they ate it raw. Whenever he hunted in this way, he always killed game, and he became forever known as Lucky Hunter. Lucky Hunter told First Woman that she must never, never follow him when he went on his hunts.

"Then it fell to First Woman to do her part in getting food. She made herself a short-handled hoe from a hickory limb, and she went out searching for food. She happened upon Horned Serpent, who was sunning himself in the morning light. First Woman struck her hoe into Horned Serpent's back, almost killing him, and—whoosh—vines and tendrils sprang forth and twined about her body, forming succulent squashes. Ever afterward, squash has been the easiest vegetable to cultivate, but because First Woman injured him, Horned Serpent has always shunned people.

"Getting squash was ridiculously easy, but after First Woman ate it, she was still hungry. She asked Lucky Hunter to build her a little storehouse up on poles that could only be reached by climbing a ladder.

The storehouse Lucky Hunter built was rectangular, about eight by twelve feet, with three poles set into the ground on each of the long sides. Then he set longer poles in the ground in the center of both ends of the house, so that a ridge pole could be set on top of them and a peaked roof built to cover it. He plastered the cane walls with clay and built a thatched roof overhanging two feet on all sides to keep the rain away from the structure. He left short stubs of limbs on one of the tall end-posts so First Woman could climb up and enter the small door to the room within. The shade beneath the storehouse was to be a refuge from the heat of the summer sun, and it was also a dry space where small cooking fires could be built.

"First Woman told him that she would never, never follow him into the woods if he would never, never follow her into her storehouse on poles. Then she climbed up the ladder into the little house, and she placed a pack basket on the floor and rubbed her navel — so — and ears of corn fell from beneath her skirt into the basket. She leaned over and rubbed her breasts — so — and beans fell into the basket, filling it to the brim. She took home this basket of food and served it to Lucky Hunter along with the squash. It was delicious and filling, though it was hard to chew because they did not possess fire and she could not cook their food. Ever afterward First Woman was called Corn Woman.

"At this time the earth was not as wet as it had been before, but it was still covered by cold fogs. There was no fire anywhere, and because they could not see in the dark, Corn Woman and Lucky Hunter became anxious whenever night fell. They also got cold every night, chilled to the bone without the heat of the Sun. Their jaws ached from eating uncooked food, and they became flatulent. The only fire came from Thunder, who hurled his flaming arrows and war clubs to earth, but with everything so sodden, the fires quickly went out. Finally, one of Thunder's clubs fell into a large hollow sycamore tree and started a fire inside. All the creatures on earth could see smoke coming out of the top of the tree, but the tree was on an island and they could not retrieve any fire from it because of the water.

"The animals took pity on Corn Woman and Lucky Hunter, and one after another of them attempted to go after fire. Crow volunteered first, and because he was so large and strong, all thought that he would surely be successful. He flew high above the water and lit on the top of the sycamore tree, but as he sat there, looking this way and that, caw-cawing, the heat from the fire scorched all of his feathers black, and he was so frightened he flew back across the water to earth. Crows have been vigilant and jittery ever since.

"Little Screech Owl was the next to try. He reached the tree and perched on top of it. But as he looked down to try to see the fire, a hot blast hit him in the face and almost put out his eyes. He could hardly see to fly back to earth, and he had poor vision for a long time afterward. This is why his eyes are red.

"Next Barred Owl flew over to the tree, but by this time the fire was burning so hot that when he looked down into the hollow tree, the smoke nearly blinded him, and ashes carried up by the smoke made white rings around his eyes. He came back a failure. Barred owls still rub the white rings around their eyes today, but they have not been able to rub them off.

"When the birds saw that they would not be able to succeed in getting fire, the snakes began volunteering. Little Black Racer volunteered first. He swam across the water and crawled through the grass to the tree, entering through a small hole at its base. But the heat and smoke inside were intense, and after darting this way and that across the hot ashes, he was almost on fire by the time he managed to get out through the same hole through which he had entered. He was scorched black from one end to the other, and little black racers to this day still have the habit of darting frantically about as if they are trapped.

"Next Great Black Snake—the climber—swam over to the island. He crawled through the grass and then went slowly up the side of the tree, wedging his body against knots and lumps of bark until he reached the top. He began crawling down inside, but the heat and smoke turned him black, and he fled for his life, climbing back up to the top and out again, falling to the ground with a thump. He slithered away from the burning tree and swam back home.

"Now it began to look bad. If all the birds and snakes had failed, what could the four-footeds expect to achieve? All the four-footeds thought up some excuse for not trying.

"At last little Water Spider said that she would try. All of the animals were surprised, and some of them laughed. This was not the water spider that looks a little like a large, skinny mosquito. It is the one with black, downy hair and red stripes on her body. 'How will you bring the fire back?' the animals all asked at once. 'I'm clever, and I'll figure out a way,' she replied. She spun a thread from her body and fashioned it up into a little bowl, which stuck tightly to her back. Then,

Water spider: shell gorget

causing not a ripple, she skipped over the surface of the water to the island. She crawled through the grass to the base of the tree, entered through the small hole, popped a little coal into her basket, and then skipped merrily back across the water. From this coal, as tinder and dry wood was carefully fed to it, a great fire was built, and Corn Woman and Lucky Hunter and all the animals danced around it. This fire has existed on earth to this very day. This is everyday fire—the fire people use to heat and illuminate their houses and to cook their food. There is another kind of fire—pure fire of the Sun—but that is another story.

"Corn Woman and Lucky Hunter had many children, but they noticed that each of the two sexes possessed something of the nature of the other. The males were outwardly males, with penises, but inside they had something of the nature of females; the females were outwardly female, with vaginas, but inside they had something of the nature of males. Corn Woman and Lucky Hunter saw that they must take measures to keep everyone from getting mixed up. They began devising ways of keeping the two sexes as separate and opposed as red blood is opposed to white saliva. When a boy was born they wrapped him in a cougar skin and placed a tiny bow and arrow in his hands; when a girl was born they wrapped her in a deerskin and placed a tiny pack basket in her hands. When boys reached puberty, they were taken out into the woods, and there they had to fast and remain awake for several nights on end, as they were hazed and instructed in the lore of men. And when girls reached puberty, they were taken to a small rude hut that was built near the town, and there they fasted and remained awake while they were instructed in the lore of women. After these rituals, the boys henceforth were required to wear breechcloths between their legs and tied about their middle with a knotted belt, and the girls were required to wear short skirts tied about their middle with a belt. The right end of the belt worn by both men and women is male and the left end is female, and the knot is the joining of the two.

"Throughout their lives, the sons and daughters of Corn Woman and Lucky Hunter were required to observe rules of behavior. Whenever the daughters menstruated, they had to remove themselves from the company of men. They were especially prohibited from placing menstrual blood in flowing water. Whenever the sons were to embark on important ventures, such as war or games with the other towns, they had to be secluded from the company of women, and they were especially enjoined from placing spittle in a fire. Placing menstrual blood in flowing water or spitting into a fire is dangerous.

"But in the course of time, it so happened that Corn Woman became careless and allowed some menstrual blood to fall into the river. Their youngest son — their baby — played near this river every day, and one day Corn Woman and Lucky Hunter thought that they heard two children talking down by the river. That night they questioned their son, and he said that he had been playing with a little boy who came out of the water. This little boy said that he was his elder brother, but that his mother had thrown him away. He was so lively and inventive, he was fun to play with. But try as they might, Lucky Hunter and Corn Woman could not catch sight of the little boy who lived in the water.

"One night they told their son that they wanted to see the little boy who came from the water. The next day he was to wrestle with the boy, and while he had him pinned down, Lucky Hunter and Corn Woman would rush out and capture the boy. The next day their son did as

Wild Thing and his brother: "spaghetti" gorget

they asked, and as he pinned down the strange boy and yelled for his mother and father, they came running out. The strange boy yelled like crazy: 'Let me go! Let me go! She threw me away!' But even though the boy shouted at the top of his lungs, they held him fast. They realized that he had been born of Corn Woman's menstrual blood in the river's water, and so they took him home to raise. They kept him in their house and fed him proper food, but he was always wild, and he was too clever by far. He had long hair, a long nose, and a forked tongue, and he talked incessantly. He was always breaking rules and getting into trouble. He became known as *Fách:aséko,* Wild Thing. They tamed him a little, but he never broke his ties to the under world, and in time Lucky Hunter and Corn Woman realized that he had extraordinary powers and abilities. He and their youngest son became the best of friends. People began referring to these two brothers as *apóókta,* the Twosome."

The Raven paused. "This is a long story," he said. "I have not yet come to the end, but I must stop and rest for a moment."

Teresa said that she was feeling ill and was afraid she might vomit. She needed some fresh air. As she walked out into the darkness, the old man tried to communicate something to me by gestures. I could not be sure what he was trying to say, but I think he was more concerned than usual about Teresa's presence on this day. Perhaps her indisposition made him suspect that her menstrual time had begun. I could not be sure. I tried to indicate to him that without her I could understand nothing he said.

When Teresa came back inside, looking none too steady, the old man eyed her for a long time, weighing the matter. I was afraid he would call an end to the session, but finally he returned to his story.

THE TWOSOME

"Lucky Hunter was amazing. Every time he went hunting, he returned with game—deer, turkey, raccoon, rabbit, duck, bobwhite quail—and all was succulent. Wild Thing and his brother went hunting with their little bows and arrows, but they seldom hit anything. They could not understand how their father could be so great a marksman, such a killer of game, so they determined to find out how he did it.

"One day Lucky Hunter struck off toward the west, and the Twosome secretly followed him. He climbed up a mountain, and at a certain place he lifted up a rock. A beautiful buck came running out, and Lucky Hunter dropped the rock to close the entrance and instantly shot the buck dead. He field-dressed it, carefully disposing of the offal, and then he set out for home.

"'Aha,' said Wild Thing, 'so that's how he does it!' The two of them ran home, reaching there before Lucky Hunter, burdened with the venison, could arrive. The boys pretended that they had been there all the while.

"A few days later they went to the special mountain, climbed up its side to the cave, and pushed away the rock that was blocking the entrance. A deer came running out, and both of the boys shot an arrow at it. Both of them missed. Then another deer ran out, and another and another. The boys became confused, unable to gather their wits, and in their frustration they both struck one of the deer's tails with their bows, knocking it into an upright position. In those days deer's

Deer

tails hung down like the tails of other four-footed animals. The boys liked this sport, and both of them struck the tails of deer after deer, and thus it is that deer carry their tails this way to this day when they are alarmed and in flight.

"Other animals began running out of the cave—raccoons, rabbits, squirrels, possums, and others. No bears ran out because there were no bears at this time. Then came the birds, great flocks of turkeys, passenger pigeons, and bobwhite quail flying up in a cloud that darkened the sky. They made such a loud roar with their wings that Lucky Hunter heard it, and when he came out of his house and saw the multitude of birds in the sky, he said to himself, 'Can my boys have done this? I must go and see.'

"Lucky Hunter went to the mountain and climbed up to the cave. He found Wild Thing and his brother standing at the entrance, blankly looking about. The entrance to the cave was open, and all the animals had escaped. Lucky Hunter was furious. He strode over to the corner of the cave where four large, lidded jars stood. He kicked the first one over and fleas swarmed out; he knocked over another and lice scurried out; from another bedbugs crawled all over the place; and from yet another gnats flew up in a cloud. The bugs crawled and flew at the boys and began biting them. The boys yelled and screamed as they flailed at the voracious insects, and they finally fell to the ground, nearly dead.

"When Lucky Hunter thought they had been punished enough, he picked them up and brushed the insects off of them. 'You boys have always had plenty to eat,' he said sternly. 'Whenever we needed food, all I had to do was come to this cave, open the door, and shoot the first animal that ran out. But from now on, whenever you want a deer or a turkey, you will have to go to the woods and hunt all over for them, and often you will not be able to kill anything. What a mess you have made! Now get out of my sight! Go home, and maybe Corn Woman will be able to get up something for you to eat.'

"The Twosome hightailed it, and when they got home tired and hungry, their bodies were covered with welts. When they asked their mother for something to eat, she said: 'We have no meat, but we have all the vegetables anyone would want. I will be back in a little while.'

"'Where does she get all this vegetable food?' asked Wild Thing. 'We've got to see this with our own eyes. Let's go.'

"They followed Corn Woman and saw her climb up a ladder to enter a small house high up on posts. They climbed up the ladder and peeped through a crack in the mud-plastered wall. They saw her place a pack basket in the middle of the floor. She stood over it and rubbed her navel, and ears of corn fell into the basket, one after another. She rubbed her breasts and beans poured into the basket. There was plenty of squash already stored in the little house because it grew in profusion from vines in their refuse heap.

"The boys were aghast. 'Only an evil sorcerer could do this,' Wild Thing said. 'Evil sorcerers must be killed. We know what we must do.' They ran home ahead of their mother.

"When Corn Woman arrived, she knew their thoughts immediately. 'So, you two half-wits are going to kill me.'

"'Oh yes, we must,' said Wild Thing and his brother, speaking in one voice.

"'It will do no good for me to tell you that you are making a big mistake,' said Corn Woman. 'So at least do as I tell you. When you have killed me, clear the weeds and bushes to make a large field in

Blue jay

front of our house. You will have to work hard to do this. Drag my body seven times around the circle of the field. Then drag my body in the four directions across the circular field. This will take a great deal more work. Then fast and stay awake all night, and the next morning you will have plenty of food growing in the field.

"'And Wild Thing,' she added, 'I bequeath to you this flute and headdress.' The headdress was decorated with ribbons and tufts of feathers, some of which were blue and white and others of which were yellow and green. 'You must always wear the headdress and you must play the flute often,' she said.

"After receiving these instructions, the boys raised their war clubs and struck their mother on her head, killing her instantly. Then they cut off her head and placed it on top of the roof of their house, facing it to the west. 'Now, Mother, keep a lookout to see your husband coming,' they said.

"Wild Thing put on the headdress and went outside with his brother. As they walked along, Wild Thing played upon his flute, and as he did—unknown to him—the feathers on his headdress turned into raucous blue jays and yellow and green Carolina parakeets, and the ribbons turned into hissing spreading vipers.

"They cleared off land in front of their house, but instead of clearing a large field, they only cleared four little spots. Instead of drag-

Carolina parakeet

ging their mother's body around and across the entire field, they only dragged it across the four spots of cleared ground, and they only did so twice. Wherever her blood fell on the ground, corn and beans sprang up. It is said that because of the Twosome's negligence, corn does not grow everywhere, but only in spots. And because they dragged her body only twice, people can get only two crops a year from a field instead of four. The boys did manage to stay awake that night, and so the next morning, just as Corn Woman had promised, the corn was full grown and ready to harvest.

"When Lucky Hunter came home, he had only been able to kill a single, scrawny rabbit. 'Where is Corn Woman?' he asked. 'Oh, she was an evil sorcerer,' said the boys, 'and we killed her with our war clubs. Her head is up on the roof, and she has been watching out for you.'

"'You fools,' Lucky Hunter thundered. 'You two are so headstrong and stupid I should kill both of you on the spot. Since I am your father, I must spare you. But I cannot bear to live with you any longer, and I am going to go and live with the wolves. Wolves are loving parents, and their cubs do not kill their mothers. In any battle they all stand so solidly with each other that none can defeat them.'

"Lucky Hunter walked away without another word. But Wild Thing transformed himself into a piece of bird's down and floated through the air and lit on Lucky Hunter's shoulder. After a while, Lucky Hunter reached the wolves' town house. The wolves were holding council inside, and Lucky Hunter strode in without noticing the piece of bird's down on his shoulder.

"'What do you want?' growled the chief of the wolves.

"Lucky Hunter replied, 'I have two boys at home who are so ignorant, heedless, and irresponsible that they are a threat to everyone. I want you and your gang to go there in seven days and play ball with them.' The wolves understood that Lucky Hunter had in mind a contest a great deal more serious than a ball game. Wild Thing understood this too, and he contrived to be blown by a breeze into the center of the town house, and the draft from the smoke carried him up and out through the smoke hole.

"Once he had drifted a safe distance from the town house, Wild Thing changed into his real shape and struck out running toward home. When he got there, he said to his brother, 'Father is sending the wolves after us. We must prepare for them.' Wild Thing knew what to do. He told his brother to run along after him, and the Twosome ran seven times in a circular path around their house. Afterward they made a great many arrows. They collected them into four large bundles and placed them in the center of the circle, pointing out at the four directions.

"A day or two later, the wolves came in a pack and silently surrounded the house. They intended to attack and kill the Twosome as soon as they showed themselves. But the boys did not show themselves. After a long wait, the wolves grew impatient. They rushed out from their hiding places and ran toward the house. As they neared the circle the boys had trod around the house, there suddenly sprang up an impenetrable thicket of thorny blackberries, honey locust trees, smilax brier, and nettles. The wolves could not get through this prickly thicket fence to reach the boys inside the house. Then the arrows from the four bundles began whirring through the air, striking the wolves and killing them. Many wolves died, but some of them ran to a nearby swamp and found refuge in a canebrake. Wild Thing and his brother followed and began running round and round the outside of the canebrake. A fire sprang up where they had run, and the cane caught fire, popping fiercely as the larger canes exploded. Many more wolves perished in the fire. Only a few of them escaped, and they are the ancestors of all the wolves in the world today. Because of their experience with

Chunkey stone

the Twosome, wolves keep away from our towns, and they shrink from people who enter the woods.

"The Twosome could not believe that Lucky Hunter had really left them. They expected him to return home. 'Where can he be?' they asked. 'Why does he avoid us?'

"Wild Thing, never at a loss, said he knew just what to do. He took the small circular stone disc they used in playing chunkey, a game the two of them had invented, and he gave it a roll toward the south. In a little while it came rolling back. He rolled it to the west and also to the north, but it kept coming back. Then he rolled it toward the east, and they waited and waited, but the stone did not return to them.

"'There's the answer,' said Wild Thing. 'Our father has gone to the Sun-land, and we must go find him.' The Twosome set off toward the east and crossed the eastern mountains, and at last they came upon Lucky Hunter, sound asleep, with their chunkey stone transformed into a little dog sitting beside him.

"'I'll just wake him up,' said Wild Thing. He untied his father's belt, pulled down his breechcloth, and rammed an arrow up his anus.

"As Lucky Hunter woke up with a start, he transformed himself into a crow and flew up shouting *Ga, ga, ga, ga!* Ever since then, crows have raided people's gardens, especially their corn, and they are frightened of men who are carrying weapons.

"After he had calmed down and pulled the arrow out, Lucky Hunter returned to his right form and asked, 'Why have you two geniuses come here?'

"'We knew that you must be lost, else you would have come home to us. So we came looking for you, and now we have found you because we are true men, full grown, and we always succeed in whatever we attempt to do.'

"'It's good to see that you have learned to be modest,' said Lucky Hunter. 'Now that you have found me, I suppose we may as well travel together. Follow me.'

"Later in the day they saw a swamp in the distance. Lucky Hunter said that they would camp for the night short of this swamp because a dangerous beast who was able to see in the dark lived there. The beast was so dangerous, he told them, that no one ever entered that swamp, especially young boys.

"At their first opportunity, the Twosome set out for the swamp, just as Lucky Hunter knew they would. They crept silently through the gloom of the swamp to its very center before they spotted the beast. It was a very large cougar, asleep, with its tail curled. 'Let's kill him,' said Wild Thing. They nocked arrows into their little bows and fired arrows one after another— *tust, tust, tust!* All the arrows struck the panther on one side of his nose. He rolled over and stretched with his feet in the air, purring loudly. Then they shot arrows into the other side of his nose— *tust, tust, tust!* But he continued to sleep contentedly.

"The Twosome returned to camp and found that Lucky Hunter had continued on without them. 'Why didn't he wait for us?' they asked. They ran along following his trail and soon caught up with him. 'You boys have caught up with me,' Lucky Hunter said. 'They don't call me lucky for nothing. Did you find the beast?'

Cougar

"'Oh, yes,' they said, 'and we gave him some whiskers to remember us by. We are men in our prime, and we always succeed.'

"Lucky Hunter again diverted the boys and went on without them. But again they followed his tracks to the very edge of the eastern earth. They got to the place where the Sun comes out. They waited for the sky-bowl to rise so the Sun could come out, and before the sky-bowl came down again, they skipped through to the other side. They climbed up on the other side, and there they came upon Corn Woman and Lucky Hunter, sitting together. Both had white hair and were pale with age. The old couple were glad to see the boys, and they doted on them. They told the boys that they could stay just a few days, and then they would have to go to live in the west.

"After seven days, the boys departed and traveled to the Darkening Land in the west, where they have lived ever since. They still love to roll their chunkey stone, and when we hear low thunder in the west, we know it is the boys playing chunkey.

"Like all of the great beings of Ancient Days, the Twosome have gone from this world to the upper world. But like all the others, the

Twosome have left small, inferior versions of themselves behind in this world. They live out in the wild, in rocky outcroppings, swamps, hollow trees, and up in the branches of living trees. They look like people, except they are very small and shy. They play tricks on people who are out in the woods. They steal small articles. They bewilder people and cause them to do strange things."

The Raven seemed to be finished, but I was unsure. His eyes were still far away, as if he might begin to spin another thread of a story. I stirred about where I was sitting, breaking his train of thought, and Teresa and I stood up to stretch our limbs.

"If Lucky Hunter and Corn Woman are your idea of Adam and Eve," I said, "they certainly made a botch of starting the human race. The two boys are ignorant, headstrong, disobedient, arrogant, and disruptive. Surely you do not hold them up as paragons for your young people to imitate."

"We do not wish for our young people to imitate the two boys," the old man said. "But young people in their heedlessness often remind us of the Twosome. Yet it is on just such brashness and energy that life depends. Besides, the Twosome still live in the west, in the Darkening Land. Much good has come from them, though not all the good that might have. Because of their headstrong actions, we take care to treat Corn Woman well, and when we hoe our cornfields, we heap the soil up around the stalks—the skirt of Corn Woman. When we do not, she becomes angry, and we have no corn. Let me continue. I have more to tell you."

Teresa and I took our seats again, and the old man continued.

HOW FARMING AND HUNTING BEGAN

"Lucky Hunter and Corn Woman had many children besides the Twosome. Most of them were still on earth, and in time they became hungry. They could not get enough food from the forest to feed their own children. They heard that the Twosome possessed a wonderful grain that was good to eat, so they traveled to the Darkening Land to search for them. Soon they heard low, rolling thunder, and the boys appeared before them, trotting along beside a little dog.

"'Let us have some of your grain so that we may live,' they said.

"When the boys gave them seven grains of corn, the people were dismayed to be given so little.

"'At the end of the day,' said the Twosome, 'plant the seven grains and sit up all night and watch over it. The next morning you will have seven plants, each with mature ears of corn. At the end of the day, shell this grain off the cobs and plant all of it, and stay up all night watching over it. Keep on doing that every night for seven nights and you will have a great quantity of corn, which forever after will grow and ripen in a single night.'

"The people set out for home. The first night they did as the Twosome had said, and the next morning they found seven stalks of corn with several ears. The next night they did the same, and the next morning they had a large field full of ripe corn. They were astonished that the cultivation of corn was so easy. They kept doing this for the next several nights. But on the seventh day the sun was hot, and they were weary from so much traveling and from not having slept for so long. They planted the corn, but they fell asleep because they were so tired. The next morning, the corn had not even sprouted. And so they reached home with only a few grains of corn, and they found that in order to cultivate it they had to work hard to prepare a field, and then they had to tend and watch over it for many months before it came to maturity. They knew it had finally ripened when the silk on the ears turned brown, the color of Corn Woman's hair. They were so relieved at having been successful, they put on a great dance and feasted on the green corn during that short period of time when it is sweet and juicy, before the grain hardens and matures. This was the first *posketa* ceremony of the green corn.

"This was not the only favor the boys did for people in the old days. After the boys released all the succulent game animals from the cave of plenty, it became very difficult for hunters to kill any of them. The animals knew that they were succulent, and they became so shy and wary that the hunters could not get close enough to shoot them. Only the Twosome were lucky at killing game, but how were they to be summoned? The people often saw faint flashes of lightning when they heard thunder in the west. So they took seven slivers of wood from a tree that had been struck by lightning. They built a house large enough to hold all the hunters, and they built a fire in the hearth in the center of the house. They threw the seven splinters of lightning-struck wood into the fire, and instantly the house was filled with blinding flashes of light, and little bolts of lightning began bouncing off the walls. The hunters were very frightened. Suddenly the flashes of light stopped. When the ashes and dust settled, the two boys were sitting by the hearth as if nothing had happened.

"'So,' the Twosome said in unison, 'you are unlucky at hunting.'

"'Yes, yes,' the people said. 'We hunt all day in the woods, and we hardly ever come home with game.'

"'What you must do to kill deer,' said Wild Thing, 'is to dance like deer and sing the songs that deer love.'

"'Yes,' his brother said, 'that is what you must do.'

"The boys then taught the hunters a deer song, and they taught them the grazing dance of deer—the nibbling, the abrupt lifting of the head, the nervous licking of the sides. They taught them to skin a deer, keeping the skin of the head and neck intact. They showed them how a hunter could drape the skin over his head and shoulders and stick one of his arms up through the neck to hold up the head and imitate the motions of a deer's grazing dance. They taught them that when deer are in their mating season, the bucks blindly compete for females and become enraged when they hear the rattle of another buck's antlers. The hunters learned to rattle antlers and wait for love-struck bucks to appear and draw near.

"In this same way the two boys taught the hunters songs to attract other succulent animals. After the hunters could sing the songs to the Twosome's satisfaction, the house again filled with blinding light and a deafening sound of thunder. When the dust and ashes had settled, the Twosome were gone.

"Today the people of Coosa have forgotten the words of some of the songs, and they no longer know the meaning of some of the words they do remember. But our hunters still sing these songs before they go on a hunt, and sometimes they are successful. Whenever they do kill a deer, they show their gratitude by cutting off a piece of the best meat and feeding it to the fire."

The Raven fell silent and seemed to be finished at last. He stretched and then rubbed his hands together. "This story of the first people reminded Robles and Feryada of Adam and Eve. But they said that the Twosome did not much resemble Cain and Able. They told me that story of Cain and Abel, but it seemed a strange tale to me. Cain had to have been crazy to slay his own brother. People of the same fire do not kill each other. It is a terrible story."

After having told me of the mad antics of the Twosome, I did not understand why the old man should have been so upset over a man who deliberately killed his own brother. And what did he mean by "the same fire"? When I pressed him, he said that it was hard to explain to Christians but that he would try to do so the next time we met.

I do not know whether Teresa was in her menses when we made our last visit to the Raven, but for three days afterward she claimed to be sick and stayed in her house. When we finally returned to the Raven, he said nothing about our absence. It seemed to me that he was glad we had stayed away.

"I have something I want to show you," the old man said. He reached beneath his bed and pulled out several split-cane baskets covered with close-fitting lids. "These are the herbs on which Horned Serpent twisted his coils on the Backbone of the Earth. They are the ones on which the Sun's blood dripped."

Holding up one herb after another, he said, "This is *páássa,* button snakeroot, the greatest of our herbs. This is *meekko hoyanéécha,* red root of willow. This is *ásse,* our beloved tea. And this beautiful leaf is *heche lopóchkee,* the tobacco we smoke in our pipes. *Heche lopóchkee* was wrested from its owners in a distant land by an ancient priest. He transformed himself into a hummingbird-hawk moth and flew silently to capture the *heche lopóchkee* under cover of darkness. The hummingbird-hawk moth is a very large red-brown moth that beats its wings like a hummingbird, but it darts aggressively about like a hawk. As a caterpillar, it is a large green worm that feeds ravenously on *heche lopóchkee* leaves, and it can eat plants that will kill ordinary caterpillars."

"These herbs are our greatest, but we have many others," he said, pulling out other baskets. "This is *weláána,* chenopodium, good for purification and purging worms. This is *achína,* cedar, for driving away ghosts. This is *kofochka-lthákko,* horsemint, good for protection against ghosts of the dead. This is *heche pakpakee,* lobelia, also good for warding off the ghosts of the dead."

Then he replaced the herbs in their baskets and put them back under his bed. Later Teresa explained to me that "herb" was perhaps not the best word for these substances because the plants have magical uses in addition to their medical use.

Hornworm and hummingbird-hawk moths

After we had drunk our usual cup of *ásse*—the taste of which I was beginning to enjoy, though it caused me to perspire—he brought out a pipe with a curiously carved bowl. "This is an ancient pipe," he said, "carved in the form of an old-fashioned war club." He stuffed a pinch of tobacco into it. Then he picked up a coal from the fire with split-cane pincers and touched it to the contents of the pipe. He inhaled deeply and blew a cloud of swirling white smoke into the room. Then he handed the pipe to me, indicating that I was to do the same. But as I inhaled the smoke, I began hacking and coughing; the smoke made me dizzy and sick to my stomach. The old man began to laugh, the first time I had seen him do so, and he reached over and took the pipe from my hand, afraid that I would drop it. It was some time before I regained my composure. Teresa, trying to reassure me, said that the young men of Coosa react the same way when they first smoke the pipe with the men.

"When you get used to it," he said, "it is wonderfully calming, and it helps you think clearly." Smiling, he said, "*Heche lopóchkee* sometimes grows in the woods where men and women make love and semen falls to the ground. The calm is like what we feel after making love."

Then his face fell serious. He rested his chin in his hands, and I knew he was about to begin another story. "I want to tell you about women and separate fires."

The Origin of Bears 〰 73

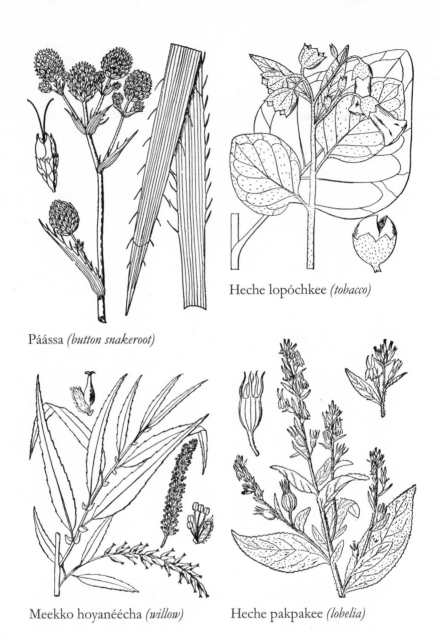

Páássa *(button snakeroot)*

Heche lopóchkee *(tobacco)*

Meekko hoyanéécha *(willow)*

Heche pakpakee *(lobelia)*

HOW THE CLANS BEGAN

"Corn Woman and Lucky Hunter had many children, and their children's children were born very rapidly and not in good order. They were Coosas, and they spoke the Coosa language, the women more fluently and volubly than the men. The children matured very quickly,

War club pipe

and the young ones were pouring out of Corn Woman's house like ants from an anthill. There was no order on earth; the people kept getting in each other's way, and they were crowding and offending the animals.

"'This will never do,' said the Sun, looking down at the swarm of people. 'I've got to slow them down, or they will overrun the earth.'

"She looked for Horned Serpent and found him lying in a swamp, with just his nose above the water, amusing himself by dunking his snout beneath the water and exhaling, so that bubbles rose up. One often sees such bubbles in a swamp today. Horned Serpent was startled when the Sun's blinding light suddenly appeared before his eyes. Angered, he began to lash about, hissing and snorting, and as he hissed and snorted, a heavy fog began to spew forth and cover the earth. Once the fog spread out, it lingered. It would not go away. The air dripped with dense, rotten-smelling moisture. Like all serpents, Horned Serpent has bad-smelling breath.

"The people and animals were in a great confusion. They could not see each other, and they had to get around by sound and touch. 'What a mess!' they said. 'We've got to overcome this stinking fog.'

"Who could oppose Horned Serpent? The men knew the location of a giant hawk's nest in a sheer cliff high above the swamp of the Horned Serpent. Since birds detest serpents of all kinds, the men knew what to do. They ran to the top of the cliff and several of them cut a stout grapevine, and when they saw that the old birds were away, one of the men climbed down the vine to the nest. Two big chicks sat in the midst of a pile of bones. The man grabbed the chicks, flung them down into the swamp, and then yelled for his comrades to pull him up to safety. When the chicks hit the water, Horned Serpent quit hissing out his fog and swam over and gobbled them up. The old hawks returned just in time to see the last of their chicks devoured. They flew down and grabbed Horned Serpent in their claws and began ripping pieces out of his body until he managed to submerge and save his life.

"Horned Serpent stayed beneath the water and tended his wounds, but his fog still lay across the land making it impossible for people to see each other. The old women sent up a cry: 'Let us all build bonfires and cluster together around them so that we can see each other.' The old women and their children raised up big piles of wood, and then each was lit to make a roaring bonfire. Together these fires defeated the fog, causing it to lift, and as a wind began to blow the fog away, the clusters of people who were feeding each fire took names from the first creature or thing they saw. One old woman and her sons and daughters took the name *Nokosâlke* (Bear people). Other mothers and their children took other names: *Fuswâlke* (Bird people), *Echaaswâlke* (Beaver people), *Cholâlke* (Fox people), *Wootkâlke* (Raccoon people), *Ahalakâlke* (Potato people), *Penwâlke* (Turkey people), *Yahâlke* (Wolf people), and so on. In the end, only one old woman and her children remained nameless. After looking about, and looking about some more, she said, 'We will take the name *Hotalkâlke,* Wind people, in memory of the sweet breeze that blew that stinking fog away.'

"After Horned Serpent's fog, a woman had to carry a child nine months before it was born, and after her child was born it took many years of care and support until it could act as a grown-up person. The people realized that they would have to stick together to raise children. So they agreed that each named group would be a clan, and each clan would take its household fire from the bonfire its old ancestress had built. In this way, the various clans had fires separate from each other.

"Merely by uttering the words *Nokosâlke, Fuswâlke, Cholâlke,* and so on, the clans had been called into existence. 'We must stick together and use the same fire,' they each said to their fellow clansmen. 'All who are birthed by our women will belong to us, and any who kills one of our number shall pay with his life. The souls of the slain shall haunt the eaves of our houses until equal blood is shed by the clan of the killer.'"

"This is why Coosa families are held together by women," said the Raven, pausing in his story to emphasize this point. "A person's closest relatives are traced through women, never through men. This puzzled Feryada and Robles. They could not get over the fact that a man's own children are not of his clan. Rather, a man's sister's children are the ones who are closest to him. Feryada and Robles could not believe it could be true that a person would not be related by blood to his father's side of the family. 'Blood is traced equally through both father and mother,' they said. But in time, after making many mistakes, they began to see that this is not so in Coosa. Once they began to grasp our rules, they saw that it is a good way to live."

He fell silent for a moment, almost in challenge, as if he expected the same objection from me. But I knew better than to argue. I looked at him blankly, and so, finding the way clear, he returned to his story. Clearly, kinship through clans was a great advance in bringing order to the way they lived.

THE CLANS AND THEIR RULES

"'Whatever we do,' the ancient ones agreed, 'we must avoid the Moon's mistake. We do not want to be marred forever by having soot smudged on our faces.' So they all agreed that no brother would lie with his sister, and as an extra measure, a man would not lie with *any* woman of his clan, no matter how distant his line of descent from hers. Ever afterward, when a man wanted the intimacy of a woman, it had to be a woman from some clan other than his own. But this made for a problem, because even though there was now good order within the clans, there still was strife between the clans.

"How were the clans to be kept in amity? First, one of the ancients spoke and then another. There was one idea offered and then another, but all of their ideas seemed silly or impractical. Finally, the spider, the little fire carrier, said: 'The clans must be woven together. I'll show you how.'

"The fire-carrier spider asked the women to drive two wooden stakes solidly into the ground. This done, she spun out a strong thread from one stake to the other, and then from this top thread she hung several warp threads. 'These warp threads represent the clans—the women and their children who stay together in one place.' Then she wove other threads crosswise, binding the threads together into a fabric. 'These crosswise threads are the men who move from the houses of their mothers to the houses of the women they marry. Together the warp threads and the crosswise threads make the fabric.' All of the people were amazed at the cleverness of the spider. They tugged at the fabric she had woven, pulling on one corner after another, but the fabric held together. Today, when Coosa women weave their suspended warps, they think of the fire-carrier spider. Thanks to her wisdom, the clans have to stay in at least enough harmony for their men and women to get together. Coosas sometimes say, 'We marry the people we fight.'

"In the marriage ceremony, the gardener is wedded to the hunter, which is another kind of weaving. The groom wears a tuft of oak leaves tied to his hair to show that he is not afraid to enter the forests. In his left hand he holds a bow and arrow to show that he will provide for and defend his wife and children. The bride holds a sprig of laurel in her left hand to show that she will always be true to her husband, and in her right hand she holds an ear of corn to show that she will garden and cook.

"'Weaving is like the words of the Master of Breath,' the fire-carrier told the ancient ones. 'Once the words fall beside each other, their meaning is apparent and cannot be changed. Language is like weaving.'

"So all of the people began talking excitedly. 'We need special words to weave us together,' they said, and they began to think up words to refer to each other. They agreed that all of their ancestors, whether by blood or by marriage, were to be honored. If it is a grandmother she will be called *póse,* and if it is a grandfather he will be *pochaa.* They all agreed that they would call their mother *échke,* and that they would call all of her sisters by the same term. The men said, 'Our own sisters we will call *eewánwa* and treat them with respect because they are the carriers of our own blood and fire. We will call our elder brother *lthába* because he was born first, and our younger brother we will call *chóse* because he was born after us. We will also call our mother's sister's children by these same terms. These people we will support and protect against all injury.'

"The ancients agreed that the daughters of those women whom they called *eewánwa* (sister), they would call *enhakpatee,* and *eewánwa*'s sons they would call *hopwéwa.* These were the children they would tend with particular care, and from whom in return they would look for particular respect and obedience.

"'Our wives we will call *héywa.* But the children of our wives,' said the men, 'though we have fathered them, are of the fire of their mothers, not of ours. We must distinguish them from our sisters' children. We will call the children of our wives *ekpoche* (son) and *echhóste* (daughter). And we will call our brothers' children by the same terms. And the children will call their father and their father's brothers *élthke*.'

"Then a little boy raised a question that no one had yet considered. 'If our fathers are to be mindful of their sisters' children,' the boy said, 'what adult will we look up to for support and correction?' The people saw the problem and talked it over among themselves. They mentioned one relative, and then another. But the mother's brother was the logical choice. They all agreed that he would be called *páwa* because he was special and had to be treated with special politeness. His wife was respectfully called *hachawa*. The mother's brother's children, however, are of his wife's fire—not of his own—and the speaker will therefore refer to them not as *eewánwa, lthába,* and *chóse,* but as *ekpoche* if a male and *echhóste* if a female."

"Enough!" I said. "This is all too complicated. I cannot keep all of these words and their meanings in mind."

"Why, it is easy," the old man said. "I have told you only a few of our kinship terms, and Coosa children of even four winters learn to use these words with no errors." The old man cackled and slapped his leg. He turned a merry face toward Teresa, who responded with a blank-faced demeanor. For a moment, in the darkening room, the old man made me think of Rabbit. In spite of myself, I was beginning to think a little like a Coosa.

I could see that the kinship words the old man was giving me had to be understood in relation to each other. It was clear that Coosas distinguish their "blood" relatives—the people of their fire—from all others. But to master the use of these words would take a great deal of study and practice. I thought about how some future priest might translate "our Father in heaven" into the Coosa language. Perhaps *élthke* would do for "our Father" if it could be made plain that God has no brothers or cousins who would be referred to with the same word. For the Coosas "our Mother in heaven" would seem more appropriate, though such a rendering of the name of Our Lord would, of course, be heresy.

The old man regained his composure, and now he cleared his throat, indicating that he had more to say.

"The sons and daughters of Corn Woman and Lucky Hunter thought up many rules, but it did not occur to them that some rules might be hard to keep. More than anything else, it is the keeping of rules that separates people from animals. Nevertheless, people have trouble keeping rules—particularly the rules of proper food.

"In ancient time, soon after the clans were devised, a boy of the Groundhog clan began leaving home and going into the mountains to spend time. First he would spend a half a day, then an entire day. As time went on, he went more and more often, and he stayed longer and longer. He stopped eating the food his mother cooked for him, and he was gone from dawn to dusk. His mother scolded him, but he paid her no attention.

"When his relatives began to see long, brown hair growing all over his body, they asked him why he spent so much time in the mountains and why he refused to eat the food his mother cooked. 'I find plenty of food there, and it is better than the corn and beans I get at home. My looks are continually improving,' he said, stroking his hairy arms, 'and soon I will spend full time in the mountains. Come with me. There is plenty of food for all, and the very best part is that we do not have to work for it. But if you want to come with me, you must fast for seven days.'

"The Groundhog clan talked it over. 'Here we must all work hard in the hot sun. Rain may be withheld from us, or late or early frosts may come, and then we may not have enough corn and beans to last the winter. The boy says that in the mountains there is plenty of food and no one has to work. We will go with him.' They fasted for seven days, and on the seventh day, they all started out, following the hairy boy into the woods.

"When the people of the other clans heard of this, they became sad, and they sent their headmen to try to talk the Groundhog clan into staying in the village and working for their food along with the others. When the headmen of the other clans caught sight of the Ground-hog clan, they saw that long brown hair had already begun to grow on their bodies. The people of the Groundhog clan had gone without human food for seven days, and they were beginning to change into four-footeds.

"'We are not coming back,' they said to the headmen. 'We are sick and tired of working in the fields. We are going where there is always plenty of food, and where we do not have to work. After this, you may call us *nokóse*—bears. When you are hungry you may come to the woods and kill us and eat our flesh. You need not fear killing us, for our spirits shall live always.'

"The Groundhog clan then sat down with the headmen of the other clans and taught them a song. Whenever hunters would sing this song, the bears would come. After they had memorized the song, the headmen started back to their villages. When they looked back, they saw a large drove of bears loping on all fours into the woods.

"Ever afterward when bear hunters are about to go on a hunt, they fast all day and do not eat until it is almost evening. When they start out, first thing in the morning, they sing the bear song. They sing it only once in a day, never twice.

> For the love of sweet grapes,
>   In the northern mountains, the Backbone of
>   the Earth, you were conceived. *Yohó.*
> For the love of fat grubs,
>   In the eastern mountains—the Sun's own—
>   you were conceived. *Yohó.*
> For the love of persimmons,
>   In the southern mountains you were conceived.
>   *Yohó.*
> For the love of chestnuts,
>   In the western mountains—the Darkening Land—
>   you were conceived. *Yohó.*
> Now surely we hunters and the black, furry fat
>   things—the best of all the four-footeds—
>   shall see each other."

The Raven fell silent, his eyes distant, as if he were watching the drama of the hunters and the bears. Then he looked at me and smiled a little. "Bears resemble people in many ways. They can walk on two feet when they wish, though they are fat and waddle comically. They can pick up objects with their paws and turn them this way and that. They like the same foods that people eat, and they are particularly fond of sweets and cooked food. Their dung resembles humans'. More than one hunter has come upon bear dung in the woods and been startled, thinking it was that of a man.

"The division between bears and people is a fragile one, and it can easily be broached. Bears have great ones among them—sorcerers—just as people do. Listen now, and I will tell you a story about that."

"There once was a hunter who shot an arrow into a bear sorcerer. This happened not in Ancient Days, but in the remembered past, though it was a long time ago. The hunter was startled to see the bear sorcerer act as if nothing had happened, and so he shot another arrow into the bear, and then another. The bear merely sat back on his haunches and pulled out the arrows, one after another, as if they were nothing.

"'You can't hurt me,' the bear sorcerer said to the hunter.

"The hunter began to look for some place to run. 'This talking bear will kill me,' he thought to himself.

"'No, I won't,' said the bear sorcerer, reading the hunter's thoughts.

"Now the hunter was more than frightened of this mind-reading bear—he was terrified.

"'You look hungry,' said the bear. 'Come with me and have some food. I always have plenty.'

"The hunter *was* hungry, and this bear was so clever that the hunter saw no way to get away from him. Against his better judgment, he went along with the bear, and after a while they entered a cave. Inside, the cave opened up into a town house, all underground, and it was filled with bears of all sizes. They were eating and talking, just the way men do in their town houses. Their chief was an old bear, completely covered with white hair.

"The bears began to dance, just like people do, and they had a good time, dancing out satirical dances that made fun of people. But after a while they began to run short of food, and bears become unhappy when there is no food. The bear sorcerer stepped forward. 'Just watch,' he said. And when he rubbed his navel—much as Corn Woman had done—a great pile of chestnuts fell to the ground. Then he rubbed his body and produced sweet acorns, strawberries, and blackberries. The hunter ate some of this food, and though it was uncooked, it tasted very good.

"When they stopped dancing, the bears picked up the hunter's bow and arrow from where it lay on the floor of the cave. 'These are the things the top-knots—the people—use to kill us. Perhaps we can learn to use them to protect ourselves.' One of the bears picked up the bow and tried to nock an arrow into the string. But his claws kept getting tangled in the string, and the arrow fell to the ground. They saw that they could not use this new weapon, so they gave it back to the hunter.

"The hunter lived with the bears all winter. He kept on walking upright, like a man, but brown hair had grown all over his body. He was beginning to like this life, and he enjoyed the company of bears, who were slow-witted but jovial. They liked nothing better than to have a good time.

"But at last the hunter began to grow homesick. He wanted to see his wife again. He told the bear sorcerer that he wanted to return home. The bear sorcerer said that he could do that, but he would have to be careful, else the top-knots and split-noses would kill him. 'Just be sure to always walk erect,' said the bear sorcerer, 'and sing loudly as you walk.'

"Sure enough, the hunters did come across the hairy singer as he was making his way home, and their dogs set up a terrific racket. But the hunters recognized the hairy man and went with him back to their town. There they took him to their priest.

"'This man is half bear,' said the priest. 'He must fast for seven days and nights in isolation from everyone, so that he may become a whole man again.'

"They took the bear-man to a small house in the woods, near the edge of the town. Here they kept all food and visitors from him. But the bear-man's wife heard of what was happening, and after he had only been isolated and fasting for four or five days, she went to get him. She was lonely for him, and he for her. He went home with her, but he died almost immediately. If he had only waited the seven days, he would have lived out his full portion of time as a man."

"Bears are so much like us," said the Raven, "that we never tire of telling stories about them. When a hunter kills a bear, the whole town turns out to see it and to hear all about what happened on the hunt. We mainly hunt them in the fall, when they are fattest. Bear flesh is sweet and good, but it is the oil we treasure most. It is delicious for cooking, and when spicebush and other sweet-smelling herbs are added, we use it to dress our hair and our bodies."

I had not rubbed bear oil on myself—heaven forbid!—but I had tasted it and found it to be excellent in flavor.

"Bear skins," he said, "because of the thick brown hair, are the best skins for bedding, and they can be worn as mantles in the coldest weather. Because bears are scarce, their skins are greatly desired, and most of them are given over to the chief."

"We owe something else to the bears," the Raven said. "Just as they like the food we eat, we like some of their foods—chestnuts, sweet acorns, blackberries, and strawberries. These are good to eat and they make you strong, but eating too much of them can make you slow-witted and clumsy. The danger of losing our human qualities by living like bears is always with us. Our stories remind us to be careful of too much life in the woods."

The Raven was finished for the evening, and after a few more pleasantries, Teresa and I took our leave.

As we walked back to our quarters, Teresa was more despondent than I had ever seen her. It seemed that each day her spirits were lower and lower. I asked her why she felt so low.

"I wish I had run away in Mexico and hidden with the Sun Woman so that I could never have been brought back to Coosa," she said. "I do not know who I am when I am here. Am I the daughter of this place? Or am I a stranger? At first, my clansmen treated me as if I were a ghost. They were afraid of me. Then, when they realized that I had been taken all the way to Mexico into a world they cannot even imagine, they began looking right through me, as if I were not there. I look at them and see the people I once knew. But they look at me and see a stranger."

"Lately it has grown worse," she said. "Not only does the Raven ask me questions that should not be asked of a Christian woman, but now the women of my clan are approaching me and asking me to do them favors. My mother and my younger sister, whom I loved above all others, are now dead, and none of my clan sisters feels comfortable with me. None will extend the comfort of the clan to me. But now they are asking me to act on their behalf."

"What do they ask?" I said.

"They say that their men do not see how rapidly we are depleting Coosa's food stores," Teresa said. "All that the men see is an opportunity to ally themselves with us in a strike against the Napochín, who have broken away from the peace of the Sun Chief."

I had heard our captain, Mateo del Sauz, speak of the possibility of such an alliance. The Napochín towns lie at several days travel to the north. The Napochín were once subject to, or at least allies of, the Coosas, but recently they have broken away and they have killed several Coosas. The Coosa war leaders want Sauz to send a detachment of men with them to attack the Napochín and bring them back into line. I assured Teresa that I would inform Sauz that the Coosa women were becoming concerned about food for the winter. And I told her that if we went with the Coosas against the Napochín, we would raid the Napochín granaries. This would ease the burden on the Coosa food supply.

Teresa was somewhat relieved by these assurances. Yet there was no cure for the real cause of her affliction. She was stranded between two worlds, and she could find little comfort anywhere.

When we returned to the Raven's house the next evening, I told him that his bear stories were leading in the wrong direction. I had already heard quite enough animal stories, and I wanted no more of them. He assured me that the ones he was telling now were far more important than the simple stories he had told in the beginning. His serious intent was borne out by the humiliating questions he insisted on putting to Teresa. Indeed, if anything, his questions to her this night were even more insistent than before, and though she was in no condition for such browbeating—having already complained to me again about impossible demands being placed on her by her Coosa kinswomen—she bore up admirably. Once again, the Raven decided to proceed despite her presence, though it clearly bothered him. Poor Teresa. I tried to comfort her with my glance, but she sat stone-faced, not looking at either of us, as she waited for the old man to begin the night's conversation.

The Raven explained that the herbs he had shown me earlier were only a few of the herbs known to the people of Coosa. As he spoke, he began taking down the bunches of dried herbs that hung inside his house, naming each one and giving account of how its properties had been made known to the people of Coosa. But he talked so rapidly, and Teresa translated so badly, I could make no sense of what he said. In part this was because Teresa, having been abducted from Coosa when she was a mere girl, had no great knowledge of these plants, and she was often at a loss for words.

"Plants are good medicine against diseases caused by the vengeance of animals," the Raven said, "but they are not so good against the anger of ancestors, and they are almost entirely useless against the assaults of the great ones of the upper world and under world." Either he was deliberately talking nonsense, or else what he had told me earlier was no preparation for these strange assertions.

"Tonight," he said, "we will talk about the anger of animals and the origin of diseases, and of the kindness of plants and the origin of medicine. Finally, we will talk about death."

THE VENGEANCE OF ANIMALS

"Animals are more pure than people are. Animals, having never broken rules, do not have to labor as people do. No food is impure for animals. They eat whatever they please, without compunction. But for people it is a constant struggle to remain pure. We Coosa people have to be careful about what we eat, and some foods may be forbidden for periods of time, or even forever. This is one of the reasons we drink the *ásse* before important undertakings. And this is why we are so given to purges by vomiting. We must purge our stomachs to make sure that we have not eaten improper or bewitched food.

"In the story I told you about the ball game between the four-footeds and the birds, I said that in Ancient Days the birds and the four-footeds talked the same language. What I did not tell you is that in Ancient Days people also spoke the same language as the four-footeds and birds, and the same went for insects and plants. All living things got along famously in those olden times.

"But the people began to increase very rapidly, and their towns spread over all the world, and they began to crowd the animals. The people devised tools and weapons for killing the animals: bows and arrows, blowguns, spears, nets, snares, fish hooks, and so on. They killed the larger animals for their meat and skins; the fish for their flesh; the birds for their meat and feathers; and they killed many smaller creatures such as frogs, insects, and worms by carelessly or contemptuously stepping on them.

"The animals called a meeting in the bears' town house within a mountain of the Backbone of the Earth. The old White Bear, who was chief of the bears, presided over the meeting. 'What do men do?' he asked.

"'They kill us and eat our flesh,' said a chorus of the bears. 'They use our skins to cover their bodies.'

"'What weapons do they use?'

"'Bows and arrows, of course.'

"'And what are they made of?'

"'The bow of black locust and the bowstring of bear gut.'

"'Well,' said the old White Bear, 'we can do as well. One of us will sacrifice himself for the others and be killed for his guts.'

"So they killed a volunteer and made a bow and some arrows. But when they tried to shoot arrows from the bow, their claws became entangled in the string and the arrows fell harmlessly to the ground. Somebody suggested that the bears might trim off their claws, and in this way they might practice and become good archers. One of the bears did so, and he hit the mark with the first arrow he shot. But the old White Bear stepped in, saying that as bears they had to be able to climb trees, and they had to be able to tear apart rotten logs in search of grubs.

"'Men's weapons are not for bears,' he said. 'One of us has already sacrificed himself to provide the bowstring, and now are we all to trim off our claws? This will not do.'

"None of the bears could come up with a better plan. Shrugging their shoulders and scratching their heads, the bears then walked out of their town house and into the woods and thickets, hoping to find refuge there. They gave up on devising a way to get revenge for their losses and to stop the increase of people. Because bears do not seek vengeance, people do not ask the bears' pardon when they kill one of them. Bears were once people, but now they are such half-wits, they do not seek clan vengeance, and they pay dearly for it.

"Next the deer met together to exact vengeance on humans, and the Little White Deer, their chief, presided. They all said that it was venison on which people mainly subsisted, and if they could not come up with some way to restrain the hunters, the deer would surely perish. They agreed that they would have to punish people. They determined that they would send their spirit to punish any hunter who does not ask pardon when he kills a deer, and they would do so by inflicting him with crippling arthritis.

"The Little White Deer is the guardian of deer. Today, whenever a hunter kills a deer, the Little White Deer rushes to the spot of the killing, as fast as the wind and just as invisible, and he bends over the bloodstains and asks the spirit of the slain deer whether the hunter asked pardon. If the answer is yes, the Little White Deer goes on his way. But if the answer is no, the White Deer tracks down the hunter by following the drops of blood, and when he arrives at the hunter's house, he inflicts him with *echo pólsee,* deer sickness [crippling rheumatism and arthritis]. Or if he cannot find the hunter, he cripples a relative of the hunter, one of the people of his fire. Today, no prudent hunter fails to say words asking pardon for killing a deer.

"Next, the fishes and reptiles discussed their complaints against people. They remembered countless injuries and impertinences. They decided that they would get revenge on the people who injured them by causing them to have mucousy diseases of the stomach, liver, and lungs, and to have nightmares—the worst kind of dreams—of snakes twining about them in horrid coils, hissing their foul breath in their faces. Or they would dream of eating rotten fish, so that they would lose their appetite for food, and some of them would sicken and die. This is why people have nightmares about snakes and fish.

"Finally, the smaller animals met together with the birds and insects. The White Grubworm served as their chief. They all aired their complaints against people and tried to decide on some way of exacting vengeance. Toad led off: 'People are so numerous, they kick me about, calling me ugly, and now my back is covered with scabs.' And he showed the others the spots and blemishes on his skin. Next, Bobwhite Quail whistled for everyone's attention: 'Men are so numerous and so cruel they burn my feet off.' He was referring to the habit of some hunters who impale smaller birds on a spit as they roast them and singe off their feathers and feet. One after another of the smaller animals, birds, and insects made their complaints. Only Chipmunk put in a good word for people, who seldom injure chipmunks because they are so small. Coosas ridicule those who hunt chipmunks, saying that such people spend more effort in the hunting than they gain in the eating. Because Chipmunk had a good word to say about people, all the other animals fell upon him and clawed at him, and he bears their scratch marks on his back to this day.

"Then all of the assembly of small creatures began to think up new diseases to inflict on the spirits of people, and for a while it seemed that they would surely kill all people everywhere. The White Grubworm, as he wriggled about in front of the assembled small creatures, grew happier and happier as each new disease was called out. Finally, when one of the creatures proposed to make menstruation sometimes fatal to women, the White Grubworm began to giggle. He raised his plump little body up as high as he could and said: 'Thanks. I am glad that some more of them will die because they are becoming so numerous they tread on me.' The thought of menstruation being sometimes fatal to women made him so giddy with joy that he fell over on his back. He was unable to get to his feet again, and he wriggled off on his back, as grubworms still do.

"The vengeful animals devised so many new diseases that people would have all died out had they not gained some new allies at that time. These were the plants, who heard about what the animals were planning to do to people and decided to lend people a hand. People seldom give serious injury to plants, while the animals constantly and continually offend plants by eating their fruits, leaves, nuts, and even their roots. The plants—every one of them—declared that they would provide a cure for the animals' diseases. They said, 'People are the enemies of our enemies, and therefore, when people are in need, we will help.' And in this way medicine came into being. Each plant—shrub, herb, tree, even grasses and mosses—furnishes a medicine to counteract the vengeance of animals. Coosas have a saying that medicines are taken from the earth's skirt. I have already mentioned the four primal herbs—*páássa, meekko hoyanéécha, ásse,* and *heche lopóchkee*—and there are many others that are known by most Coosa people. Some, however, are known only to priests and healers, who, when they are baffled about how to obtain a cure, ask the spirits of the plants themselves for the best medicine to use.

"It is from events that occurred in Ancient Days that animals acquired their meaning. When people in their everyday lives encounter animals, they may be reminded of things animals did when the world was coming into being. Seeing the little black racer snake, one might think of the time when the animals were trying to wrest fire from the hollow sycamore tree. In some cases, the appearance of an animal may have particular significance to an individual. When a rattlesnake crawls near some person's house, that person becomes anxious. The rattlesnake is first among snakes, and he has a close affinity to Horned Serpent, and Coosas do not kill him. A person in the house may have injured or killed a snake, and that person might be mindful of a snake-caused illness. Or, because of Rattlesnake's friendship with Horned Serpent and Thunder, his appearance may presage a rainstorm.

"Plants do not bring this kind of meaning to us. They do not presage things that are poorly understood or yet to be, as do animals. But plants of today do bear the mark of Ancient Days. The *ásse* plant, from whose parched leaves we make our beloved drink, is a sign of people existing in harmony with each other. Cedar is a sign of longevity and good health. The sight of some plants fill people with dread. Water hemlock is often used by sorcerers to cause injury and trouble in a person's life. It is especially disturbing to find a section of deliberately cut water hemlock stalk on the path to one's house, for it almost surely means that a sorcerer is at work. This may send a person scurrying to a priest. The Ancient Days are not behind us. No, they keep coming around.

"But to return to the diseases that afflict people, many people are sickened by animals' spirits seeking revenge for being injured. More often than not, people inflict these injuries unawares. The spirits of worms and maggots, for example, can cause boils, pustulating sores, and pimples. Adolescent boys and girls, who are famous for running and tumbling about in the woods, often get pimples on their faces because of their careless tramping on worms. Many of the diseases caused by vengeful animals can be cured or lessened by herbal medicines.

"There are diseases from other causes that do not yield to such cures. Each person has four souls. The first, the soul of conscious life, resides in the top of the head. Every person's soul of conscious life is different from all others, and it is the soul that departs the body immediately upon death. This is the soul that is defiled when one is scalped by an enemy. The soul of life secretes the watery body fluids: phlegm, sexual fluids, and most especially saliva. Normally this soul lingers for a while before going to the west, the land where the Sun darkens. But some souls are stubborn and do not want to leave because they are lonely. They lurk in dark places, and they can spoil the saliva of their loved ones. A person whose saliva is spoiled loses the will to live. They become reclusive, want to stay abed all day, and cannot bear to be with neighbors and friends. Spoiled saliva can be stubborn to cure. The offending soul must be driven to the Darkening Land. But even when they are there, they can communicate with the living. Old people in particular experience this as a ringing in the ears. It is the souls of the dead calling for them.

"The second soul is the liver soul. Its secretions are black bile, yellow bile, and gastric juice. The liver soul can be damaged and destroyed, and it is a very serious illness, but I will tell you more about this at a later time. The liver soul lingers for seven days after death, and then it dissipates.

"The third soul is located in the heart. Its secretion is blood. After death, it lingers for about a month, and then it goes into the earth.

"The fourth soul is in the bones. After a person dies, the soul of the bones lives on for about a year. This is why we mourn for a year after a person dies, and this is why we bury our beloved dead in the floors of our houses and our heroes in and near our mounds and temples. When people neglect their dead ancestors, it is a bad thing. The ancestors are jealous, and their feelings can be hurt. They are capable of punishing kinsmen who are left behind in life."

I began to shift about in my seat, and the Raven fell silent, realizing perhaps that such beliefs about multiple souls and shades of ancestors are anathema to Christians. A person has but a single soul, and the soul's destination after death depends upon how he has lived his life in Christ. The old man must have gained from Robles and Feryada some inkling of how ignorant and barbaric these Coosa beliefs appear to Christians.

I regained my composure, however, and pretended interest in the nonsense he was spouting. We must know their delusions if we are to counter them. "Tell me more about sorcery," I asked.

"Sorcery is a difficult subject, and one that is hard to explain to Christians," said the Raven. "I will tell you something of what I understand about it the next time we converse. But for now, I want to discuss a further cause of illness, one that priests are almost helpless against.

"The very worst diseases are those that are caused by the first beings — the great ones, like Sun, Moon, and Thunder. These beings are so remote from us that it is hard to know their intentions, or even whether their intentions can be known at all."

THE ANGER OF THE SUN

"In Ancient Days it came about that people began to die by the hundreds. No one knew why this was happening. The priests were helpless. Finally, they used splinters from a lightning-struck tree to call in the Twosome, who revealed to the people that the Sun was angry at Coosas because she thought they had insulted her, and she meant to kill every one of them with fever.

"The people were baffled about why the Sun had taken such offense. The Twosome informed them that the Sun had her feelings hurt because she thought that the people of Coosa had insulted her; she thought they loved Brother Moon more than they loved her. The Sun had looked down and noticed that when people looked up at her, they squinted their eyes and grimaced. But when they looked up at brother Moon, they always had pleasant expressions on their faces.

"The Twosome told the people that it was the Sun's habit to stop in and visit her daughter at the doorstep of her upper-world house on her transit across the sky-bowl each day. They would sit and talk about this insult, and the Sun would get more and more angry until, in her wrath, she would send down her rays to kill people with fever.

"'We've got to set her right,' the people said, and they begged the Twosome to help them.

"The Twosome took pity on the sick and dying Coosas. They changed a Coosa man into a spreading viper snake, and they changed another into a copperhead snake, and they told them to go up into the sky to wait at the door of the Sun's daughter's house, and to bite the Sun when she next appeared. The two serpents did as they were told, hiding themselves at the door of the house of the daughter of the Sun. But when the Sun appeared, her bright light frightened the spreading viper, and he rolled over on his back and played dead, vomiting horrid yellow slime, as he does to this day. The copperhead, for his part, was so dull-witted he crawled off without trying to bite the Sun.

"The Sun continued having her daily visits with her daughter, and the people continued to die by the hundreds. The Twosome tried again. They asked for another volunteer, and they changed him into a rattlesnake. Then they called in their old friend Horned Serpent, and they sent the two of them up to ambush the Sun at the door of her daughter's house.

"The people were sure that Horned Serpent, with his huge size and frightful horns, would get the job done. But on the way to the Sun's daughter's house, Rattlesnake got ahead of Horned Serpent, and he coiled up at the door. When the Sun came by he lunged for her but missed and struck the Sun's daughter, who fell in the doorway of her house, dead as a stone. Rattlesnake hurried back to the Twosome to tell them what he had done. When Horned Serpent found out the error

Rattlesnake had made, he departed without doing anything, and he became even angrier at people than he already was. To this day he is so angry it is dangerous even to look upon him. The mere sight of Horned Serpent can cause a man or a man's relatives to sicken and die.

"As for Rattlesnake, since he performed his valiant though inept deed, people have respect for him. When he appears, people address him as *pochaa*, grandfather, and they wish him well. Rattlesnake will not bite unless a person disturbs him or does something really stupid.

"When the Sun discovered her daughter lying dead in the doorway of her house, she went inside and began to grieve. The earth fell dark because the Sun would not come out. The people stopped dying of fever, but now they became afraid that because the Sun would not show herself, every living thing would die in the darkness.

"Again the people called on the Twosome, who came and told them that they would have to send a party of men to the Darkening Land to retrieve the soul of the daughter of the Sun. They chose seven of the most valiant Coosa warriors to make the journey. They gave each of the men a sourwood rod a handbreadth long. They also gave them a lidded cane basket to take along with them. The Twosome told the men that they would find the daughter of the Sun at a dance. The seven Coosa warriors were to stand outside the dance circle, and when the daughter of the Sun danced by, they were to tap her with their sourwood rods and she would fall to the ground. Then they should put her into the basket, put the lid on securely, and carry the basket home. Above all, under no circumstances should they open the basket until they got home.

"The seven warriors set out for the Darkening Land with their rods and their basket. When they arrived at the Darkening Land, sure enough, they found many people dancing in a circle. The daughter of the Sun was in the outside circle, and as she danced by, one after another of the seven warriors tapped her with their rods, and each time she looked at the face of the man who had tapped her. She came around the circle again, and again the seven men tapped her with their rods. When the seventh tapped her, she fell down to the ground senseless. Immediately they picked her up, put her into the basket, and closed the lid.

"They set out toward the east, for home, traveling as rapidly as they could. After a while, the daughter of the Sun came to her senses. She told them that she was thirsty. But they had been told that they must

Cardinal

not open the basket. She pleaded with them to give her a drink of water, but still they ignored her, even though they felt sorry for her. As she kept on begging for just a little drink of water, her voice grew weaker, and at last she told them that she was suffocating. Fearing that it might be so, they lifted the lid of the basket just a little, but as they did, there came a fluttering sound and something red flashed by their faces. Then, from some nearby bushes, they heard a cardinal say *kwish, kwish, kwish!* They knew then that the daughter of the Sun had been transformed into a cardinal. Now the Sun would never have her daughter back as she once had been.

"This failure of the seven Coosa warriors is the reason why the souls of the dead do not want to go to the Darkening Land, a place from whence they can never return. Had the seven warriors succeeded, souls could be brought back from the Darkening Land. But now they cannot. It is partly for this reason that Coosas mourn so deeply when their loved ones die, and why they lavish such attention on them. We place their favorite food and drink in the grave with them, along with their favorite tools and weapons. And we send gifts to go with their souls to kinsmen already dead. We encourage souls to go to the west by heating cedar twigs in a dry pot, making an incense that repels lingering souls.

"The Sun had been pleased with what the seven Coosa warriors were attempting to do. But when they came back with an empty basket, she began grieving all over again. 'My daughter, my daughter,' she wept. Thunder became so sad at the spectacle of his mother weeping, he began weeping as well, and it rained and rained, until people became afraid that the darkened earth would be covered by water.

"Finally, the people selected their most attractive young men and women to dance for the Sun. They gathered in two circles, one inside the other—the dance formation that most pleases the Sun—and as the drummer drummed, they danced in their circles and looked up at the sky with pleasant expressions on their faces. But still the Sun grieved and rain fell from the sky. At last the drummer changed the tempo of his drumming. This caught the Sun's attention, and she looked down. She was pleased with what she saw, and she ceased grieving and smiled upon her grandchildren down below, and the rain stopped."

"It is so difficult," the old man said, "to know the intentions and motives of the Sun, a being who is so distant from people. When we go to water in the early morning to purify ourselves, we try to do it at a spot where we can see the Sun reflected in the water as she first rises above the edge of the horizon. Occasionally, we see an omen in the water—a leaf falls, a fish rises—and when this occurs in the reflected Sun, it is an omen of important things to come."

I pressed him to elaborate, but he would not. "Seeing into the future and into the causes of things is a long story." He said that he would have to fast and purge himself and that we should not return to his house until he had done so.

Here at last was the subject of sorcery. I would have liked for him to continue, but I knew from the way he talked that he was finished for the evening. These matters would have to wait until the next time Teresa and I visited his house.

The Raven had informed me that the subject of our next conversation was both difficult and dangerous, and that he had to fast for four days before we could meet again. When Teresa and I went to his house on the appointed night, we found him sitting in his customary place. He showed the effects of his fast, and he did not rise as we entered his house. The room was dark, but when Teresa went to add some wood to the fire, the old man insisted that I do it.

As I have already written, Coosa people believe that a person's character and spiritual condition are affected by what he eats. Many foods are forbidden, such as carnivorous birds and mammals (except the bear), creatures that burrow underground, and certain aquatic animals, such as eels. Thus, on those occasions when Coosas think they might be sullied by unwanted influences, they consider it only prudent that they fast and purge themselves by vomiting. They even examine the vomitus in the absurd belief that they can discover in it evidence of occult influences. This is why the old man began every session by vomiting up the *ásse* he drank, and why on this night he preceded our talk with a severe fast of four days. I gathered that he was striving for utmost purity as he approached a topic about which he had, if not actual fear, at least a respectful wariness.

The old man's voice was weaker than before, although he rallied a bit after we drank the *ásse*.

"We Coosas learn from everyday life what you Christians learn from your bundle of thin white cloths. [He meant the Bible.] We see events in Ancient Days reenacted before us in everyday happenings. Some Coosas see more significance in such occurrences than others, but any Coosa can see the Sun follow her blazing trail across the sky. Any Coosa can see the soot-besmirched Moon take his course at night. Any Coosa can see the black racer snake, cinder-colored, darting nervously this way and that. Any can see the flashes of light and hear the awful sound as Thunder shoots his arrows and hurls his war clubs to earth, and any can hear the faint rolling sounds as the Twosome play chunkey in the Darkening Land. Anyone can see in the sky the drawn bow of rainbow colors in which Thunder is clothed.

"No Coosa will fail to note the appearance of the creatures who were active in Ancient Days, though some people are better than others at interpreting their meaning. All will ponder the meaning of the appearance of a rattlesnake, particularly a large one; or a bear; or a terrapin; or the sounds of a certain owl at night. Beings that cannot be seen are always behind the beings that can be seen, and any thoughtful person is attentive to this. Every Coosa has heard the ancient beloved stories, and every Coosa is aware of the events in Ancient Days that keep on occurring in the time in which we live.

"Beyond this, there are times in every Coosa's life when he will be particularly interested in trying to discover unseen causes. This is particularly so when things are going badly for him. In those times, the ordinary observance of everyday life is not enough to help a man understand his problems. On those occasions he will go to a priest, to one who is particularly skilled at discovering hidden causes. Since the under world teems with the hidden causes of things, a priest may take a person to the bank of a river, the watery path to the under world. The person stands facing the river while the sun rises above the edge of the earth. The moment of daybreak is the most special time. The priest cuts a branch from an oak tree and makes it into a switch. He stands out in the water and moistens one end of the switch with his saliva and sticks the other end into the water to about half its length, and while standing still he moves the stick opposite to the course of the sun [he means counterclockwise] to make a circle in the water. The priest pays close attention to this circle of water, and if anything intrudes itself into the circle, whether the shadow of a bird flying over-head, or a minnow breaking the surface, or a leaf floating through, or a bubble floating up to the surface, the priest can sometimes divine from this what is at work in the man's life. Most promising of all for the outcome of things is a circle of water that remains unsullied.

"Going to water, however, is not an altogether trustworthy way of discovering hidden causes. It is a method known to all Coosas, and all of us resort to it in the course of our lives. Often we do so on the occurrence of a new moon, when we wish to learn whether we will have good health in the coming month.

"A more reliable way is the beads."

The Raven stopped his narration and reached into a pouch that hung from his belt. He pulled out two beads, one red and one black.

"Have you a question you would like to put to the beads?" he asked.

What a dilemma he had put me in! Inquiring into the hidden causes of things by such means was satanic—no doubting it—and my giving assent to his doing so on my behalf would be a sin. Yet if I did not *seem* to give assent to what he was telling me, I would undermine his confidence in me, and then I should never learn about some of those things that are clearly taken seriously by Coosas and that we must know about if we are to counter them with the true gospel. And so, while praying silently for God's understanding and forgiveness, I pretended to take the offer seriously.

"Yes, I have a question," I said. "According to rumors coming from our camp at the Port of Ochuse, our chief, Don Tristán de Luna, has been acting strangely, and I fear that his sanity is being tested by a demon. Can your beads tell me who will prevail in this contest—Luna or the demon?"

The old man held up the red bead between the thumb and index finger of his right hand and said, "This bead is Chief Luna." He held up the black bead in a similar manner in his left hand. "This bead is the demon Satan," the old rogue said with a sly smile.

I nodded as if I accepted these premises completely, and in truth I did find myself more interested in the proceedings than I expected to be. Praying silently for God's nearness and protection, I watched the two beads in the dim light as they began to move, ever so slightly at first. Gathering strength, they moved along the first two joints of his index fingers, and then, stronger still, all the way down to the lower joints of his fingers. They moved up and down, following an irregular path. At first the red bead was more active, but then the black bead picked up strength and began to follow a serpentine movement. The red bead meanwhile became weaker and weaker until at last it lay still against his finger. The black bead still moved vigorously in the other hand. I could not see how the beads were impelled to move. It seemed not so much that his fingers caused the beads to move, but rather that the beads caused his fingers to move.

The old man's face was grim. "I am afraid that your chief may indeed be beset by the demon Satan, and the outcome does not look good. It is possible, of course, that something else of which we are un-

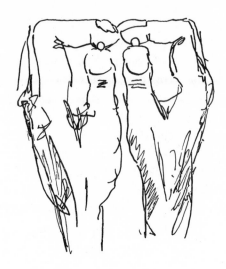

aware has caused the beads to behave falsely. There is a more reliable method I can use for an answer, if you wish for me to proceed."

It was most curious to me that I took seriously what the old man was saying. If the beads spoke with the voice of Satan, then I should have continued to regard their activity with the greatest mistrust. But now a deeper sense told me that the Raven was actually sincere—that he was on the side of Luna, not of Satan. And if he were against Satan in this matter, then perhaps in this instance his divination was somehow on the side of God. As Our Lord himself said, "If Satan works against Satan, he is divided against himself; so how can his kingdom last?"

That is the best explanation I can offer for the feeling I had that God was truly present as I replied to the Raven, "Yes, please do inquire further if you are able. The more we know about this matter with Don Tristán de Luna, the more prepared we will be to meet the danger."

"Then I must go and fetch what I need," said the old man. "It lives in an underground place." He got up and left the house. I fully expected him to return with some creature in tow, but when, after a while, he came back into the house, he was carrying only a small object wrapped in what appeared to be a piece of dressed deerskin.

He whispered some words to the object which I could not make out, and I looked to Teresa for a translation. She sat looking at the old man wide-eyed and rather pale around her mouth; then she gave me the shrug and blank face she reserved for such occasions.

"This is my *sapeya*," he said as he unwrapped a circular piece of deerskin revealing a rather large, reddish-colored crystal. It was partly encased in a small piece of deerskin, sewn to fit it exactly, as if it were the crystal's dress, and the casing appeared to be encrusted with dried blood as well as with a quantity of red ocher pigment.

"*Sapeya* crystals come from horned serpents," he said. "Some of them come from their scales, and they are rare, though I have known them to be found in the sand and gravel along rivers and creeks. This is not Horned Serpent—the great one—of the stories I have told you; these are from the small horned serpents that exist on earth today. *Sapeya* are capable of movement, and I have even heard of them spinning round and round in the sand in which they are discovered. My *sapeya* is one of the rarest of all. It is larger than most *sapeya,* and after I found it, I dreamed that it had come from the forehead of a horned serpent, where a diadem is located that gives off dazzling flashes of light. *Sapeya* must be tended with care. On every darkening moon, when the moon just disappears from the sky, I feed mine deer's blood, rubbing the blood over the *sapeya*'s clothing.

"*Sapeya* are prized by hunters because they are irresistible to deer. Often a hunter will keep red ocher pigment in with his *sapeya*. Before a hunt he will take a small amount of this pigment and rub it across his eyes like the eye markings of a peregrine falcon." Demonstrating, he dipped the end of his finger into the pigment and made horizontal V-shaped marks around each eye.

"Now I will inquire further into Chief Luna's struggle," he said.

My heart was pounding. Horned serpents' scales and deer's blood were surely tools of the Devil. My sense of trust had vanished, and I now feared that I was placing my soul, and Teresa's too, in real peril. I silently prayed again for God's presence and protection and crossed myself. That calmed me and gave me courage. I nodded for him to proceed.

"First, you must give me a white dressed deerskin," he said. "My *sapeya* wants more clothing."

I had no deerskin, and I had no cloth, but Teresa had a piece of cotton cloth tied to her belt for carrying small objects. She handed it to me, and I offered it to him, thinking that after he returned it to me, I would burn it and give Teresa a replacement. But later it became clear that the cloth now belonged to the old man.

He took the cloth and placed it on the floor. Then he placed his horrid, gore-stained crystal in the middle of it and wrapped the crystal in the cloth, saying words that Teresa was unable to translate. He carried the bundle to a jar of water, unwrapped the crystal, and immersed it for a moment. Next, he passed it several times through the smoke of the fire that burned in the hearth, holding it quite close to the coals to warm it.

Finally, he stood up and turned his back to us as he gazed into the depths of his crystal. He looked intently at it while softly talking to it. I looked at Teresa, who said that she could only understand a few of the archaic words he was using but that he seemed to be saying sweet, imploring words to the crystal, much as a man would use flattery to seduce a woman. I crossed myself again. My courage was holding steady now.

The old man moved toward the light of the doorway to get a clear look at the crystal, and as he studied it I saw his shoulders slump. Finally, he turned around, with the crystal held out of sight, and he said that Chief Luna must be warned at once that his well-being was in peril. The old man seemed to be utterly confident about what he was saying, and, God help me, it made me so uneasy that I shivered.

The old man told us that he must go outside for a little while to put his *sapeya* to sleep. Before he left, he said a few words to Teresa, and quite out of character, he laughed heartily. After he went out I asked her what he said. She blushed, and I almost wished I had not asked. But she was accustomed now to telling me everything. What he had said was that he hoped she had either a husband or a lover to go home to, because to bring a *sapeya* into a house in which a woman was present would make her behave like a doe in rut. This time I was more embarrassed than Teresa, perhaps because in her Coosa upbringing such subjects were commonplace, even when children were present. For her this was a mild affront compared to the mortification she had suffered earlier from his grotesque questions.

After what seemed a long time, the old man came back into the house. He returned to his favorite seat and indicated that he had more to say. He seemed stronger than before, perhaps because he was rising to his subject, which clearly enthralled him, or perhaps he was feeling the effects of the *ásse*. As always, the beverage was making me perspire. But I was as attentive to hearing his satanic stories as he was in telling them.

"Coosas not only seek to discover the spirits that cause things to happen in their lives," said the Raven, "but they also seek to influence them—to affect these spirits for their own purposes. I will explain what I mean.

"I have already told you how vengeful animals inflict diseases on the people who needlessly injure and kill them. Last week a Coosa man, a famous hunter, came to me complaining of pain and stiffness in his knees. His pain was worse in the morning, when he got out of bed, and the pain was lingering longer and longer as the day went on. I questioned him about his obligations to his ancestors, and it seemed he had not failed them. He had honored all his clansmen, both alive and dead.

"I asked him about his hunting. He told me that he is always careful to ask pardon of deer when he kills them, but he revealed that several moons ago, in early spring, in the time when deer give birth to their young, he had killed a doe, and nearby he had found her fawn, which he also killed. He had asked pardon for killing the doe, but he had neglected to do so when he killed the fawn. Could the spirit of such a young and insignificant creature be the cause of his affliction? I thought that it could be. I told him that he must take my treatment. The angry deer spirit had to be expunged.

"I prepared a medicine by immersing in water the roots of bear's bed fern and crow's shin fern as well as cedar. Both the hunter and I fasted for the duration of my treatment. We only ate a little thin *sááfke* after sundown.

"I performed the first part of my treatment just as the Sun was rising above the edge of the earth. I prepared a place for the hunter to lie down, and nearby I placed a terrapin shell containing two white beads. I asked him to remove his clothing. As he lay there, I rubbed the medicine all over his body—particularly on his knees and other joints— and as I did so I recited beloved words from Ancient Days. It is not enough to merely discover why a man is ill, or to prepare the correct medicines. One must utter the correct words. If the medicine is not empowered, imbued with the correct words, it will be useless. And it goes without saying that words uttered by one who is impure will be to no effect. This is why sorcerers are sometimes called *este poskâlke,* fasting men.

"These are the words I uttered:

Listen! Ha! In the Sun Land you repose, O Red Dog. O, now you have swiftly drawn near to hearken. O great knower, you never fail in anything. O, appear and draw near running, for your prey never escapes. You are now come to remove the intruder. Ha! You have carried a small part of it far off there at the edge of island earth.

Listen! Ha! In the Frigid Land you repose, O Blue Dog. O, now you have swiftly drawn near to hearken. O great knower, you never fail in anything. O, appear and draw near running, for your prey never escapes. You are now come to remove the intruder. Ha! You have carried a small part of it far off there at the edge of island earth.

Listen! Ha! In the Darkening Land you repose, O Black Dog. O, now you have swiftly drawn near to hearken. O great knower, you never fail in anything. O, appear and draw near running, for your prey never escapes. You are now come to remove the intruder. Ha! You have carried a small part of it far off there at the edge of island earth.

Listen! On the Southern Hills you repose, O White Dog. O, now you have swiftly drawn near to hearken. O great knower, you never fail in anything. O, appear and draw near running, for your prey never escapes. You are now come to remove the intruder. Ha! You have carried a small part of it far off there at the edge of island earth.

Listen! On the Southern Hills you repose, O White Terrapin. O, now you have swiftly drawn near to hearken. O great knower, you never fail in anything. Ha! It is for you to loosen its hold on the bone. Relief is accomplished.

After I said these words, I blew my breath onto the man's body, particularly onto his knees, suffusing them with my words. I repeated all of this for a second time when the Sun was above the rim of the earth, then for a third time a bit later, and for the fourth time when the sun was directly overhead.

"I gave the man one of the white beads that lay in the terrapin's shell, the one that represents good health; and then I gave him the other one, the one that represents the happiness that good health brings. These were his to keep, and perhaps to attach to his person. I advised him to avoid using too much salt or wood ash lye to season his food, and I told him it is dangerous for anyone with deer-vengeance disease to eat hot food. As well, I cautioned him to avoid eating the flesh of squirrel, an animal that humps its back like a person with severe deer-vengeance disease. This completed my cure."

I silently asked the Lord's forgiveness for my having listened to this pagan nonsense and for pretending to be seriously interested. But had I not done so, I am sure that the old man would not have revealed his beliefs to me. Indeed, I asked him to elaborate and explain the sense of the words he uttered over the man's body.

"Why do you pray to dogs when you have a patient so seriously ill?" I asked.

"It is not to actual dogs I pray," he replied, "but to spirit dogs. Remember that it is an angry deer's spirit I was trying to expunge from the sick hunter, and the ability of dogs—especially in a pack—to frighten and chase deer is known to all."

"But why call on dogs of many colors?" I asked.

"The dogs are from the four directions, and their colors hearken back to the four cords that suspend the earth on top of the waters. Just as these four cords keep the earth from sinking into a watery chaos, I want these spirit dogs to keep my patient from a similar fate. Notice that I brought the dogs in from east, north, west, and then south, always moving opposite the course of the Sun. The Sun always starts her day by moving to her left, and she gets angry at anyone she thinks is mimicking her. You should know by now that no one in his right mind risks incurring the Sun's wrath. She will not be mocked."

"But if all of these spirit dogs have carried a piece of the offending spirit deer to the edge of the earth in the four directions, why do you need to invoke the White Terrapin?" And with this question, imply-ing that I acknowledged the validity of the old man's assumptions, I began to wonder if I were losing hold of my sanity.

"Oh, we must always call the White Terrapin in such cases," he said. "Because deer-vengeance pain in the joints is so stubborn, a cure re-quires an adversary who is patient and will pull and tug on it for a very long time. As you should know from the stories I have already told you, that is terrapin exactly."

The old man seemed to have an answer for everything. I had only one more question. "Why do you refer to the spirit dogs and the spirit terrapin as 'great knowers who never fail'?"

"It is simple," he said. "If we want them to help us, we must flatter them. Flattery makes them come to us boldly and do the most that they can do."

It was disconcerting that I was beginning to see that the many fantastical things the old man had been telling me for all these nights were not just a pack of disconnected lies. There was a barbaric regularity behind his stories. Individually, they were nonsense, but taken altogether even I was beginning to see a certain logic in them. I could not deny it.

The Raven was ready to tell me more, and I, God help me, was ready to listen.

"Coosas not only seek to gain advantage over the unseen forces that affect our health, we seek advantage over the forces that affect the world at large. Coosas have a saying that when Old Lady Corn is growing in the fields, she is supreme. If our corn does not thrive, we do not thrive. Corn needs rain, in the right amounts and at the right times in spring and summer. A drought can cause the corn to fail, and too much rain can drown it.

"Controlling rain is difficult, tricky. I myself have little ability to control rain. It is only rare individuals who possess this ability, seemingly from birth. We call such an individual a *kéélth:a,* a knower. They have a special relationship with Horned Serpent; they do not fear Horned Serpent, and Horned Serpent seems to like them. A *kéélth:a* fasts and goes out to a quiet place in the woods where he throws beads toward the south to persuade the White Person to bring rain. He puts some clay in a basin of water, and when the clay floats to the top of the water, it means that it is going to rain.

"A famous old *kéélth:a* I once knew would take pieces of red sumac wood to the Coosa River and feed them to Horned Serpent, who would pay him back by causing the White Person in the south to bring rain.

"I have seen this *kéélth:a* turn a storm. Several years ago, some very dark clouds came rolling in from the west at a time when the corn was newly sprouted and vulnerable to drowning. This *kéélth:a* faced the storm, and stretching out his hands toward it, he said:

Listen! O now you want to make love. Ha! I am exceedingly afraid of you. But yet you are only tracking your wife. Her footprints can

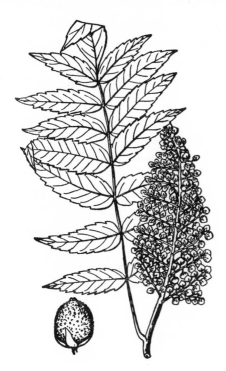

Red sumac

be seen over there, directed upward toward the heavens. I have pointed them out for you. Let your paths stretch out along the tree tops on the lofty mountains and you shall have paths to where you two can lie together without being disturbed. Let the paths you follow be where the waving branches meet. Listen!

Then the *kéélth:a* pulled off a blade of the small corn and waved it while he blew his breath in the direction in which the rain was to go. As it turned out, it did rain, but the young corn was not damaged."

"But why," I asked, "did he address the storm as looking for his wife?"

"All beings understand the attraction of one sex for the other—how strong the pull is. The *kéélth:a* meant to cajole the storm into taking a path through the mountains north of our settlements, to its loved one in the forest, where they would not be disturbed while they made love.

"People adore a *kéélth:a* who can bring rain to a drought," he said, "and they regale him with stacks of firewood and other gifts. But being a rain *kéélth:a* can be dangerous. A famous *kéélth:a* was once asked to bring rain to end a drought, and he brought a frightening storm that drowned half of our corn crop. Coosas were so angry with him that he became afraid to show his face in the plaza. For his part, he blamed the storm on Coosas who persistently violated rules and avoidances."

"Is a *kéélth:a* the same as a sorcerer?" I asked. I had heard the old man refer to sorcerers when he told the story of the bear-man. Now I wanted him to elaborate because sorcery surely betokened the work of the Devil.

"No, a *kéélth:a* is a *kéélth:a*," said the old man. "A sorcerer has a different nature. A sorcerer is one who causes things to happen by saying words or thinking thoughts. Sorcery is not a rare or unusual matter in Coosa. Any Coosa woman might utter words to make her food cook more rapidly. Any man might utter words to help him kill a deer to feed his family. Any Coosa of almost any age might utter words for good health upon seeing a new moon. Such words are common knowledge to the people of Coosa, and the saying of them is an everyday matter."

I pressed the old man to give me some examples of such words.

"It sometimes happens that a man will begin to worry about his wife's affections," he said. "He may begin to think that a rival is interested in her, or she in him. I will recite for you a saying that ensures her affections and detracts from the rival. The worried husband says this at night, after his wife has fallen asleep:

Listen! O, now you have drawn near to hearken. Your spittle, I take it, I eat it. Your body, I take it, I eat it. Your flesh, I take it, I eat it. Your heart, I take it, I eat it.

Listen! O, now you have drawn near to hearken, O, Ancient One. This woman's soul has come to rest at the edge of your body. You are never to let go your hold upon it. It is ordained that you shall do just as you are requested to do. Let her never think upon any other place. His soul has faded within him. He is bound by black threads.

The man says this for four successive nights, and each time he moistens his fingers with his saliva and rubs it on his wife's breast. The would-be seducer is wrapped about with black threads, as if caught by a spider."

"Do such sayings always have their intended effect?" I asked the Raven.

"Of course not," he said. "But frequently the wife stays faithful."

"Then the words in themselves do not have any power."

"Of course they do," said the Raven. "If the words fail, it may only mean that the rival lover, or his sorcerer, is using words of his own that are stronger. Or the strongest words may be those of a third person who has no interest in the woman but who wants to cause distress to the couple by rupturing their marriage.

"Let me give you an example of an act of sorcery that did have its intended effect, an act that I myself set in motion. It took place after Soto came here. It occurred after the battle at Mabila, when so many of our young men died. Because of the distress and disorder, Coosa was full of sorcery and counter-sorcery for a long time afterward.

"There was one old man of the Bird clan who was much disliked in Coosa. Even his own clansmen disliked him. We had suspected for a long time that he was using sorcery against people in a wild and irresponsible way. After the battle at Mabila, rumor had it that this man had uttered words intended to strengthen Soto. To test him, in a very indirect way, I implied such to him on one occasion, and from his response, I concluded that the rumor must be true. Such a black heart could not be allowed to continue among us. I determined to remove this man from this world by uttering some strong words.

"Truly serious sorcery is always worked by means of one of the four sacred plants—*heche lapóchkee*—tobacco. It is specially grown in very small patches, out in the forest. The ground is prepared by piling up wood from a lightning-struck tree. The wood is then set afire, and as it burns it kills the weed seeds that lie in the soil. The tiny seeds of tobacco are planted in this burned area. The mature tobacco is harvested, dried, and preserved. Then the tobacco is empowered. That is, the sorcerer's words are infused into it, and the tobacco is then used to convey their power to the intended target.

"I empowered some tobacco at dawn on the bank of the river, when the three worlds were coming distinct in the first light of the Sun. I held the tobacco in my left hand, and as I uttered the words, I kneaded the tobacco counter to the sun's direction with my right hand. And finally I blew my breath into the tobacco and rubbed some of my spittle on it. I meant for this evil sorcerer to go mad. To that end I said these words:

Your pathways are black. You are wood, not a human being! Dog dung will cling nastily to you.

You will be living intermittently. *Auuuuuu!* you will be saying as you walk along toward the Darkening Land.

Your black guts will be lying all about. You will be lonely.

You will be like a brown dog in heat. You are changed. You have just become old, you of the Bird clan.

In the very middle of the wilderness, changed, you will be wearing a necklace of dog dung around your neck. *Auuuuuuu!* you will be saying.

Your pathway lies toward the Darkening Land!

"These words were meant to spoil the evil sorcerer's soul, transforming him into a wooden person, with none of the feelings of a normal person. From that state he would turn into the semblance of a dog, befouled in his own shit, entangled in his own guts, made mad by dog desire, howling crazily in the night. I smoked some of the tobacco and blew the smoke in his direction. Then I sprinkled a few pieces of the empowered tobacco near the door of his house, where he was likely to step on it. Finally, I contrived to smoke the last of it in his presence, and he actually breathed in some of the smoke."

The Raven paused and looked at me grimly. "That is what sorcery is," he said.

Mother of God! Do they live with such black oaths and satanic incantations on all sides, every day of their lives? I tried to hide my dismay.

"And did your words cause the man to go mad?" I asked.

"Not immediately. But as time went on, and as the awareness of the man's evil nature became known to every Coosa, including the people of his own Bird clan, the man became thoroughly isolated. No one would have anything to do with him. His own clansmen were loathe to speak to him. He stopped showing his face in the plaza. He remained inside his house, and he lost his appetite and became emaciated. He began to talk to himself, and to do bizarre things. At last, he killed himself by eating water hemlock."

All of us fell silent. Teresa sat wide-eyed, forgetting to keep up her careful demeanor, and I am not sure how much I was able to conceal my horror at the old man's words.

"If I may say so," the Raven said at last, "a sorcerer among your own people has aimed such words at Chief Luna. From what you tell me, he is filled with blueness. His soul is spoiled. That is why he is acting so strangely. And that is why I advise you to warn him about it at once. If you do not, you may expect terrible things to befall him and his people. But if you warn him, he can take steps."

"Our steps are to pray to God Most High," I answered.

The Raven shrugged and said nothing.

I thought that by now I had plumbed the depths of Coosa deviltry and depravity, but the old man was not through. What he told me next reeked of the putrid fumes of hell. Even though he was suffering from hunger, lack of sleep, and the exhaustion of a long night of conversation, he sat bolt upright as he continued, enthralled by what he was telling me.

"Sorcery is no stranger to Coosas. If anything, it is too familiar. It can be difficult to discover the motives of particular sorcerers. But witches (*póólth:a*) are another matter. Witches are inherently vicious. One cannot discover their motives by the usual means because they do not have motives in the usual sense. Sorcerers are human; witches are not. Witches steal the health and lives of people by stealing their liver souls, and they add to their own lives the time their victim might have lived. When witches attack one's liver soul, it causes yellow skin, great pain, and terrible lassitude.

"They can cause other kinds of mischief—such as injecting objects undetected into the bodies of their victims—but death is what Coosas particularly fear from witches. The corpse of a person killed by a witch may be seen to have a bluish color in the face. A witch may be of either sex. They may be old or young, but almost always they are old. What is truly frightening about witches is that they can assume the shape and form of anyone. When we are out in the woods, away from our settlements, we are especially apprehensive about suddenly happening upon anyone. Is this a well-loved cousin coming along the path, or is it a hideous witch who has taken on the shape and appearance of a well-loved cousin?

"Coosas gossip and speculate endlessly about witches. We do not understand how witches came to be among us. None of the great spirits, so far as we know, created them. A famous witch—Spearfinger—lived in ancient time, but no one knows how she came to exist."

"Long, long ago there dwelt in the mountains a terrible monster whose food was human livers. She could take on any shape or appearance to suit her purpose, but in her right form she looked very much like an old woman, except that her whole body was covered with a skin as hard as a rock—so hard no weapon could wound or penetrate it—and on her right hand she had a long, stony forefinger of bone, like an awl or spearpoint. With this she stabbed anyone to whom she could get near enough and stole their liver souls. On account of this finger she was called 'Spearfinger,' and on account of her stony skin she was sometimes called 'Stone-dress.' When Coosas first heard of the *Nokfilaki* and their hard clothing, some thought they might be the children of Spearfinger.

"Spearfinger had such powers over stone that she could easily lift and carry immense rocks, and could cement them together by merely striking one against another. To get over the mountainous country more easily she undertook to build a great rock bridge across the head of the river running through Coosa. She had it well started when lightning struck it and scattered the fragments along the whole ridge, where the pieces can still be seen by those who go there. She used to range all over the mountains about the heads of the streams and in the dark passes, always hungry and looking for victims. Her favorite haunt was the trail at the head of Talking Rock Creek.

"Sometimes an old woman would approach along the trail where children were picking strawberries or playing near the village and would say to them coaxingly, 'Come, my grandchildren, come to your *póse* and let *póse* dress your hair.' When some little girl ran up and laid her head on the old woman's lap to be petted and combed, the old witch gently ran her fingers through the child's hair until she went to sleep. Then the witch stabbed the little one through the heart or back of the neck with her long awl finger, which she had kept hidden under her robe, and she took out the child's liver soul and consumed it.

"She would enter someone's house by taking the appearance of one of the family who happened to have gone out for a short time, and once inside and unsuspected, she watched for her chance to stab someone with her long finger and take out his liver soul. She could stab him without being noticed, and often the victim did not even know it himself at the time—for it left no wound and caused no pain—but went on about his affairs, until all at once he felt weak and began gradually to pine away, and he was always sure to die, because Spearfinger had taken out his liver soul.

"When the Coosas went out in the fall, according to their custom, to burn the leaves off from the mountain in order to collect the chestnuts that had fallen to the ground, they were never safe. The old witch was always on the lookout, and as soon as she saw the smoke rise, she knew Coosas were there and would sneak up to try to surprise one of them alone. So, as well as they could, they tried to keep together and were very cautious of allowing any stranger to approach the camp. But if one went down to a spring for a drink, they never knew but it might be the witch that came back and sat with them.

"Sometimes she took her proper form, and every now and then, when far out from the settlements, a solitary hunter would see an old woman with a queer-looking hand, going through the woods, singing low to herself:

> Liver, I eat it.
> *Yahóóla, yahóóla.*

It seemed at first a pretty little tune, but when he made out the words it chilled his blood, for he knew it was the witch, and he would hurry away, silently, before she might see him.

"At last a great council was held to devise some means to get rid of Spearfinger before she should destroy everybody. The people came from all around, and after much talk they decided that the best way would be to trap her in a pitfall where all the warriors could attack her at once. So they dug a deep pitfall across the trail and covered it over with brush, earth, and grass so that it looked as if the ground had never been disturbed. Then they kindled a large brushfire near the trail and hid themselves in the laurels; they knew she would come as soon as she saw the smoke, thinking she could find some people gathering chestnuts.

"Sure enough, they soon saw an old woman coming along the trail. She looked like an old woman whom they knew well, and although several of the men wanted to shoot at her, the others interfered because they did not want to hurt one of their own people. The old woman came slowly along the trail, with one hand under her blanket, until she stepped upon the pitfall and tumbled through the brush and earth covering the deep hole below. At once she showed her true nature, and

instead of the feeble old woman there was the raging Spearfinger with her stony skin and her sharp awl finger lashing out in every direction for someone to stab.

"The hunters rushed out from the thicket and surrounded the pit, but shoot as true and as often as they could, their arrows struck the stony skin of the witch only to break and fall useless at her feet, while she taunted them and tried to climb out of the pit to get at them. They kept out of her way, but they were only wasting their arrows until a small bird, the tufted titmouse, perched on a tree overhead and began to sing. They thought this bird was singing the word 'heart,' indicating that they should aim at the heart of the stone witch. They directed their arrows where the heart should be, but the arrows only glanced off with their flint heads broken.

"Then they caught the titmouse and cut off its tongue, so that ever since its tongue is short and everybody knows it is a liar. When the hunters let it go, it flew straight up into the sky until it was out of sight and never came back again. The titmouse that we know today is only a miniature of the other.

"They kept up the fight without result until another bird, the little chickadee, flew down from a tree and alighted momentarily upon the witch's right hand. The warriors took this as a sign that they must aim there, and they were right, for Spearfinger's heart was on the inside of her hand, which she kept doubled into a fist, this same awl hand with which she had stabbed so many people. Now she was really frightened. She began to rush furiously at them with her long awl finger

and to jump about in the pit to dodge the arrows, until at last a lucky arrow struck just where the awl hand joined her wrist, and she fell down dead."

"That is the story of Spearfinger. The chickadee is a messenger bird. Warriors who are out on a raid listen for it particularly. Often when a chickadee comes near camp and sings persistently, it means that an enemy is approaching. And sometimes a chickadee will fly near a house to announce the same thing.

"It always gladdens the heart of a Coosa to hear the song of the chickadee because it can be trusted to tell the truth. But is the song we hear truly that of a chickadee? The fact is, the song of the chickadee sounds very much like the song of the tufted titmouse. Is it the truth-teller we hear, or is it the liar? And isn't the same true of Spearfinger? Is it our beloved grandmother we see, or is it the dreaded Spearfinger, whose very heart is not located in her body where it should be?

"Coosas understand that one cannot see into a person the way you can see into an open-weave basket. All one can see is the outside, and a pleasant and attractive exterior can mask a monstrous interior.

The great Horned Serpent lived in Ancient Days, but smaller, inferior versions of him live on earth today; the same is true of Spearfinger. Witches—Spearfinger's descendants—exist in Coosa today. A witch may be anyone—a kinsman, a spouse, or a next-door neighbor—and may have a perfectly pleasant exterior, but the blackest of interiors. Why do witches exist? They exist because Spearfinger existed. Why did she exist? No one knows.

"Witches sometimes take the appearance of ravens—they only pretend to be ravens—in the light of day, and they transform themselves into owls in the dark of night. Pruk, I am happy to say, is able to recognize these raven-mockers. When he sees one flying overhead, he flies up in a rage and attacks it. Afterward it takes him some time to unruffle his feathers.

"Before they take on the appearance of a raven or transform themselves into an owl, witches must vomit up their guts and leave them behind, and when they return they swallow them and reassume their human form. The smell of guts often gives witches away. Witches cannot be explained, but they can be discovered. And when they are found out, they die, because they cannot exist when ambiguity and duplicity are stripped away.

"Witches can cause almost anything to go wrong in a person's life, but the most despicable thing they do is to steal life from the sick and dying. They are as attracted to seriously ill people as maggot flies to a dead dog. When a person lies gravely ill, and especially if he is at death's door, it is the most dangerous time for being attacked by witches, who can enter a house invisibly and steal life from the sick person.

"A priest or a healer will take strict precautions with a patient who is seriously ill. He scans the sky for raven-mockers and listens for their cries. Just as one can divine with a circle of white water, one can also divine with red fire. The fire in a hearth is an old woman who wishes to protect members of the household from harm. A healer will rake the coals of a fire in a hearth into a four-sided heap, the same shape as the mounds alongside our plaza. He will then sprinkle a pinch of tobacco on this heap of coals. Whenever a spark flares up, it indicates the direction from which a witch is approaching. If the particles of tobacco cling together and fall onto the top of the mound, igniting with a pop, it means that the witch is already inside the house. This unmasks the witch, and often that is enough to kill him or her. If the

Great horned owl

unmasked witch does not soon die, the people of a town may have to kill this person, just as Spearfinger had to be killed. This is particularly so for people who have been repeatedly accused. After they are killed, their bodies are cut up and left to be devoured by animals, or else they are buried separately, apart from other people."

The old man's voice began to falter. He was weakened from his prolonged fast, and he had talked far longer into the night than was his custom. It was as if he had pushed himself to this extraordinary length in order to finish telling everything that he wanted to communicate to me on this night's subject.

"Robles, the black-skinned man, had some understanding of witches," the old man said. "He told me that people in his homeland knew about witches. He had not heard about Spearfinger before, but he thought it was reasonable that a witch named Spearfinger had

Water hemlock

existed in Coosa in Ancient Days. Feryada also knew of the existence of witches, but he insisted that they were the work of the spirit Satan. I knew this to be false. Coosas had experience with witches long before any of us ever heard of the existence of Satan."

All of us were tired. We sat in silence for a few moments. I myself was gathering strength to stand up and leave. But when I made a motion to do so, Teresa did not follow me. She sat with her shoulders slumped, looking down at her hands.

"What is it?" I asked her.

"I am afraid that someone is working sorcery on me," she said, and she pulled out from the belt of her skirt a short length of a weed stalk. "I found this today at the entrance to my house. By the manner in which it lay against the doorway, I thought it unusual, and I picked it up and brought it with me. I wanted to show it to the Raven."

She repeated this in the Coosa language and handed it to the old man, who turned it around in his fingers.

"Yes," he said, "this is a piece of water hemlock stalk. Be sure to wash your hands before you put food in your mouth. The poison is very strong."

He peeled the hollow stalk open and examined its contents. "Here are splinters from a lightning-struck tree, mud-dauber dirt, crushed wasps. It is certain some Coosa has enmity for another and wishes illness for that person, perhaps even death. But for whom is it intended and why?" He looked narrowly at Teresa. "Are you feeling ill?"

"No worse than usual," she replied.

"Then it may be intended for someone else, or it may be that it is more a warning than a true act of sorcery. This hemlock may not have been empowered by words. Have you offended someone?"

"I have not intended to offend anyone. But after first treating me like a stray dog, my mothers now come to me asking me to intercede on their behalf with the *Nokfilaki*. How can I, who am little better than a slave among the *Nokfilaki*, do what my mothers ask?"

"Perhaps you cannot," the Raven said. "But you must appease your mothers. If you cannot do as they wish, at least give them soothing words and let them know that you are truly their daughter. As a precaution, it would be good to put some cedar boughs into a fire and rub the smoke onto your body." He rummaged around under his bed and came out with a buckskin thong to which was tied the foot of a bird of prey. "Here. Wear this owl's foot around your neck. It will put sorcerers on notice. They will know their words could come back on them. If you begin to feel ill or have more difficulties, let me know at once."

Teresa nodded and gave him a small, grateful smile. After all their earlier difficulties, I was glad to see her receive from him a measure of kindness and protection. It seemed to me that the love of Christ was beginning to bond the three of us together, as strange as that may seem, given the nature of this dark Coosa world. But Our Lord himself, after the Cross, descended into hell before his Rising, and in that dreadful place, which was even darker than this one, he drew souls to himself through the power of his love. At that moment I thanked God for sending me here on this mission.

Teresa rose to her feet, but the old man remained seated, as if he had something more to say. We waited politely, though we were very tired now and wanted to go home to our beds. He, too, was weary but deep in thought. At last he looked up and added: "As much as Coosas know about the world and about themselves, every Coosa man and woman encloses a small or even a large mystery. Coosas know many things. Our knowledge is a great tree with many branches, but as is true of every tree, there is a knothole, an opening in this tree that leads to a rotted place within. That rot within is Spearfinger and her kind."

At the end of our last conversation, as the Raven bid us good night at the door of his house, we agreed that we would allow him two days to rest and repair the effects of his fast. Teresa and I were surprised when he instructed us that on our next visit we should come to his house in the light of day. Nevertheless, we returned on the designated day at just past high noon, as the Sun was beginning her decline toward the west. Pruk was perched on the top of the house, perhaps on the look-out for raven-mocker witches, and the old man was sitting just inside the door, shaded from the sun but still near the light. He had a piece of dressed deerskin in his lap, and he was using a bone tool to flake a flint arrow point. "My eyes are not what they used to be," he said. "I am making this point just to see if I can still do it, but it is not a very good one." He held up the small triangular point and turned it in his fingers.

For the first time since we had begun conversing, he greeted Teresa in a friendly manner. Though I could not understand what they were saying, it was clear enough that they were exchanging pleasantries. I asked Teresa what was the substance of their conversation. She said that in light of their last conversation, he had asked about her health. Then he told her that he could remember her as a young girl, running through the house-yards and gardens of Coosa, climbing trees, and teasing the boys. Her grandmother, he said, had named her the Climber.

I asked him why we were meeting in the light of day and why he had not interrogated Teresa about her menses as had become his practice. "Today," he said, "I want to tell you about things that happened long ago, but not in Ancient Days. I want to speak of certain occurrences when the world was young. With these stories we do not have to be so careful. Still, it would be best to go inside where we will not be disturbed." Once we were inside, he propped a thorny branch of honey locust against the open doorway, presumably a sign that no one else should come in.

The fire in his hearth had burned down to a few coals so that the only light came in through the doorway and down through the smoke hole in the roof. It took several minutes for our eyes to adjust to the dim light. "Today," he said, "I want to speak about a certain brother and sister of the Wind clan—Sun Chief and Sun Woman."

SUN CHIEF AND SUN WOMAN

"Long ago, in the earliest days, there was great, unruly disorder among the clans. From the time when the mothers built their fires to disperse Horned Serpent's fog, the clans had been jealous of their own. For people of all the clans, as for all creatures except the bear, vengeance was both a high virtue and a binding duty. If anyone injured a member of your clan, it was your duty to inflict an injury upon the offender, or if not on the offender, then on a blood relative of the offender. And this was especially so when an offender killed a member of your clan.

"The problem was that when the offender or a relative of the offender was killed in retaliation, that in turn would touch off another round of killings. Coosa was in disorder. People began to fear and distance themselves from each other. People even began speaking different languages. It looked very bad for all people. They had no way to rise above vengeance.

"The Sun had not particularly intended to create Corn Woman or Lucky Hunter, but it so happened that she did create them, and her progeny pleased her when they sang songs and danced in her honor. But now there was so much strife between them, they rarely sang or danced for her.

"The Sun knew that the clans did not recognize any power higher than themselves. No one could restrain the actions of anyone in another clan. The Sun, who sees all, examined each and every Coosa until she came to a brother and sister of the Wind clan who were living in the ancient village of Etowah. Both of them were extraordinarily handsome, and they were wise in the ways of people. It was not that the Sun's light fell only on them, but the two were so dazzling to the eyes that all Coosas knew they were different—set apart. Just to make sure that people realized this man and woman were special, the Sun conferred some of her fire on them.

"The young man kept this purest of fires always burning inside his house, feeding it with logs of oak and hickory from deadened trees in his cornfield. He purified the wood by peeling off its bark. This fire was never used for everyday purposes. It was not for heating or cooking, or even for lighting pipes. Nothing was ever thrown into it. It was never to be doused with water. It was kept burning for its presence, as an earthly representative of the Sun herself, and its smoke was a kind of umbilical cord to the Sun. People began coming to the young man's house to see this pure fire—people of all the clans, not just Wind— and they began to realize that this young man was wise beyond all experience. He spoke so fluently and beautifully, and with such authority and persuasion, it was as if the upper world were speaking through him. Whatever he said, the people heeded and remembered.

"The elders of the clans asked the young man how they might lessen the disorder that was among them. He told them that they must possess a white way of rising above the red strife that is the fate of the earth's vengeful clans. As a first step, he gave them the Law of Blood. Namely, if a man of one clan killed a person of a second clan, the people of the injured clan had the duty of killing the killer, or if not him, one of his blood kinsmen. Then the matter was at rest. It was settled forever. Further killings were abhorred by the Sun. In this way, the principle of vengeance could do its work, but at the same time it could be held in bounds.

"Moreover, the young man told the elders that they needed a white refuge from the red strife of life. Henceforth, he said, his own house would be a white house of peace. Any who had killed another could flee to his house, where the sacred fire burned, and there find refuge until some way of satisfying the fury of the aggrieved clan could be sought. Not all killings were willful acts requiring another killing. If, after a time, however, the aggrieved clan could not be persuaded to accept compensation for their loss, then the blood revenge would have to be taken.

"The elders went away well satisfied with what the young man had said. Far fewer killings occurred among Coosas after the Law of Blood was instituted, and some revenge killings were set aside after the young man's house became the white house of peace. The people of Coosa became more trusting of each other. They found, moreover, that the young man was persuasive. He could stand between angry clansmen and say one soothing thing to one and another soothing thing to a second, and often they could all be satisfied. He persuaded them to bring out their better sides. He rose above the opposites. He never used angry words to achieve his end, and because of this he never incurred anger.

"The young man's sister was as admirable as he was. She wore her hair pinned up in an elaborate bun, with strings of small white beads woven into it. The other women admired it, but they were hard put to duplicate it, and they decreed that this way of wearing the hair was to be reserved for her and her daughters. She was a wonderfully clever and attentive mother. And she was an extraordinary gardener, raising corn that was as good for admiring as it was for eating. All of the people of Coosa praised her garden.

"The young woman invented many customs that pertained to the lives of women. She grew tired of her brother's incessant questioning about her menses. He always reminded her of the carelessness of Corn Woman, whose menstrual blood in a river had given birth to Wild Thing—a mixed blessing, at best. The young woman built a small hut on the edge of town, and when she was menstruating she would abandon her house and garden and enjoy the rustic solitude of this hut. If the men wanted food, they knew where the cooking pots were. If they wanted the weeds cleared from the garden, they knew where the hoes were. The women of Coosa were well pleased with the menstrual hut.

"Indeed, the clan elders, both men and women, were well satisfied with all the new customs invented by the young man and his sister, and they began referring to them as Sun Chief and Sun Woman. The elders brought another vexing problem to them. It sometimes happens, they said, that a particular clan or clan lineage will suffer from lack of food or clothing, while other clans may have plenty. Sometimes a clan's food is destroyed in a fire; sometimes the disaster is war; sometimes it is flood or drought. The clans always look after their own, but when a clan has lost everything, how can the needy be helped?

"Sun Chief said to them: 'I will build a white storehouse—a storehouse of the Sun. Bring to me the first fruits of what you hunt and collect and of each crop you raise, and I will store them. When any of the clans of Coosa are short of food or clothing, they may come to me, and I will help them. Moreover, the people of Coosa should always bring to me the seeds they are about to plant, and I will enliven them with the Sun's warmth.'

"The people were well pleased with these new customs, and in gratitude they began to bring Sun Chief gifts of food beyond first fruits. They brought him all bear and cougar skins and some dressed deerskins as well, and all of this bounty went into the Sun's storehouse to be given out as needed.

"Sun Chief was always devising festive and pleasant ways to bring Coosas together. As time went on, they brought him not only the first corn they grew in their gardens but also a portion of the wild foods on which they depended. Sun Chief said that it would be good to have a feast on these occasions. People are never more content than when they are eating good food. Many of these were feasts the people had celebrated in their own way for a long time, but Sun Chief embraced these old festivals and made them his own.

"The first feast of the year came in the Deer Moon, in early spring, and it celebrates the animal from which Coosas get their most valued meat.

"The second feast is the Strawberry Moon, when the women and children go out and gather large quantities of strawberries. The men go out and kill a number of wood ducks. Wood ducks are unusual because, unlike other ducks, they both nest in trees and stay here the year around.

"The third festival is the Pokeweed Moon, when the first shoots of pokeweed come up in spring and can be stewed. Coosas greatly anticipate this feast because they have endured the cold season with no green vegetables, and they hunger for them.

"The fourth festival is the Squash Moon. During this month in early summer delicious small fish run in the rivers and are caught in quantity.

"The fifth festival is the Plum Moon. Large quantities of the red fruit are gathered, and some of them are dried to be eaten later.

"The sixth festival is the Mulberry Moon in the hottest part of summer. For this festival, many doves are killed and taken to Sun Chief.

"The seventh festival is the *posketa*—the fasting—or Great Corn Moon. This is a very important feast in late summer when the bread corn comes ripe and can be taken from the stalk and stored for use during the coming winter. The *posketa* is a rite of renewal and reconciliation, and the people endure a long fast in preparation for it.

"The eighth festival is the Turkey Moon, which comes at that time in early fall when the leaves put on their greatest show of color. At this time turkeys come out of the deep forest to more open country, where they feast on nettle seeds.

"The ninth festival is the Rabbit Moon. Many rabbits are snared.

They are eaten, and some of their skins are preserved for use. Quantities of persimmons can be picked up and their pulp dried for use through the winter.

"The tenth festival is Bear Moon, when the days are short and the bears are at their fattest before their winter sleep. Bears are not numerous among animals, but every year Coosas kill several of them and they hold small feasts.

"The eleventh festival is the Cold Meal Moon. This is in the coldest days of winter, when our stored food begins to run low. It is, however, a time when ducks and geese stop in for short visits and can be killed by hunters.

"The twelfth festival is the Chestnut Moon. Coosas relish these nuts, and they collect them in early fall, but this time in winter is when they taste especially good. Food is in short supply at this time of the year.

"The thirteenth festival is the Hickory Nut Moon. Hickory nuts preserve very well in their thick, hard shells, and we relish them in these last days before spring when there is nothing else left but corn. We crush the nutmeats and mix them with cornmeal to make a delicious bread.

"The clan elders were mighty well pleased with these new customs and festivals. They went to Sun Chief and asked him how his new leadership might be perpetuated always. Sun Chief told them that by Coosa clan custom he could not pass his office to his own son, but only to the son of his sister, Sun Woman. Hereafter, he said, Sun Chief shall be the eldest son of the eldest sister of the former Sun Chief. If it happens that a future Sun Chief has no sister, then the position of Sun Woman will pass to the eldest woman in the Sun Woman's line. In this way, no matter how many cousins there are, the successor of the Sun Chief will always be chosen by birth.

"This was a good solution because from ancient time Coosa men distinguished elder brother from younger brother and Coosa women distinguished elder sister from younger sister. The clan elders were so pleased with this rule of succession that they wanted to further elevate Sun Chief. They called out the people of Coosa to build an earthen mound at the edge of the *paaskóófa* (plaza) at the village of Etowah. On top of it they would put a temple for the Sun's fire. This would be Sun Chief's home. The mound was to be built out of new earth dug from a pit. The people referred to this mound in a roundabout way,

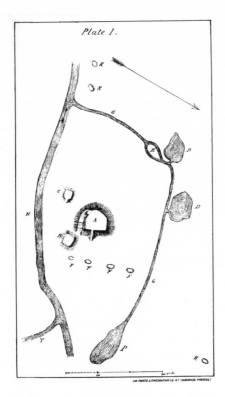

Plate 1.

calling it 'the high place.' They built the temple on top of it, and on the front of the temple they built a porch, where Sun Chief could meet in the shade with his principal men and warriors. Thus elevated, he could more easily converse with the Sun. As the years passed and the Sun Chiefs succeeded each other, this mound at Etowah was enlarged with new earth many times until it became a high hill. Other mounds were built there also, but they are not as large.

"Sun Chief liked his new house atop the mound. He began coming out of his door each morning to greet his mother, the Sun, shouting *hou!* to her several times in a loud voice. He blew a puff of tobacco smoke from his pipe to her and then puffs to the other three directions, and he indicated with his arm the path the Sun was to take across the heavens. From his high place he could see the point on the horizon at which she rose, and mark the changes of the seasons.

"The clan elders decreed that the sacred fire would be maintained by fire-keepers, eight in number, representing the principal clans. These were the people who had the fullest knowledge of traditions. They served in shifts, two at a time, and on penalty of death they were to take pains that the fire was never to go out. Sacred fire was never to be removed from the temple and mixed with ordinary fire. Nothing was to be put into the fire except the sacred logs. The ashes are cleaned out and kept in a special container, and periodically they are piled up at a special place near the temple called 'the place of spirits.' People are not to go there. When children sometimes do so, they are punished by being dry-scratched—by having their dry skin scratched with the sharp teeth in a section of garfish jaw.

"If the fire ever went out, it was understood that it would cut the people of Coosa off from the favor of the Sun, and horrendous things would happen to them. To oversee the fire-keepers and to be the protector of Coosa knowledge and traditions, there would be a High Priest, who would serve at the pleasure of the Sun Chief. Unlike Sun Chief, a priest is not born to his position. He must achieve it. He must learn a great deal, and he must know and understand the ways of people. I am now teaching what I know to several young men, and each full moon I examine them to see if they have learned anything. When a young man finishes this instruction, he is buried in a shallow grave, in which he breathes through a hollow length of cane, and a small fire is built on top of his grave. Before he can serve the sacred fire, he must himself 'die' and pass through fire, and when the earth is renewed he emerges as a new man. Unlike Sun Chief, a priest seldom wears special clothing, as you can plainly see from the way I am dressed.

"We still follow the ways given to us by the first Sun Chief. As for Etowah itself, although the mounds still stand, only a few people live there anymore, and it is no longer a great place. Etowah lies at some distance upstream from Ulibahali. As you *Nokfilaki* traveled from Ulibahali to Coosa you bypassed Etowah. Today Coosa is in the center, although the Sun Chief's mound, as you have seen, is not yet very high. In time it will grow larger. Every time a Sun Chief dies, a layer of new earth is added.

"The mound at Etowah is so very high because Etowah was the center for so long. It was a very great town. In the earliest days the clan elders agreed that because Sun Chief lived in the glow of the heat of the Sun, he must not sweat as ordinary people do, else he would surely perish. He was not to do work that would cause him to sweat in the heat of the day. He was entitled, therefore, to draw his sustenance from the food that his people brought to him. Moreover, all bear and panther skins, being rare, were to be given to him to use as he wished. Only he and his blood relatives were entitled to wear otterskin robes, the most beautiful skins of all. And the same was true of Thunder's metal, of which he was very fond. He decorated himself with large pieces of it, wearing it on his head and also on his body. Thunder's metal is both of the water and of the Sun. On hot moist days the rays of the Sun can be seen in the sky—they are Thunder's metal made liquid.

"The clan elders of Etowah freely instituted other customs that enhanced the standing of Sun Chief. When Sun Chief speaks to any person, that person, before answering, must hold up his arms, spread them wide, and thrice utter the sound *hou*. If it is an ordinary Sun, not Sun Chief but a relative, they say *hou* only once. And when Sun Chief has finished speaking to them, they retire by walking backward. When the Coosa people approach Sun Chief on their own initiative, they get down and place their hands on the ground and utter *hou* three times. They teach their children to bend over and touch their foreheads to the ground when they come near Sun Chief, and they punish them severely when they do not. From the beginning it has been decreed that only men of distinction may enter Sun Chief's house—women and children who are not related to him never enter his house. And no one ever touches his bed or his possessions except for his own wife. None ever stands between Sun Chief and a fire that is lit for illumination.

"Moreover, on certain festival days and when other chiefs come visiting, Sun Chief's subjects carry him about on a litter, the poles of which they bear on their shoulders. While carried thus, other retainers walk along extolling him by singing songs and playing music on cane flutes.

"Sun Chief stands at the center of the world. He stands between the forces that are opposed to each other on earth—especially the clans, with their ferocious self-interest. He also stands between the opposed fires of the above and the below—the upper world and the under world. It is said that Sun Chief stands at the center of the four directions and the three levels. Sun Chief has an ally in the Master of Breath. When people become disobedient or violate the rules of the clans, the four winds punish them, as when the blue wind comes from the north and destroys the early corn.

Horned serpent (Citico gorget)

"From the beginning, Sun Chief was on the best of terms with the Sun, mistress of the above, but he was also on good terms with Horned Serpent, master of the under world. Sun Chief was fond of swimming in the river that ran by Etowah. He could stay underwater for very long periods of time. In fact, whenever he swam he was communing with Horned Serpent. All of the Suns have a special relationship with Horned Serpent. That is why you have seen Sun women wearing shell gorgets around their necks depicting a big-eyed Horned Serpent.

"It is said that Sun Chief could charm Horned Serpent to surface and come to land by shaking his rattle and singing four songs. He always did this at dusk, when the birds had retired for the night, to keep them from raising such a fuss when Horned Serpent roiled and splashed in the water. At the edge of the water, Sun Chief would lay down a length of green wood on which Horned Serpent would rest his head. Then he would feed him short lengths of *tawa cháátee,* red sumac. While Horned Serpent fed on this, Sun Chief would scrape and cut off small pieces of his horns so that they fell upon a circular piece of white buckskin laid on the ground. This is the most powerful hunting medicine, and it will attract women like nothing else.

"The leaves of *tawa chááte* turn bright red in early autumn, and we mix them in with the tobacco we smoke. The fragrant fruit of *tawa chááte* makes a pleasant drink or a good-smelling perfume, and a drowsy person can touch it to his lips and stay awake.

"The first Sun Chief and his sister Sun Woman were magnificent people. They were the first Coosas who were white leaders above the struggle of the red clansmen down below. Sun Chief spoke so beautifully that no one with a self-seeking argument could prevail against him. He knew how to use just enough force and no more. He took just enough tribute and no more. And the first Sun Woman was his equal. Sun Chief discussed all important matters with his sister, and he always listened to her advice. She was a superb mother, raising up the boy and girl who were in line to be the next Sun Chief and Sun Woman.

"Sun Chief and Sun Woman lived a very long time. Sun Chief governed well, and the people prospered. Sun Woman married a man of the Cougar clan, and they had many children. After they died, the most skilled stoneworker in Coosa made statues of them. The likeness was so good that some people believed they had been miraculously transformed into stone. A special alcove was prepared for them inside the temple, and the statues resided there side by side, Sun Chief sitting with his legs crossed in front, as all Coosa men do today, and Sun Woman sitting with her legs tucked beneath her, as all Coosa women do to this day. On certain festival days, the two of them were taken out and carried about on a litter for all the people to see."

This was the first that I had heard of idolatry in Coosa. I interrupted the old man and pressed him to tell me more about the stone figures.

"I have never set my eyes on them," he said. "I only wish that we could carry them about at our own festivals and hearken back to those best of days of long ago."

"But you are the High Priest, and no mysteries are kept from you."

"The stone figures of the first Sun Chief and Sun Woman were buried near the edge of one of the mounds at Etowah many years ago," he said. "We Coosas are much ashamed of the events that led to their burial."

I suppose I should have been happy at this news, but it did not seem from the way he spoke that the idols had actually been denounced. I suspected that the motives that prompted the burial of the statues would not engender Christian joy.

"Why on earth," I asked, "should the people of Coosa have buried such sacred objects?"

"It is a very sad story," the old man said.

THE NEGLIGENT FIRE-KEEPER

"Many generations ago, while Etowah was still the center of the chiefdom, the sacred fire was burning low in the temple on a sultry, summer night. It so happened that one of the two fire-keepers in the temple heard that his sister had suddenly fallen ill. He thought that it would be all right to leave the fire to the other fire-keeper while he himself went to see about his sister. But with no one to converse with, in the stillness of the summer night, the other fire-keeper dozed off. When he awoke, he found to his horror that the fire had gone out. Though he blew as hard as he could on the charred wood in the hearth, he could not raise a spark.

"He went outside the temple and asked a passerby to bring him a hot coal of a fire to light his pipe. It was well known to all that it was forbidden for him to light his pipe from the sacred fire. The passerby obliged by bringing him an ember from a household fire, and the fire-keeper lit his pipe. Then he took the ember inside the temple and lit a profane fire in the hearth. He revealed what he had done to no one.

"Terrible calamities began to occur almost at once. A mysterious illness began to afflict the Suns, and several of them died. None of the priests could do the least bit of good for those who were ill. A terrible drought set in and the corn withered in the field. It was the most severe drought anyone could remember. Finally, the fire-keeper himself fell ill, and he feared that if he died without confessing his crime, everyone else would die. Already so many people were buried along the margin of the burying mound at Etowah, they were running out of space.

"The fire-keeper went to Sun Chief and prostrated himself before him, touching his forehead to the ground. He trembled and had difficulty speaking. At last he managed to say, 'I am the cause of our people's distress. For what I have done, I deserve execution. All I ask is that my body not be thrown out for the dogs to eat.'

"Sun Chief realized that the man must have committed a very great offense. Since only the fire-keeper knew what that offense was, he could take it to his grave. In order to help the man confess what he had done, Sun Chief assured him that he would never throw his body to the dogs.

"The fire-keeper confessed his crime to Sun Chief, who immediately called a meeting of his council of elders. They ordered the fire in the temple to be extinguished. Sun Chief poured water on the fire, and then he went outside the temple and sang a death cry. All in the town knew immediately what had happened, and the word spread far and wide among the towns of Coosa. All of the people fell absolutely silent, remaining in their houses.

"Sun Chief himself executed the evil fire-keeper. He struck him a blow on the back of his head with his falcon club, and the man died instantly. Sun Chief kept his promise about not feeding him to the dogs. Instead, he ordered that his body be cut into pieces and hung up in the trees for the birds to eat.

"Sun Chief, fully expecting to die himself, stood atop the mound singing his death song. A storm blew up and Thunder hurled a war club down and struck the ball post in the center of the plaza. The ball post splintered into many pieces, and its resinous heart pine center caught fire, burning with a hot flame even though it was raining. Sun Chief took this as a sign that this was fire of the Sun. But he understood that this fire had to be *wrested* from where it burned; it could not merely be taken. Blood had to be spilled before Sun's fire could again burn in the temple. The High Priest, who perhaps wished to atone for his own inability to discover the cause of the calamity, stepped forward and offered his own blood. Though it pained Sun Chief to allow it, the head warrior stepped forward and executed him. Sun Chief then took a burning splinter from the ball post and carried it into the temple and relit the sacred fire.

"The sickness ended, and so did the drought. But the damage to Etowah was never fully overcome, and Sun Chief began declining in health. When he died, he was buried with all his finery. Four of his favorite retainers were executed and buried with headdresses, ear discs, and war clubs made of Thunder's metal. They razed the temple and buried its contents—including the two stone statues—in a separate pit, along with the dismembered bodies of the temple keepers. It so happened that Sun Woman's son was living here in the village of Coosa, and when Sun Chief's mantle passed to him, he did not return to Etowah. A mound and temple were built beside the plaza here, where we sit today, and it was at this time that the reign of Coosa began."

If the stone statues were gone, I wondered, what had replaced them? I was most anxious to learn of the present existence of any graven images. Trying not to reveal my abhorrence of such things, I asked, "After the stone Sun Chief and the stone Sun Woman were buried, was this an end to sacred objects in the temple?"

The old man balked, and I knew he had said all that he was going to say on this day. He may have been uneasy discussing such matters in front of Teresa.

"I cannot say," he said, steering a careful course around my question. "It is dark inside the temple. It may be that I once caught sight of the image of Horned Serpent. And the temple is a place where one might put a *sapeya* safely to sleep."

He said this as if he, the High Priest, did not know everything there was to know about the temple. But I knew not to argue with him. When he indicated that this would be a good place to end our conversation, Teresa and I got to our feet and, after a few moments of polite talk, took our leave.

When we returned to the Raven's house the next day, he seemed glad to see Teresa, and the two of them exchanged pleasantries. From the way she responded, I gathered that he was teasing her in a friendly way. When I asked her to tell me what had passed between them, she explained that he had asked her whether her "mothers" and "sisters" were treating her better. It turns out that he himself had put in a good word for her with some of her kinswomen, using his prestige to ease her predicament.

Then the old man said something more to her, and she blushed deeply and held her hands in front of her face. Reluctantly, she told me that he had learned that a certain young warrior had lost his heart to her. I was not surprised, for I had often noticed this young man as Teresa and I walked back and forth between our encampment and the Raven's house. He was a handsome, intelligent-seeming fellow with a pleasant countenance.

Teresa told me that she had thanked the Raven for interceding on her behalf with her kinswomen, but as for the other matter, she told him that she is a Christian woman and the young man should develop other interests. Though I worried that these improved relationships between Teresa and the people of Coosa might lead to difficulties of a different kind, I kept my silence, and turned my attention to the Raven, who was settling down to begin our conversation.

"Today I am going to tell you about another great man from the early days," he said. "His name was Tastanáke, and I think you will be especially interested in how he came into this world. Robles said Tastanáke reminded him of Christ. But Feryada said he was more like another of your holy men, the one named Moses." The old man's eyes twinkled as he saw how much his words captured my attention.

"Sun Chief is not the only leader in Coosa. He is a white chief, Coosas also have a red chief. The person who is Sun Chief can only ι the first-born son of the first-born woman of the Sun clan, but the rea chief may be of any clan. He is not born to his position—he rises to it by being skillful and brave in warfare. However, this has not always been so.

"Long ago, the red chiefs, who were the war chiefs of Coosa, all came from the Cougar clan. Some were good leaders, and some were not. Skill in combat is not equally attained by all. In fact, it is a very rare ability.

"It so happened that in those early days, a particularly inept war chief came into power. He inherited his position, but he had no understanding of the skills of a warrior—the finesse of the bow and arrow, the crippling club, the stalking approach, the lightning ambush, or the heedless, mad attack. Instead, he relied on his sorcerers and his informers. He called himself Lightning Bolt, as if he were the earthly representative of Thunder. He thwarted Sun Chief's every move.

"Sun Woman's daughter gave birth to a new generation of Suns, including a girl named Dogwood Flower. While still young, Dogwood Flower's mother died, and because the girl was an orphan her clansmen took advantage of her. Whenever there was a task to be done, they would say: 'Dogwood Flower do this, do that, do the other,' and she would do it.

"They were always sending her to the spring in the Dark Swamp to fetch water. When alone at the spring, she would talk to herself. In time, she began hearing another voice. She had never heard such sweet words. They rippled through the air and at times came dripping down sweetly like spring rain. When this mysterious speaker finally showed himself, he was a beast of diverse parts. Mostly he was a serpent, but he had a cougar's head and teeth, a deer's horns on his head, and a falcon's wings—and a ravishingly handsome beast he was. As he twisted and turned, his muscles rippled and his colorful scales glittered. It was Thunder in the guise of a beast of odd parts. Dogwood Flower could not resist his advances, and she became pregnant.

"She concealed her pregnancy, and when the baby was born, she placed him in a canebrake. But she could not evade the stealthy ways and sharp eyes of Cougar, Bear, and Blue Jay, who lived in the canebrake. They found the baby and took him to Sun Chief, who tickled him under the chin. Sun Chief ordered Cougar, Bear, and Blue Jay to take him back to the canebrake and to rear him there in secret.

"As the boy grew up, he became as handsome as his father, and the girls of Coosa began finding reasons to go to the canebrake, where they hoped to see him, and even more, to be seen by him. The boy inherited more than good looks from his father; he possessed a remarkable power over water in every form. He knew just the words to cause a flooded stream to retreat back into its banks. Even in a drought he could bring rain; he could beckon a fog, and he could make that same fog lift. When he was twelve years old, some people began referring to him as Chief of the Waters.

"As Chief of the Waters, he was a fierce and determined competitor. He was uncanny at the game of chunkey. Wherever his pole slid to a stop, the chunkey stone meekly rolled over to it, as a fawn is drawn to a doe, and then fell over on the pole. Whenever he shot an arrow, it found its mark. When he took up the war club, the graceful moves he made were more dance than combat. When he was twenty years old, people changed his name to Tastanáke. He was the first one to hold that title.

"Now, Lightning Bolt had a diviner who was renowned throughout Coosa. This diviner came to him one day with a prophesy. His prophesy was that a baby had been found by Cougar, Bear, and Blue Jay, and that the baby had grown into a young man who was destined to kill Lightning Bolt. This was no ordinary prophesy, and Lightning Bolt was filled with apprehension. He suspected that this young man was the one people were calling Tastanáke, the child of Dogwood Flower and great-grandson of the reigning Sun Woman. He determined that he would set some traps for Tastanáke, and one of them would surely do him in.

"When Lightning Bolt next encountered Tastanáke, as senior to junior, he commanded Tastanáke to go to a certain deep pool in the Dark Swamp, dive into the water, and bring up some nodules of flint. But Sun Chief had gotten wind of what was going on and had warned Tastanáke that he had better be wary of Lightning Bolt. When Tastanáke told Sun Chief about what he had been commanded to do, Sun Chief gave him some shell beads and told him that at the deep pool in the Dark Swamp, he would see a small bird with a fish spear — it was a kingfisher. As everyone knew, kingfishers are fond of beads, and they will do anything to get them, even if it means diving to the bottom of the deep pool.

"Tastanáke went to the deep pool in the Dark Swamp, and he tossed one of the shell beads up into the air. The kingfisher flew over and caught it in his beak. The kingfisher wanted the rest of the beads for a necklace, and so the two soon struck a bargain. As Tastanáke waited on the bank, the kingfisher flew high in the air and then hurled himself into the water. In a little while, he surfaced, flapped the water off his feathers, and brought a flint nodule to Tastanáke, who exchanged it for a bead. The kingfisher then brought up another and another. Finally, the kingfisher's bead necklace was complete. Tastanáke had all the flint he needed, and he took it to Lightning Bolt.

"'Now you must do a second thing for me,' said Lightning Bolt. 'I need some cane for making arrows, but none will do except that which comes from the canebrake in the Dark Swamp.'

"Tastanáke had no choice but to obey. As before, he told Sun Chief what he had been commanded to do. Sun Chief warned him to take great care, for this part of the swamp was the home of dangerous poisonous snakes. Tastanáke should take some lengths of grapevine with him, and before he got near the cane, he should make them into hoops. When it came time to use them, he would know what to do.

"Tastanáke did as he was told, and as he ventured into the Dark Swamp and drew near the canebrake, sure enough there were rattlesnakes and water moccasins coiled and ready to strike. But he knew what to do. He took the grapevine hoops and rolled them past the snakes. As the hoops rolled along, it seemed to the snakes that they moved in an even more fluid motion than they themselves made when they crawled, and fascinated, they slithered off, watching the hoops roll. With the snakes distracted, Tastanáke ran quickly into the canebrake, cut down some small canes, snatched them up in his arms, and took to his heels.

"Lightning Bolt turned glum when Tastanáke handed him the bundle of canes. He then gave Tastanáke a third task. 'In the Dark Swamp there is a large tree with an eagle's nest on top. Kill the old eagles and bring me their fledglings.' As always, Tastanáke went to Sun Chief for advice. 'Find yourself a bottle-gourd vine,' he said. 'Make a lariat, and from the gourds make a helmet for your head and coverings for your hands to protect yourself from the eagles' claws. When the old eagles attack you, you will know what to do with the lariat.' Tastanáke did just as Sun Chief had said and went into the Dark Swamp to raid the eagle's nest. In no time at all the old ones flew down and attacked the gourds that were attached to his head and hands. With the birds flapping about him, he could not reach the nest. But he knew what to do. With his gourd-vine lariat, he caught both eagles and bound them together. Tastanáke knew of the respect which all birds accorded the old eagles, and so he did not kill them. Rather, he tied them up and hid them in the Dark Swamp, knowing he would have to do his work and get away before their allies found them and set them free.

"So Tastanáke shimmied up the tall tree, took the fledglings from the nest, and made it home safely from the Dark Swamp. He delivered the fledglings to Lightning Bolt, who was so beside himself with anger at Tastanáke's success that he grabbed up the fledglings and wrung their necks, killing every one of them. Had Tastanáke not taken the precaution of preserving the lives of the old ones, the lineage of eagles would have ended then and there."

The Raven could see that I was beginning to get restless. He had tantalized me with comparisons to Moses and Our Lord, but except for Tastanáke's conception and infancy, there was little similarity between him and Christ or Moses. The story of Tastanáke seemed to be just another wonder story, much like the ones he had already told.

"Just listen," the old man said. "We Coosas are not like you Christians. For you, Christ represents all that is good. You say all other spirits are evil and must be stamped out—spirits such as Satan and the serpent who tempted Eve. But we Coosas know that the world is moved by the clash of opposites. The Red and the White. These are in opposition, yes, but it is not that one of them is simply evil. Each has its place. The Red is different from the White, it is true, but it is also similar to it. Having a white leader like Sun Chief is not enough. We must also have good red leaders, men of action. Let me continue."

Of course I let him continue, but I no longer had any hope that Tastanáke's story would contain a link between the Coosa world and Christian truth.

THE CONTEST BETWEEN TASTANÁKE
AND LIGHTNING BOLT

"Lightning Bolt's three trials had failed to kill Tastanáke. Lightning Bolt was furious, and he was more frightened than ever. For his fourth trial, he challenged Tastanáke to a game that he modeled after the contest between the four-footeds and the flyers in Ancient Days. He instructed Tastanáke to prepare a playing field in the town plaza and to show up with a team of players on a certain day. Lightning Bolt would bring a team of his own to play against him.

"Tastanáke was to set up a tall pole in the center of the plaza and mount a basket on top of it. Lightning Bolt also commanded him to prepare a ball that could be spanned within the circle of a man's thumb and forefinger. Play would begin when the ball was tossed up into the air among two teams of players. A player could grasp the ball in his hand, or even put it in his mouth, but he could only score a point if he dropped the ball and kicked it with his foot to hit the post. If he succeeded in hitting the post, he scored one point, but if the ball fell into the basket on top of the pole, that counted as two points. The first team to score eleven points would win the game. Weapons were banned from the playing field, but a player could use both his hands and feet to dislodge the ball from a player who possessed it.

"Tastanáke did as he was told. He erected a pole in the center of the plaza, and when he attached a basket to the top of it, he secretly dedicated it to the eagles whose nest he had robbed. He made the ball from the leather of a deer's foot, that being the most vigorous part of the deer. He stuffed it with clay and deer hair.

"Then Tastanáke called together all of his allies—the Cougar, Bear, and Wolf clansmen. That night Sun Chief told Tastanáke that he himself would back Tastanáke's team against Lightning Bolt, who was the cause of so much mischief. Then he told Tastanáke and his allies what to do if they wished to win.

"During the night before the pole was to be raised, the women who supported them were to be compliant with any man's advances. If anyone wished to touch or fondle any woman, even if she were married, she must let him do so without complaint. If any woman refused to comply, the pole they planted would give the advantage to their opponent. The ball players, however, were not to join in these activities. In summoning the will to stay away from the women, they would increase their strength and sharpen their forces for the game.

"Both Sun Chief and his heir apparent would remain in the temple on top of the mound and fast from the night before the game until after the game had been played. They would drink only a very small amount of thin *sááfke* after the Sun had gone down. The fire on which it had been cooked would be a new fire, and this fire would only be used for cooking this *sáɑ́fke* and for lighting pipes of tobacco—nothing else. The tobacco they smoked would be the sacred tobacco mixed with red sumac leaves.

"The players also spent the night in the temple. They sat on low benches, facing in the direction of the town of the team they were to play. Sun Chief sat on a bench behind them, instructing them and admonishing them to acquit themselves as true men. If they got hold of the ball, they should not let go of it, even if they were beaten to death. He said this to them many times. Sun Chief drank *ásse* all night, and he vomited frequently. When he was not drinking *ásse,* he smoked tobacco.

"After midnight, the players howled like wolves from time to time, to show how devoted they were to each other. The dogs of the village joined in the howling.

"Sun Chief told them to be careful of magic being worked against them by their opponents. So Tastanáke brought in diviners of his own, who worked through the night to discern what their opponents' magic was and to frustrate or undo it. To work against their rival's fast for purity, Tastanáke and his players killed a possum and cooked it down until it was a sodden mess. They would use this vile stuff to moisten the pigments they smeared on their bodies for the ball game. The mere smell of it would be enough to weaken their opponents. In addition, they would rub on their bodies some mud from a yellow jacket nest mixed with water to give them the potency of that horrid little bug. They also cooked up some rabbits' hamstrings and sprinkled the stew on the path their opponents would take to the game.

"Some of the old diviners slept that night in order to see what their dreams had to say. If any of them dreamed something that betokened good or ill for particular locations around the field where their benches might be placed, they acted accordingly, always seeking to place their benches where the omens were most favorable.

"A final act of magic was performed just before the game. Before members of the opposing team made their appearance, Tastanáke and his players cooked up a big pot of *ásse.* They counted the number of players on the opposing team, and they made up a bundle of finger-length sticks of sourwood, one for each player on the opposing team. Then they threw the bundle of sticks into the boiling water. This would make the opposing players soft and compliant. The *ásse* leaves for this brew were gathered from near the village, not from the Dark Swamp, where they were ordinarily collected. This helped ensure that the leaves had not been spoiled by sorcery.

"At last Sun Chief's team approached the ball field. Sun Chief told them to pretend that they were several men short of their intended strength. When Lightning Bolt's team of Deer, Foxes, and other swift-animal clansmen were counted, Sun Chief's team came up short, and they asked several men who were lounging about the field to come and play on their team. One of these was Tastanáke in disguise, dressed in an old feather cloak and seemingly ill. He had been leaning against a post as if to hold himself erect. When summoned, he limped over to join the team.

"The two teams took to the field. Lightning Bolt's players had painted themselves red, while those of Sun Chief had painted themselves white. The red team quickly scored six points, and it seemed as if the whites would go scoreless, and Tastanáke would perhaps be killed. But when the reds scored a seventh point, Tastanáke flexed his muscles, doubled up his fists, snapped his forearms and fists back against his shoulders so violently his joints popped, and he let loose a roar that was as loud as thunder. In answer there came from the west the low sound of thunder, and then peals of thunder that grew louder and louder, though there was not a cloud in the sky.

"The next time the ball was tossed up, Tastanáke grabbed it and ran down the field, knocking players this way and that. Approaching the goalpost, he gave the ball a little toss and kicked it high into the air, and it fell down into the basket. The score was seven to two. The next time the ball was tossed in the air, Tastanáke repeated his performance, and he continued in this way, scoring again and again until he scored the winning point.

"The game was over and Tastanáke had triumphed over Lightning Bolt once again. Lightning Bolt was now terrified that the diviner's prophecy was coming true, that the time was approaching when Tastanáke would take his life. Lightning Bolt was desperate. 'I now challenge you to a game of chunkey,' he said. 'I will bet my life against your life.'

"Lightning Bolt had always been a champion chunkey player, and he felt sure he could best Tastanáke at this game, and then he would send him out of this world forever. Everyone gathered around to watch as the two players rolled the stone wheel and cast their poles after it, over and over again. Lightning Bolt was indeed a good player, and the rolling stone often came to stop right beside his pole. But Tastanáke was even better, and he skunked him again.

"'All right,' said Lightning Bolt. 'You won the game. My life is yours. But let me have a drink of water before I die.' He was trying to find a way to escape. But Tastanáke took his chunkey pole and stuck the end of it against the ground, and a clear spring came bubbling up. Lightning Bolt drank a long drink from it. 'That was a wonderful drink of water,' he said, wiping his mouth with his hand, 'but now I have to pee.'

"So Tastanáke shaved off a few splinters from his chunky pole and threw them to the ground, where a thicket sprang up. 'You can pee in that thicket,' he said, and Lightning Bolt walked into the thicket and relieved himself. He stayed in there a long time, but with everyone standing around, he could not get away, and so at last he came out again.

"'If only I could have one more pipe of tobacco before I die,' said Lightning Bolt.

"'All right,' said Tastanáke, 'you can light your pipe from the fire in my house.' Lightning Bolt walked into Tastanáke's house while everyone waited outside the door. Again he took his time. Everyone was waiting, but he stayed and stayed. When Tastanáke finally went inside to look for him, he saw that Lightning Bolt had knocked a hole through the back wall and was long gone.

"Tastanáke and his allies set off in hot pursuit. Lightning Bolt ran a great distance through heavy rain, fogs, cold mists, even frost. But Tastanáke possessed the formidable powers of the beast of diverse parts. As a serpent he was undeterred by water, as a deer he was fleet and long-winded, as a panther he was unafraid of the dark, and as a falcon he could swoop onto his prey with unfailing vision. With his bipointed knife he could stab and slash in all directions. Lightning Bolt was doomed. In due time, Tastanáke caught up with him, and as soon as he laid hands on him, he killed and beheaded him.

"Because of his splendid performance against Lightning Bolt, Tastanáke was afterward recognized as the true earthly representative of Thunder through his ally, Horned Serpent. His color is red, and he is greatly revered to this day. Before he left this world at the end of his life, Tastanáke laid down the qualifications of the warrior who was to succeed him. He had to be a mighty swimmer—a friend of water.

He had to be a master of the chunkey game. Even more, he had to be an unexcelled champion at the ball game, a game that is so rough it is nicknamed 'the little brother of war.' In one-on-one combat he had to have killed seven warriors and three war captains.

"Before his death, Tastanáke asked that his body be placed on a pyre, along with pumpkins filled with water. As the fire burned, the pumpkins would pop open, and he would ascend to the upper world in a cloud of steam. 'Whenever you hear thunder,' he said, 'you will know that it is me.' Thunder partakes of both fire and water, and he is a great friend of the Coosas."

I have seen the ball game played in Coosa much as the Raven described it. It is most interesting, and I have taken careful note of it, since the regulation of this game will pose a great problem for future missionaries. They only play it in the summer season, and—perversely it seems to me—they play it just after noon, during the hottest hours of the day. One town will challenge another town to a game by sending a courier who is most strangely garbed in something of the guise of a raccoon, with a raccoon tail, but with his body painted black with red streaks, and with horns on his head. He looks like the Devil himself. If the town he visits accepts the challenge, he comes back home with a great show, shouting and making a commotion with a rattle. But if the challenge is not taken up, he comes slinking back into town with his costume and his rattle slung from his shoulder on a little stick.

Except for a deerskin breechcloth, they play the game naked, and they wear their hair braided. After the start of play, they clump together in a mass that looks like a huge pinecone. And when the ball is thrown up, it is a melee. They climb over each other as if they were so many pieces of firewood; they step on bellies and faces; they kick and claw at each other. If anyone puts the ball in his mouth, the others will choke him, or jump on his stomach, to make him disgorge the ball. When the play moves away from the pileup, as many as three or four players may be lying on the ground, out of breath or prostrate from the heat, with their faces flushed bright red. Bystanders do no more than pour water on them to bring them to their senses so they can get back in the game.

They are careful to "sleep the ball" the night before the game, staying awake all night, talking softly among themselves. They always make new fire, which they take to the game, carrying it as coals smoldering in some bundles of fiber. They continually pay their respects to Sun Chief and Sun Woman, and most particularly to Thunder. They greet the goalpost by holding their hands together and saying *hou* three times in just the way they pay respect to their chief. And all but the players are utterly lascivious the night before the game, the women seemingly offering not the least resistance.

The coals of new fire they carry to their game are used to kindle a small fire in front of the players' bench. It is carefully guarded by their magicians, who pretend to discover by divination the thoughts and concealed actions of the opposing team. And they try to devise ways of polluting the fire of their opponents by, for example, throwing a bit of the scalp of a slain enemy into the fire, or sprinkling it with a brew made from cooked rabbits' hamstrings. They call this by a word that means "sorcery opposing sorcery."

It is a barbarous game, not only because it occasions lasciviousness and sorcery but also because of the physical mayhem that ensues in the actual play. Nothing could be more contrary to the peace of Christ, except war itself. From the mad disorder on the field, the players sometimes come away with broken arms, ribs, or legs, or are blinded in one eye, and even death is not unknown. The people pamper and spoil their best players, laboring for them in their cornfields and building houses and storage houses for them. When a game is to be played, with its days of preparation beforehand, everyone is so totally absorbed that they often let their fields go neglected. Of course, they gamble heavily, sometimes losing everything they own. That fellow Lightning Bolt, who invented this game, was surely the Devil himself.

On reading back through my transcriptions of our conversations, I was struck with what the old man had said about the meaning Coosas find in animals when they encounter them in dreams or in waking life. It is obvious that such animals could remind Coosas of events that occurred in their stories of Ancient Days, but he seemed to be saying more than this. He implied that the meaning of life is revealed to Coosa people through the events in their everyday experience. If this is true, it could prove to be very difficult to persuade them of the truth contained in the Holy Scriptures. If everyday life is their instruction, how might they ever be persuaded to undergo the difficult preparation for learning to read the Holy Book? Or, more practically, how might they be taught to respect and obey those who are able to read the Scriptures?

On my next visit to the Raven's house, I asked him whether a coal popping in the hearth isn't merely a coal popping; whether the sound of water rushing over a shoal isn't merely the sound that water makes; whether a serpent that crawls near one's house isn't merely a serpent; whether an owl hooting near one's house at night isn't merely an owl? Is nothing trivial? As usual, Teresa translated as he gave me his answer.

"Thoughtful Coosas reflect on the events of each day," he said. "The same forces and relationships exist in the large and in the small, and the one reveals the other.

"For example, you should understand by now that opposites exist everywhere in life. The red is opposed to the white. This can be seen in one's body, where blood is red and spittle is white."

To dramatize his point, he picked up a small piece of cast-off cane matting and spat on it. He removed a bag—made from the whole skin of an otter—that he carried tucked under his belt, and he drew from it the arrow point he had made the day before. He pricked his finger so that a drop of blood fell on the piece of cane matting. The white and red drops lay side by side on the piece of woven cane.

"Both blood and spittle are necessary for life," he explained, "and if either is spoiled or lacking, life can end. Any warrior knows that if he is injured or loses too much blood, he will die. All Coosas know, as well, that if their saliva is spoiled by malevolent spirits, especially if it turns murky and yellow, they will sicken, and if the offending spirit is not appeased or driven away, the person may die. You may have noticed that after telling a story, Coosas spit to show that their saliva is clear.

"May not the same contraries be seen in the house we are now in? Can you see that the floor is red from the clay into which the floor is dug? And though the walls are much darkened by smoke, they were once white. A house needs both a floor and walls.

"What of the town of Coosa? On one side of the plaza are the white clans, and on the other side of the plaza are the red clans. They never marry among themselves; white always marries red in the union of opposites. And I remind you that the temple of the Sun Chief is a white house of peace and a refuge that exists above the red strife among the clans of the town.

"What of life on earth? Life on earth could not exist without red fire and its opposite, white water. They do not tolerate each other; water extinguishes fire, and fire dissolves water into mist. Fire is like blood, the warmth of the body, and water in streams is like cool saliva. And just as saliva comes from the mouth, many streams have their headwaters in springs that come forth from the hills and mountains.

"Need I speak of the upper world? Red Sun and White Moon were created at the beginning of Ancient Days by the Master of Breath. Coosas who listen to the stories of their elders—and all do—can see in everyday life the same order that exists everywhere, and it has been thus since Ancient Days.

"So you see, if we begin with the small, my own blood and spittle, we can progress to the large, the Sun and Moon. But the order that is in the world can also be seen by beginning with the large and working down to the small. Listen.

"When Crawfish dove down beneath the ancient waters and brought up a bit of mud, it grew and spread rapidly to form island earth. When the new earth threatened to sink down beneath the water, it was suspended from the upper world by four cords, and together these four cords were two opposed twosomes. The red cord was in the east, the direction of the Sun's rising, a place of life and striving, and its opposite, the black cord of the west, was in the direction of the

Sun's descent, a place of dissolution and death. To the north was the blue cord, the direction of cold deceit and witchcraft, and its opposite was the white cord of the south, the direction of warm peace and trust. In the upper world, a full cohort of spiritual beings exists in blue north, black west, white south, and red east. On this earth, with Coosa at its center — and the ball pole in the center of the plaza is the center of Coosa — the four directions stretch out to the horizon.

"In the town, the temple is situated so that the door faces to the southeast, toward the Sun's rising. One can stand atop the mound and follow the progress of the seasons by the changing position of the Sun at her rising against the palisade and other structures. In this way we know when the days will begin to lengthen in the dark of late winter and when they begin to shorten in the long days of summer.

"But what about inside the temple, when the mound beneath it can no longer be seen and the Sun's light is closed out? I can tell you that the four directions can still be seen even there in the roof-support posts in the middle of the temple. Each direction is represented by a pair of posts. In the center of the temple, the sacred fire is fed by four pure logs arranged in the form of a cross, with the fire burning in the center, where the four logs meet.

"Are the four to be seen here inside my house? The floor of this house is as square as is the island earth. And the middle of my house is another square contained within the four support posts holding up the roof. Each of them represents one of the cords attaching island earth to the upper world. And the beds along the four walls are each the resting place of the various members of the household, just as the spiritual beings rest in the four directions of the upper world. The square interior, with its hearth, stands in the same relation to my house as the plaza stands in relation to the town of Coosa.

"Are the four directions to be seen in me? As I stand here facing in the direction of the red sunrise, I have the black west to my back. And as I raise my two arms, my right hand points to the white south and my left hand points to the blue north. From the small to the large, and from the large to the small, the same relationships can be seen everywhere.

"This is not to say that the four ways are equally present in all individuals. Each person contains all four colors, but in any person it is usual for one color to be stronger than the others. Red individuals are lively and active; black individuals are slow and withdrawn. White individuals are level and direct in their behavior; blue individuals are devious and vexing.

"I can show that the same is true of the three worlds—the upper world above us, this earth on which we stand, and the under world beneath us. In the town, the plaza represents the earth where people play out their lives. It is kept clean and orderly, and Coosas never allow refuse to clutter it. It is here that some of the most important rituals of Coosa are observed. The temple on top of the mound represents the upper world, where the sacred fire burns. The steps up the face of the mound lead to the upper world. In the temple the sacred fire is connected to the Sun by an umbilical cord of smoke. Sacred fire in the temple is to the plaza what the Sun is to the earth.

"The under world is down below, where we place the bodies of those who have died. The Suns are buried in the most honored place, in the temple floor and in and around the mound. Notable persons are buried in special places in the plaza. Ordinary people are buried in the floors of their houses or in the family compound. It is fitting that the bodies of the dead be buried in the under world, for death creates disorder, and the under world is a place of disorder.

"Like all Coosa houses, my house perfectly reflects the three worlds. The earth lies within the walls of the house, and the roof is the upper world. Beneath the floor is the under world.

"Would it surprise you to learn that Coosas see the three worlds in the body of a person? The feet are the under world. The body, along with the arms and legs, are the earth. And the head is the upper world."

Interrupting the old man, I challenged him, saying that the resemblances he had described are games of riddles and similes that any child can play. I told him that I could not see how the matters he had discussed—such as the existence of the opposites—had any bearing on everyday life in Coosa.

"Show me," I said, "how the opposites have meaning for everyday Coosa life in the same way the Holy Book gives meaning to the lives of Christians."

He answered me at once.

"Men and women are opposites, are they not? They are not born opposites—each has a little of the nature of the other—but Coosas hold up Corn Woman and Lucky Hunter as ideals for Coosa people to imitate. Corn Woman is the mistress of the garden, and Lucky Hunter is the master of the forest. Girls and boys spend their lives mastering the arts of gardening and hunting. Their lives are separate, and yet they are a unity in life. Remember the belt they wear about their waists? The right side of the belt is male, the left side is female, and the knot is the unity.

"When women are not out in their gardens, they are ordinarily to be found in their houses and in their lineage courtyards, along with other clanswomen, as well as with their brothers and unmarried sons. Each household compound has its rectangular storehouse, raised up on eight posts, in which corn is kept, as well as other foods, dressed deerskins, and such things that must be stored with care. Here the stored stuff is beyond the reach of rodents, who have difficulty climbing the posts. The women like to sit in the shade beneath these store houses, and the small fires they build send smoke up through the cracks in the floor, discouraging insects. This storehouse is Corn Woman's house where she first gave birth to corn and beans. It is also a safe place where young girls sometimes go for trysts with their lovers.

"Women are the red sex. They are never happier than when they are with the people of their fire, their clansmen. These are the people with whom they are most comfortable. Men are the white sex. They prefer to be in the company of other men—men of all clans. If animosity exists between the men of two clans, they have to find a white path to overcome it because success in the hunt and in warfare depends on it.

"In the plaza, males are represented by the ball pole in the middle of the plaza. Around the base of this pole is a small mounded area that represents the female. Again, the ball pole and the small mound at its base represents the union of opposites. In many everyday endeavors it is the same. In gardening it is the men who clear the land of vegetation and prepare the soil for planting, but it is the women who do the planting and tend the crops to maturity. In the hunt it is the men who kill the game and who field-dress it, but it is the women who cure the skins and cook the meat.

"There are times when men and women must be kept separate. When men are about to embark on endeavors such as war and the ball game, they must keep apart from women, else their powers would be diminished, for at that time they must be completely men. Men who are to embark on a raid or a ball game must withdraw into the temple or some other sequestered place, and they ordinarily fast. Women, when they menstruate or give birth, also sequester themselves in the clan menstrual hut, so as to be kept from men, else their health would be endangered."

This, I had to admit, was a kind of answer to my question. But the old man's idea of holiness was so different from mine. I could see nothing sacred in this Coosa religion, nothing to tie man to the deity. As best I could, I told him so. I am not sure he understood, but, as usual, he had a ready response.

"Robles and Feryada once told me that Coosa fire reminded them of the bread and wine of the Christian ritual.

"Fire is the gift of the Sun, thrown down to the Coosa people by her son, Thunder, and brought to us across the water by the clever water spider.

"Fire can be spoiled by contact with impure things, or by the bad behavior of people. The fire that burns in the hearth inside the temple is the purest fire. As I have told you, it is kept pure by fire-keepers who have this as their responsibility.

"Like water, fire purifies, but in a different way from water. Fire purifies by obliterating. When the matriarch of a household dies, we bury her in the floor of her house and then set fire to it, and on this same spot we build another house for the next matriarch in line. And we do the same when a Sun Chief dies, except we burn his house atop the mound and bury it beneath a layer of new earth over the entire mound before building a new house for the next Sun Chief in line.

"Each house in Coosa also has a sacred fire burning in its hearth. The ancestral spirits of the household are attentive to how people behave in the presence of the hearth, just as the Sun is attentive to how people behave in the presence of the temple fire. However, the fire of households is less pure than that of temple fire. It is exposed to bits of food, or drops of saliva that find their way into the hearth. Women who are just beginning their menses may come near the fire. It follows that as time goes on, household fires become less and less pure.

"This is why, on certain occasions, as when it is necessary to brew *ásse* before some important undertaking, such as curing an illness, the men will kindle a new fire with a fire drill. It is everyday fire, but it has not been made impure by any human act or failure to act."

I did not even attempt to address his comparison of Coosa fire with the Body and Blood of Christ. He was right in seeing a similarity in the sacred regard accorded to each, but this was no time to try to show him the difference by explaining the meaning of the Mass. Much thought must be given to how the Coosas perceive their spiritual world before such an attempt could possibly have any real effect. For this reason I was careful to stay with the Raven's view of things.

"It follows," I said to him, "that household fires must become more and more impure as time goes by. They must eventually become dung heaps of impurity."

"In a few days," he said, "you will see how household fires are purified in Coosa." And with that, his eyes twinkling and his voice still full of energy, he brought our session to a close. I wondered what he meant, but with the Raven I had learned to wait and see.

As we said our goodbyes, the old man called Teresa over and whispered something in her ear. She flinched and blushed and was more flustered than I had ever seen her. The old man slapped his leg and laughed.

As we walked back to our quarters, I asked Teresa to tell me what he had said. She refused, but I kept insisting until finally she began to speak.

"He said to me, 'I hear you have been trying to chase the fox from the storehouse.'"

I could see nothing at all offensive or embarrassing in that, and I kept after her to explain why it had so discomfited her.

"The young man who has been dogging my heels is named Chola Háácho, Crazy Fox," she said, as if that explained everything.

"But what is it about the storehouse?"

"If you must know," she said, "two nights ago Chola Háácho and I met in a storehouse for an innocent conversation. One of my clan sisters saw us coming out together, and now the story must be all over Coosa. Everybody knows everything in Coosa, and they always think the worst of every piece of gossip they hear."

I myself was endeavoring not to think the worst. "Have you sinned with this man?" I asked her carefully, trying not to impart to her my sense of alarm.

"No," said Teresa. "It is just that he is a handsome man, much honored in Coosa, and it pleases me that he likes me. In fact, it pleases me so much that I have to keep reminding myself that I am a Christian woman, not a Coosa. But, no, I have not sinned with him."

13 Posketa

The day after my most recent conversation with the Raven, I noticed extraordinary activity everywhere in the town. On all sides, people were bustling about, cleaning and refurbishing. They were feasting prodigiously, as if they were trying to eat up all of the remaining food in their larders from the previous year. The women were cleaning their houses, and the men worked alongside them, making long-neglected repairs. I noticed, as well, that the men were making similar repairs to the temple and portico on top of the mound. They even swept the plaza clean, piling up the old dirt and litter around the margins of the space. I could see that this practice of piling up old earth over the years had formed a notable earthen ridge along the margins of the plaza. I recalled that the mound, in contrast, had been made of new earth. The women were making pottery, weaving a great many split-cane mats, and fashioning new clothing.

I asked Teresa what was afoot, and she said that an important festival and ritual was about to begin. It had to do with the corn coming ripe, she said. She remembered it from her childhood as an especially happy time. When we next went to the Raven's house, a few days later, he met us at the door, gaunt again, obviously fasting. Pruk was perched on his shoulder, waggling his great beak about, cocking his head, looking us up and down with a baleful eye. The old man told us that these were the "broken days," explaining that several days ago, Sun Chief had sent runners out with identical bundles of small pieces of switch cane to the several towns of Coosa. Each day the headman of a town pulled one stick from the bundle, broke it, and threw it away, and on the day the last stick remained, all the people of Coosa, from far and wide, were to come and encamp at the principal town. That would be tomorrow morning.

He told us that this was the *posketa*—the great fast of the green corn celebrated when the bread corn was ripe enough to be eaten green. It would go on for four days, and the last of these—*nettaa hátkee,* the white day—was the most important. With this great fast—he himself was already fasting—the world of Coosa would be made new again. Sun Chief had ordered beloved old men to go out and collect the roots and leaves that would be used in medicines in the ceremony. He cautioned Teresa and me that we should not so much as chew on a leaf of the new corn, we should speak to each other in low voices, and we should not eat any meat or salt until the white day. He reminded me that in our last conversation I asked how fire was purified, and he said that if I would only keep my eyes open I would see.

Then he excused himself and said that he would not be able to talk to me again until after the *posketa* was over. Except during ceremonial acts, he had to remain isolated with other men inside the temple and on the temple porch until the *posketa* ended. He said that Teresa would be able to explain to me in a general way what was going on, and he would answer specific questions later. "This is Thunder's tree," he said, propping up a branch of thorny honey locust across the entrance to his house as he went back inside.

It was late afternoon, and as Teresa and I walked back past the plaza, we saw that a dance had just begun. The only dancers were women, and they were forming their usual patterns of circles, spirals, and lines. But their motions seemed lascivious to me, and Teresa said that this was the smudge-faced dance in honor of the Moon. I asked whether it had anything to do with the Moon's illicit affair with the Sun, and she said that it did. She said this dance is similar to what occurred before the ball game I had seen. The customary rules regarding proper behavior between the men and women had been relaxed, and that is putting it mildly. The dance seemed to express the notion that their social order was in a shambles and needed to be remade.

Tomorrow, Teresa explained, everything would be different. Men and women would be forbidden even to go near each other. They could not speak to each other, and they had to remain strictly segregated. All had to begin a fast that would last for three days. It was particularly enforced from sunup to sundown, and it was most strictly observed by Sun Chief, the priests, the honored warriors, and the principal men. After sundown, some of them would drink a little bit of thin hominy. The young men tried to observe the fast, but many of them violated this and other prohibitions. All were prohibited from eating meat and from adding salt or ashes to their food for the duration of the ceremony. And most especially, until the end of the festival, they were not to eat even a taste of the newly ripened green bread corn. Teresa said she especially remembered from her childhood how anxious she had been to eat the sweet, new corn—it was so tempting to sneak out into the fields and take an ear. But the old bread corn had to be purged before the new bread corn could be eaten. If any violated this prohibition in a public way, he would be whipped, his house would be burned, all of his property would be seized and placed in Sun Chief's storehouse, and he would be banished from Coosa as a defiled person. If any person secretly violated this prohibition, he would surely fall ill with intestinal worms, and the people of the town might be subject to famine in the coming year. These threats were enough to frighten the children and keep them away from the cornfields.

Teresa and I lingered about the plaza, and as the afternoon wore on, she began remembering more and more details of the festival. When I asked her about the strongly scented herbs with which the people had festooned their refurbished houses, Teresa remembered that it was *weláána,* wormseed or chenopodium, one of the more important herbals the Raven had shown us. She said that on this night the old people would tell their restless children many animal stories. But the unmarried men and women would be out and about, and I might expect to hear them laughing and teasing each other. At dawn the following day, everything would change. If any of the men broke any of the prohibitions, they would be punished by dry-scratching.

We stayed at the plaza until sundown and then went home to our beds. It was indeed a restless night. Everyone in the town was stirred up with anticipation, and I myself was able to sleep very little. I was anxious to see what would happen in the next few days. Already I had been able to understand so much more than I would have been able to do before my many conversations with the Raven. Teresa had promised to stay near me during the festival to help me take in all that unfolded, which she subsequently did. My intent is to describe here all that I saw and learned.

First day. The people were up at dawn to decorate and refurbish the temple. They painted it inside and out with white clay mixed with water. They brought in new split-cane mats the women had woven to be used on the beds and, I presume, the floor.

Early in the morning, the men gathered in the plaza to drink *ásse.* Before drinking, they dipped the first two fingers of the right hand into the cup and then flipped a few drops in each of the four directions. The principals among them assembled at the foot of the mound. Sun Chief came out of the temple, dressed in an otter-skin shawl draped loosely about his shoulders and wearing a polished copper disk with a cross embossed on it. On his head he wore a crown of white feathers, with the tallest in front, and descending in length on both sides to smaller ones. Two of his beloved old principal men stood near him with short staffs to which a half-circle fan of eagle feathers had been attached. Periodically, they would swoop these feathered staffs near his body. When Sun Chief wished to sit down, he did so on a special seat reserved for him in the portico.

The *ásse* was served from shell cups to the men in a strict order. Sun Chief was served the white-frothed tea first from an ancient shell cup that was used by him alone. The attendant dipped up a full cup and uttered the word *choh!* Then, bending low, he ran up to Sun Chief and held the cup to his lips, and as Sun Chief drank the white-frothed tea, the attendant uttered three drawn-out sounds—*yah-hóó-la!* Sun Chief drank the tea just as long as the man uttered the sounds. Then, using other shell and gourd cups, the *ásse* was served to the other men according to their rank. The *yah-hóó-la* cry was only accorded to men of high status. First, the red and white leaders lined up in two rows, facing each other, and the drink was served to them, all in strict order of rank. Then the cups were passed to all the other men who were present. It was a startling sight when, after a few minutes passed, all of the men regurgitated what they had drunk, hugging their arms across their stomachs, spewing the clear liquid on the ground to a distance of as much as six feet. The Raven had always gone outside to vomit up his *ásse,* and so I had never witnessed the act.

I asked Teresa what the *yah-hóó-la* cry meant. She said it is a title of respect, a respect that enters the men as they drink the *ásse* and hear the sounds uttered.

All others—women, children, and undistinguished men—were served very small portions of the herbal they call *heche pakpakee,* "tobacco foam." This is lobelia, a plant that in small amounts induces euphoria. A greater amount causes vomiting, and Teresa said that too much of it can even cause coma and death.

In the afternoon the adult men and women, forming separate groups, assembled on the plaza in front of the mound. Children and onlookers, including myself, Teresa, and some of the Christian sol-

Looped square gorget

diers, stood around the margins of the plaza. Out of the temple and
down the steps came the Raven, dressed completely in new white deerskin clothing—moccasins, leggings, breechclout, and an entire white
deerskin worn around his back with the four legs wrapped around and
tied in an X in front. He wore a large white circular gorget, cut from a
conch shell and suspended around his neck, and a white swan's skin on
his head. Beside him was a fine-looking man who was likewise dressed
in impressive clothing.

The people fell silent, and the old man prepared to speak. As was
his custom before speaking formally, the Raven first spat in each of
the four directions. When he began, his voice was so low that no one
at any distance could make out what he was saying. But the man beside
him boomed out in a strong, staccato voice what the Raven was saying, and it seemed that for every ten words the old man used, the man

standing beside him elaborated into fifty. Teresa said that this man was a *yatéka*—a speaker or translator—who was gifted both in the Coosa language and also in foreign languages.

After some time, Teresa informed me that the old man was telling some of the same stories he had told us. As the afternoon wore on, she told me which stories were being related: the emergence of the earth from the waters, the Master of Breath and the creation of Sun and Moon, the birth of Thunder and Rabbit, and how Rabbit was father to Horned Serpent. Teresa said that these stories were told in the light of day only when everyone was observing a strict fast.

After the telling of the stories by the old man and his *yatéka,* a pot full of *páássa*—button snakeroot—was brought out. The Raven immersed one end of a two-foot length of hollowed river cane into it and blew his breath into the liquid a few times. The men all drank some of this *páássa,* and later they vomited, though all they had on their stomachs was this liquid, and not much of that. Then they brought out a great quantity of *meekko hoyanéécha*—willow root—which they drank, rubbed onto their bodies, and sprinkled inside the temple and portico, around the plaza, and on the persons of all who had touched corpses the previous year. Afterward, the men ate small amounts of *heche pakpakee.*

For their part, the adult women went to the river and bathed. They returned to the plaza with single red circles painted on either cheek and with long trailing ribbons tied to their hair, and they danced a dance to the Sun—*icha opánka*—one of the circular dances that they believe pleases the Sun so much. Moving counterclockwise around the plaza, they would look up and smile at the Sun, singing as they danced, and I kept hearing them whistling the song of a bird call we often heard in Coosa. It sounded like *what-cheer, cheer, cheer.* I asked Teresa about it, and she said it is the song of the cardinal—the daughter of the Sun. Later she pointed out this bird to me. Its feathers are a brilliant red color, and it has a black face and a pointed crest. Some of the small children of the women who were dancing on the plaza wanted to go out to be with their mothers, but they were strictly forbidden to do so.

As the women were concluding their dance and hymn to the Sun, a wretched-looking creature, a man in the costume of a rabbit, with absurd long ears and a white, fluffy tail, flounced onto the plaza and began pestering the women. "What do you want?" the people shouted. "Girls! I want girls!" the creature squeaked, and he began flaunting an obscene gourd phallus. But the women ran at him, cuffing him when they could, and they pretended to be disgusted by him. Finally, another masked actor came onto the field in a great, intimidating rush, brandishing an old-fashioned war club. He was mostly dressed in red but had also rainbow colors in his costume, which contained some serpentine elements. He continually flicked his tongue in and out like a serpent. Teresa said that he was portraying the first Tastanáke, Thunder's son. Tastanáke got after Rabbit with his club, striking him in mock combat, and Rabbit shrieked, turned tail, and hopped off, to the great amusement of everyone.

As night came on, the men erected several large, tightly bound bundles of dry canes around the plaza and set their tops on fire. They burned with a bright flame, producing very little smoke. Some old men assembled and began dancing. These were *henehas,* lesser noblemen, rather like Spanish magistrates. We watched them for a while, but it was a monotonous dance, and Teresa and I were tired. We returned to our quarters, she to hers and I to mine, and retired for the night.

Second day. The men were up early in the morning, assembling at the plaza. As they had done the day before, the men drank *ásse* and ate small portions of *heche pakpakee,* and the women bathed in the river.

The men decorated the men's house, an open-air porch attached to the front of the temple. Using a white pigment, they decorated the posts with drawings of creatures I could not make out. Teresa asked around about the animals and learned that they were all martial animals such as the cougar, the peregrine falcon, and most especially the rattlesnake.

At midmorning the women came onto the plaza, and the men moved to the margins, still keeping a strict separation between the sexes. The women began dancing the arrow dance, celebrating in their own way the martial spirit of the Coosas, repeatedly forming up in three circles. Sun Chief came out of the temple and stood at the top of the steps, watching with pleasure as the women danced.

Then the Raven came out of the temple with his *yatéka,* and the two of them told more stories. They told about the Sun's inadvertent genesis of Corn Woman and Lucky Hunter, and of what these two brought to the Coosa way of life. They told of the origin of corn and beans, and about how hunting songs were obtained by Coosas. To everyone's great entertainment, they told stories about the Twosome, Corn Woman's son and "blood-clot boy," and about both the advantages and the disorder that their immature antics brought to Coosa life. And they told of the origin of bears, the origin of the clans, and the institution of marriage.

When the sun began to decline, the men drank *meekko hoyanéécha,* and again they vomited, purging anything that might remain in their stomachs. Again they ate a bit of *heche pakpakee.*

Later in the afternoon, the young warriors ran onto the plaza in several organized troops, each following a leader carrying a length of cane with white feathers tied to its end, and they began a dance celebrating the martial arts. Sun Chief appeared at the top of the mound dressed in regalia. He and some of his old principal men held weapons and copper and shell objects, which Teresa said were old and hallowed and the subjects of many stories. Ordinarily they were kept inside the temple, but now the retainers held them up for all the people to see.

Then Sun Chief descended the steps as if to review the assembled warriors. Unbeknownst to me, the men had placed manikins made of straw at each of the four corners of the plaza, seemingly as sentinels. I asked Teresa about these straw men, but she did not know their significance. A drummer began to beat time on a drum made of a large ceramic pot, and others joined in with rattles made of gourds containing pebbles. The dances that ensued were vigorous and athletic. The warrior-dancers engaged each other in mock battle, particularly with wooden war clubs, which they wielded with clever, artful movements. I gathered that the ways in which they wielded their clubs in the dance were the same as when they were actually fighting.

Then, suddenly, as if from nowhere, a troop of men appeared, dressed as enemies, shouting fierce turkey-gobble war cries. The enemy troop attacked the straw men sentinels with their war clubs and pretended to knock them to the ground and behead them. Then, screaming the death cry, they rushed across the plaza, taking aggressive postures with their bows and arrows and war clubs, and the warrior-dancers drew back, pretending to be confused. To the horror of the spectators, the attackers seized Sun Chief bodily and carried him away.

Before they had gone far, the warrior-dancers on the plaza rushed to overtake them. The two groups clashed in mock combat, with the invaders at first shouting cries of victory and their pursuers shouting cries of defeat. Onto the field came the Tastanáke warrior, dressed as a peregrine falcon, wearing a half-mask with a curved beak and a cape in the guise of wings. He grasped a rattle carved in the form of a human head and a special war club with falcon talons carved on its end, and as he shook the rattle and waved the club, the enemies began to give way. So much did they fear him that if he made so much as a motion at them with his war club, they would fall down and pretend to be dead. So many were lost in this way that the enemy troops began uttering cries of defeat and ran into a nearby canebrake for refuge. Then Tastanáke escorted Sun Chief back to the plaza, accompanied by the victorious warrior-dancers. They danced until late at night celebrating Sun Chief, Tastanáke, warriors, and the art of war.

That night the people again set up burning bundles of dry canes around the plaza. In the flickering light, the war leader, still in falcon dress, stepped forward and shouted out a man's name in long drawn-out syllables. Then he shouted it again at normal length. A young warrior who, Teresa explained to me, had distinguished himself in battle the previous year stood up, seized his war club, and ran over to Tastanáke. When Tastanáke stuck a feather in the young man's hair, the young warrior whooped ferociously and ran a circuitous route back to his place, crying *youh, youh!* Several other young men were honored in the same way. The names by which they were called to come forward were new names reflecting the particular valor of each, and they would be known by these names from now on.

The night was wearing on, but the festivities were not over. Now there began a series of dances celebrating various animals. The music was verse and response, with the dance leaders shouting out words and lines of a song, to which the dancers responded with other words and lines. They danced on and on, celebrating animals that are useful as well as others that seemed to me to be quite useless. These included animals after which the clans were named, as well as several others. For each of these, they danced mimicking its supposed characteristics.

The bear dance came last, and it seemed to be the featured dance, with the performers imitating the ungainly gait of the bear as it stands on two legs and walks with its forepaws folded in front. Instead of admiring these strong and dangerous creatures, the onlookers heaped scorn on the bears because, as is well known, bears are too stupid to seek revenge.

Having stayed at the plaza until the last dance of the evening, I was

*Tastanáke warrior dressed as a falcon: embossed copper plate from Mound C,
Etowah site*

exhausted when I returned to my quarters. But I had to admit, tired as I was, that I was enjoying the festival. Because of all the Raven had taught me, these goings-on did not seem as strange as they would have had I witnessed them when I first arrived in Coosa. It seemed to me that, lacking the light of Our Lord Jesus, these people had fashioned a life for themselves that, though misguided in many ways, had served to sustain them until the light of Christ could reach them. I could see God's mercy in that. I believe He takes care of all His children, whether or not the Gospel has reached them. He loves them even as they languish in darkness.

With these thoughts, I fell asleep, tired but happy that two more days of festivities lay ahead.

Third day. Perhaps I would have been less sanguine the second night had I known how little sleep was in store for me. Just before dawn Teresa came to my quarters and awoke me, saying that the people were all still up because the ball pole was down. We went immediately to the plaza, and sure enough there was only a large hole near the middle where the pole had stood. Some of the young warriors had come during the night and dug out the old pole and carried it away.

Teresa asked around and learned that at the same time the young warriors were taking down the old ball pole, the senior warriors had gone out and cut down a large pine tree to make a new one, taking care that it did not touch the ground as it fell. They propped it up with forked poles, cut off all its limbs, and replaced the uppermost limbs with sassafras sticks, each with a tassel on the end. They attached a basket to the top of the post in honor of the eagle's nest Tastanáke had raided, and they placed a carved wooden eagle in the nest. This was meant to honor the eagles that Tastanáke had offended in order to satisfy Lightning Bolt.

The people helped guard the pole until dawn approached, aligning it so that the eagle's nest faced in the direction of the rising sun. They attached wild grapevines—in remembrance of Tastanáke's hoops—to the top of the pole. Half of the vines were held by men and the other half by women.

As the first light came into the sky, a large number of people carried the pole to the plaza, holding it up off the ground. Several of the warriors ran over to the hole in the center of the plaza, tossing in some flowers of *heche pakpakee* and several scalps from slain enemies.

Everyone had turned out for the raising of the new ball pole. Many of the young warriors commenced to dance, howling like wolves to show their bonds with each other. Just as the sky became red with dawn, six fine-looking young men and six fine young women came into the plaza, where they performed an intricate dance in a circle, accompanied by drum and rattle. Then Sun Woman came out to dance while holding a length of split hickory that had been heated, its end folded over into a loop, and deerskin lacing put in the loop. It was an implement the women used in playing a special ball game of their own.

Just as the sun peeped above the horizon, the end of the new ball pole was put into the hole, and the men and women tugged on their grapevines to pull the pole erect, with the eagle facing toward the direction of the setting sun, the direction of death. As the pole was being pulled up straight, the young man who was next in line to be Sun Chief placed his hands together and showed his obeisance to the present Sun Chief by uttering the sound *hou* three times. When the pole was firmly in place, the Tastanáke warrior came out with a shell cup full of *ásse* and poured it upon the pole.

At that point, all present were startled to hear a shrill cry of *weeee* pierce the air, coming, as I soon discovered, from a young man who stood on top of the mound, holding up a short length of cane with four white feathers tied to the end. He made the cry four times. Teresa explained that he was a member of the Bird clan, and he was calling down all the birds for the feather dance. Several members of the Bird clan then brought out lengths of river cane about six feet long with various kinds of feathers fluttering loosely from their upper ends. As they danced, a leader sang songs to the birds while the dancers moved the canes up and down, making it seem as if a flock of many different kinds of birds were hovering over the corps of dancers. They repeated this dance at each of the four directions around the plaza. The songs were melodic and the dances quite pleasing overall.

Next a small group of pretty girls came out onto the plaza. They were dressed in newly made clothing and wore strings of white shell beads against their dark skin. Teresa said that none of them had had their first menses. They danced around the plaza, paying particular attention to the four corners. Teresa said that they were renewing the four cords because they had become worn in the course of the year. She said the earth had to be made new again. It occurred to me that the pattern they were dancing resembled the square with looped corners the Raven had drawn on the dirt floor of his house. This was a stately dance, and both sexes and all ages stood around the perimeter of the plaza admiring the young dancers, and occasionally they joined in singing the song the girls were singing.

The Raven appeared on the steps of the mound with his *yatéka,* as before. By this time I understood that the stories he was reciting were much the same ones he had told me, and he was reciting them in much the same order. I marveled that, in the pagan drama of the *posketa,* I was beginning to anticipate what came next. Much as I expected, the old man began to tell stories about the enmity between people and animals, and about the vengeance of the latter in the form of diseases of all sorts. He told of the amicable relations between plants and people, and of the origin of many Coosa herbal medicines. Last of all, he told of the anger of the Sun, of how she inflicted a terrible plague on the people, of the accidental killing of her daughter, and of the botched effort of the Twosome to retrieve the soul of the Sun's daughter from the western Darkening Land and the origin of the red bird. In so doing he told of the origin of death, the place where all must go and from whence none returns. None, that is, except our Lord Jesus Christ.

After the sun passed its zenith, the men drank a great brew made out of several of the principal medicinal plants. After this, all of the able-bodied men went out into the forests to hunt and fish. They were most assiduous at this, Teresa explained, because what they obtained from this hunt would presage their success at hunting and fishing in the coming year.

There was a lull in the festival until late afternoon, when the hunters and fishermen returned. It soon became clear that they meant to renew and repair not only their material goods but also their society. Sun Chief and his principal men proceeded to hold court. According to Teresa, they would try to resolve as many disputes and issues as they could.

They began by punishing those who had broken the rules of the *posketa.* The offenders were all young men who had eaten food when they should have been fasting, or who had touched a prohibited woman, or had violated any of the myriad rules of Coosa life. Teresa said that from what she could find out, it was almost always young men who came afoul of the *posketa,* not because they were the only ones who broke the rules, but because they were the ones whom the older men held most accountable. Later, the Raven told me that he might as well talk to the posts in the temple as to admonish young men to behave well.

The miscreants, six sheepish-looking young men, were taken to the temple porch where the Tastanáke warrior dry-scratched their legs. He did this by taking a comb-like implement made of a short section of the jaw of a large garfish. He scratched their legs deeply enough that blood oozed out of the scratches. While this punishment was inflicted on them, the young men stood stone-faced, showing not the least concern for the pain they were feeling. After the scratching was done, each of them ran his cupped hand up the scratches on his legs, and then flung the pooled blood in their hands onto the ground, seemingly as a point of honor. I wondered whether this act in some way commemorated the Sun's blood falling to earth.

Next, the *henehas* presided over the resolution of a number of small quarrels and misunderstandings of the kind that occur in villages everywhere. They listened as the disputants stood before them and made their complaints. In some cases, the act of standing up before everyone and making their cases public was enough to satisfy the aggrieved parties. The *henehas* admonished the disputants to uphold the morality of the Coosa people and to act better in the future. In some instances interested members of the public chimed in, stating their own opinions over how the issue or dispute should be resolved. In almost every case, it seemed to me, the disputants came away with a resolution or relaxation of their complaints against each other. In one instance, two old matrons of different clans embraced each other, weeping, after a dispute caused by their young people had been resolved.

The last to be heard was a case of witchcraft, and this was heard by the Raven and some of the other priests, with the *henehas* also present. Teresa said that these were always the most difficult cases to resolve. The accusation of witchcraft came from an older woman, a first wife, against a younger co-wife, who had recently entered into a polygynous union, a practice that, regrettably, is not rare in Coosa. To make matters worse, the two women were sisters. The older woman complained that she began having violent headaches soon after the younger sister had entered the household, and she was sure that she had been bewitched.

The clansmen of both the husband and the two women were present, and the Raven and the other priests circulated among them, asking questions and listening closely to the answers they heard. Teresa followed it all, and reported it to me as coherently as she could. It turned out that the man of the house had been married to his first wife for a long time before taking her younger sister as a co-wife. The man was much in love with the younger woman. She was his favorite, and he concealed his feelings very poorly. The young woman had for many years secretly felt oppressed by her older sister. The older woman had been deeply wounded by the marriage and her diminished status, but she tried to conceal her hurt from everyone.

Armed with this information, the old priest first addressed the clansmen of the husband. He berated them, asking why they had allowed one of their own to so openly show his true feelings for one wife over the other. Then he berated the clansmen of the women. How could they allow the young woman to incite her sister to such secret rage and jealousy? Didn't they understand that they were no longer merely sisters but co-wives? The old man walked over to the fire where they had served *ásse* and the various medicines. He dropped a pinch of tobacco onto the coals, and because it burned evenly and did not pop or flare up, he concluded that no witch was present. He gave doses of the "great medicine" to the two women, and also to their husband. (I later saw them make this medicine, which I will describe in due time.) He admonished them all to take better care of each other, and the crowd joined in, agreeing as a kind of chorus. The Raven then spoke to all assembled, urging them to be kind to each other, and he especially admonished the women not to speak ill of each other.

The *henehas* asked the assembled people if anything remained to be resolved. When nothing more was brought forth, they then put the torch to a heap of old clothing, tools, implements, and such that had been piled up by the edge of the plaza. All the worn-out trappings of the past year were being expunged from memory.

The men again swept aside the litter that had accumulated on the plaza. A large number of mature women appeared with pack baskets full of moist, dark soil they had taken from their gardens. They scattered this new earth over the surface of the plaza. Near the ball pole, in the exact center of the plaza, a small wooden stake had been driven, and around this stake the women made a little mound of new earth. Once they had completed this task, all were forbidden from setting foot on the plaza. They stationed dog-whippers—including the six scratched miscreants—along the edge of the plaza, armed with cane switches. They had to keep a sharp eye out for children and dogs who might stray in. Any dog that evaded their efforts and strayed onto the plaza was immediately killed.

After the new earth had been scattered over the plaza and the sun had gone down, the men were allowed, for the first time in three days, to eat small portions of food. Many of them were looking thin and somewhat weak.

Fourth day. There was no dancing on the third night. The Coosa people disappeared into their houses, and I thought the *posketa* was coming to an end. But I could not have been more mistaken. In the half-light before dawn, I was awakened by a terrible cry. It was Sun Chief standing atop the mound, uttering a death cry. At this signal, all of the people immediately poured water on their household fires, extinguishing them to the last spark. Stranger still was the complete silence. It was as if time had stopped in Coosa. All of the people, including the youngest of children, fell absolutely mute. In this eerie quiet, they began busily cleaning out and repairing their hearths.

Teresa and I walked over to the plaza, where the people were beginning to assemble in a large, silent crowd. Up on the mound I saw the Raven, still dressed in the white deerskin clothing. He squatted on a deerskin laid at the top of the steps that led up the face of the mound, and he began to make new fire by twirling between the palms of his hands a short sassafras stick, the pointed end of which he had placed in a hole in a small poplar board. He was uttering what seemed to be an invocation, but the language sounded so old-fashioned to Teresa that she could not understand much of it, except a reference to the water spider's rejoicing. Just as the sun was peeping above the horizon, he dropped the stick of wood and grabbed up a white swan's wing, and, as he fanned gently, he added pinches of tinder to the spot where he had been drilling. Then he dropped onto it a loose wad of fibrous dry hickory bark and fanned it with the swan's wing.

Suddenly, in the dim light of early dawn, the mass of bark fiber burst into flame, and as it did, a triumphant shout went up from the people. It seemed to me almost as if they were expressing their relief that fire had saved the world from cold disorder and darkness, and life and time had begun again. It was as if Sun had prevailed over Moon, day had prevailed over night, and light over darkness. A fresh new year of order had prevailed over the tangled disorder of the past year. The Raven stood before the fire with the white wing in one hand and an ancient pottery bowl in the other, and he spoke fervently to the fire in an archaic tongue that Teresa could not understand.

A small arbor with a roof made of green willow boughs collected by the young warriors had been erected over the little mound that the women had made in the center of the plaza. In came four young men, each reverently bearing a peeled oak log about the length of one's outstretched arms, and they placed the four pieces of wood beneath the rude arbor with four ends touching, forming a cross aligned with the four directions. For each of the logs they called out the name of a direction: first North! *honíltha;* next its opposite, South! *wahála;* then West! *hasakláátka;* and then its opposite, East! *hasóóssa.* The Raven came down the steps of the mound carrying the new fire and brought it over to the four logs, where he placed it in some split-cane kindling that had been piled in the center where the ends of the logs touched. The fire flared up, and again a shout went up from the people.

I had been so preoccupied with the kindling of the new fire in the plaza that I had ceased to pay attention to what was happening on top of the mound. I was taken aback when I saw two almost life-size wooden statues, a male sitting cross-legged and a female seated with her legs tucked beneath her. They were much the same, I presumed, as the stone representations of the first Sun Chief and Sun Woman that had been buried at Etowah. So, the Coosas had not, as I had assumed, rid themselves of idolatry. The two statues were guarded by a group of warriors and principal men, who stood behind them. The existence of these two idols had been unknown to Teresa also. When she asked bystanders about them, they said that the statues were brought out to oversee the making of new fire. They were also brought out when seeds were blessed and on a few other occasions.

The old principal men placed a little of each kind of food and medicine into the Raven's earthenware bowl to be fed to the new fire. They laid four perfect ears of the new corn in the center of the fire, each with a *heche pakpakee* blossom stuck in one end. They were careful to lay down the ears of corn in a counterclockwise direction. They sprinkled a little *ásse* and *meekko hoyanéécha* onto the fire, and then they fed it bear oil along with slivers of meat, which Teresa was told came from the right sides of tips of deer tongues. This caused the fire to flare up brightly, and the old man bent down to study the fire closely. Teresa

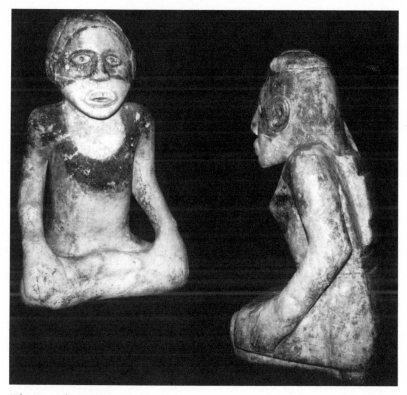

The Etowah statues

learned from those around her that the old man was looking for omens in the blackened, curling meat.

The priests then took pots of *páássa* and *meekko hoyanéécha* and, taking care not to step into the plaza itself, sprinkled some of each on the four corners of the plaza; then they sprinkled both medicines on the seats inside the temple and in the men's portico. Finally, they served small portions of *meekko hoyanéécha* to all who wanted it, both male and female, young and old.

Now came a much anticipated moment. Everyone watched attentively as the principal men standing atop the mound placed the two idols on Sun Chief's litter. This litter consisted of a seat centered on an equal-armed cross made of four poles, with two parallel poles in each direction, and covered with a white cloth. Hoisting the poles to their shoulders, a company of bearers carried the litter around the perimeter of the plaza, and as they proceeded, a troop of principal men walked along singing and playing music on cane flutes. This procession made a complete circuit around the sides of the plaza, and its members were the first ones to step onto the prepared surface of the "new earth," as if to say that the earth was the dominion of the Sun clan. The idols were then carried back up the steps of the mound and into the temple. Next, seated on the same litter, Sun Woman and Sun Chief were carried around the plaza. Sun Chief held up a white war club through the entire parade.

While Sun Chief and Sun Woman were carried on their circuit, the Raven took coals from the new fire that burned beneath the makeshift arbor in the center of the plaza and placed them into a number of small pots, all of which appeared to be old and well used, not new like the rest of the pottery seen at the festival. These little pots of fire were topped off lightly with ashes, and they were given to principal men to be carried to the several towns of Coosa. Teresa said that in each of these towns a fire would be kindled from the coals, and from this fire all of the clans would take their new fire, and finally each of the houses belonging to the various clans would light their new household fire. This, it seemed to me, implied that the various clans had their own separate fires, hearkening back to the origin of the clans in Ancient Days, but at the same time all of the clans were united in the fire of Coosa.

After Sun Chief and Sun Woman made their circuit around "the world," the men drank some of the great medicine, which included the most important of the Coosa herbs. To prepare it, the priests crushed the leaves, pounded them in a mortar, and put them into cold water. Then the priests took cane tubes and blew their breath into the medicines so that they bubbled up a great deal.

In the early afternoon, a small number of the senior matrons of the clans danced onto the plaza, followed by a like number of senior men from the clans. Both sexes were dressed in clean white deerskin clothing. Both had adorned their hair and bodies with bear grease perfumed with sassafras and spicebush. The women had attached to their legs several tortoise shells containing pebbles, so that when they danced their rattles provided an exact accompaniment. Each of the old men carried in one hand a cane with two white feathers attached to the upper end of it, and in the other a green willow bough taken from the roof of the arbor over the new fire. A man sat at the side of the plaza beating time on a drum, and the drum and rattles together made a pleasing sound. The women danced very sedately, and the men danced a counterpoint to their dance. Perhaps owing to the high spirits of this part of the festival, while the women endeavored to preserve a formal demeanor, the old men began making abrupt utterances, which Teresa had trouble translating, but which she said were meant to cause the old women to lose their composure. I gathered that these were bawdy comments. At times they succeeded in causing the women to break down and laugh, much to the merriment of the onlookers.

At the conclusion of this dance that had been by turns sedate and hilarious, a line of young men came boisterously onto the plaza. They formed up single file, each person clasping with his right hand the left hand of the person in front of him, and they took an S-shaped path as they moved along. They represented Horned Serpent, with the man at the front of the line holding up the head of a monstrous snake, very grotesque, with a carnivore's teeth and deer horns on its head. They had contrived in some manner to make a large forked tongue that flicked in and out. All of the several dozen young men who were the body of the serpent had their bodies smeared with identical patterns of color—red, white, blue, and black. Four boys at the tail of the snake held large gourd rattles, which they rattled as the only accompaniment to Horned Serpent's antics. The leader contrived to coil the body of the serpent and then uncoil it, making it difficult for the boys at the tail to keep up as the movement grew rapid.

Horned Serpent took over the plaza. All of the people had moved to the sides, fascinated at the spectacle of Horned Serpent tossing his grotesque head, flicking his tongue, and rattling his tail in triumph at his serpentine capture of the plaza.

Then, moving at a fast tempo that was suddenly beaten on a large drum, two rather small young men made their appearance. Their movements were vigorous and acrobatic. One was good at jumping into the air and doing a flip, landing on his feet. The other specialized in cartwheels and in jumping up into the air and then landing on his hands and walking about upside down. They were both painted red all over their bodies. The one who made the flips wore a headdress on which blue jay and Carolina parakeet skins had been attached, and from which dangled several greenish cords representing snakes. They were acting the parts of Wild Thing and his brother—the Twosome— and they made a great racket yelling and imitating the raucous cries of the blue jay and the Carolina parakeet. This caught the attention of Horned Serpent, and when the Twosome began rolling grotesque grapevine hoops about the plaza, Horned Serpent became fascinated, his great head moving to follow every move of the hoops. At the close of this drama, the Twosome rolled their hoops off the plaza toward the canebrake, and Horned Serpent followed in docile fascination as a great cheer went up from the crowd. Both the Twosome and Horned Serpent disappeared into the canebrake. After a little while, bereft of their costumes, all of them came back to join the people at the plaza.

In the middle of the afternoon, the festival moved toward an activity that had seemed very long in coming—the eating of the new green corn. A great many cooking fires were started in the area surrounding the plaza. Teresa said that the members of the clans cooked together and ate together, in their several localities. They put unshucked ears of green corn in the ashes to roast; in addition, all of the game and fish killed by the men the previous day was cooked on frameworks over the coals of the fires, imparting a delicious smoky flavor to the meat. In addition, they had other foods of every sort, including berries and fruits in season.

While the food was being cooked, the men played ball games against the women. Bets were placed on the outcome of these games, with men betting dried venison and women betting bread they had cooked. The men bet against women who were members of their wives' clans. The ball games were played in the plaza, with the ball post as the goal, but the women did not have the same rules as the men. To score a point the women did not have to kick the ball to hit the post. They were allowed to throw it with their hands, which was considerably easier to do, and thereby they generally succeeded in defeating the men, though it seemed to me that the men were not exerting themselves to win as much as they might have. When they ran, the women were surprisingly skillful at tripping the men, causing them to fall and, in fact, making them seem inept.

In the hours in which some were cooking and others were playing the ball game, Teresa informed me that the "forgiven ones" were returning to Coosa—that is, the men and women who had committed such serious infractions during the previous year that they had been forced to leave the towns in exile, living wherever they could, sometimes in makeshift shelters in the forests. Theft and adultery were infractions great enough to warrant such measures. At the time the new fire was created, however, all crimes from the previous year, excepting a man-killing, were forgiven. And the rule was that no one should mention or allude to these crimes ever again. The forgiven ones rejoined the people unobtrusively. It was as if they had never been away.

At long last, the *posketa* feast began. Although they served a prodigious variety of food—now including meat and salt—the food they honored most was roasted green corn seasoned with bear oil. This is their nectar, their food fit for pagan gods. Before the men ate any of this green corn, they took a bit of it in their fingers and rubbed it on their faces and on their breasts. As they ate the corn, they made a careful collection of the empty cobs. Teresa learned that they take these cobs home and keep them inside their houses for four days in memory of Corn Woman's sacrifice.

During the course of the feast, Teresa was visibly moved when two of her clan sisters—both handsome young women—came over to her, bringing roasted corn and meat for her. They conversed with her for a time, and Teresa informed me that they had invited her to join in the last episode of the *posketa*. It was the first time that she had been invited back into the inner circle, so to speak. Teresa looked to me for some visible sign, and I nodded. I did not see what the harm would be if she joined her relatives when that particular moment, whatever it was, arrived.

We were ready now for the closing ceremony. In preparation, there had to be assembled several substances whose meanings Teresa could not adequately explain to me. For one of these, the women made ashes by setting pots filled with old corncobs and pinecones on hot fires. Then four girls who had not had their first menses brought small quantities of ashes from their homes and mixed them into the ashes in the pots. From what I could gather, these ashes symbolize life as it is lived in reality, some of which conforms to the highest morals or aspirations and some of which does not.

The men, for their part, mixed up several pots of white clay with water—the very same paint they used on the temple. This color, it was clear to me, symbolized peace, purity, and good behavior.

They had on hand several little baskets filled with the flowers of *heche pakpakee*. Teresa was not clear on the significance of these flowers, but she thought that they might represent fertility and procreation. They resemble tobacco flowers, she said, which are strongly associated with the sexual union of men and women.

These substances were assembled in the plaza and then taken to the temple and the men's portico. Here, all of the people of Coosa, including Teresa, who went at this point to join her sisters, smeared their bodies first with ashes and then with white paint, and then each ate a small portion of the flowers.

The Raven strode to the base of the mound and stuck into the ground a length of cane with two white feathers tied to the end. When he uttered a death cry, Sun Chief and some of the Coosa principal men and elders appeared, all smeared with ashes and white clay, and they walked down the steps and stood beside the planted cane pole. Then the young warriors appeared, likewise smeared with ashes and clay. Finally, the townspeople, wearing ashes and clay, crowded around to stand with the others.

As the sun began to disappear below the horizon, the Raven took up the cane pole and began leading the crowd as a body out of the town and down to the river. The people gradually drew out into a single-file line, the men first, then the women and children. As they made their way to the riverbank, the Raven uttered the death cry three more times. Upon reaching the river, he stuck the pole into the ground at the edge of the water, and the men crowded up close to each other.

Each man put a small pinch of *heche pakpakee* on his own head and in each ear. Then, at a signal given four times, they threw pieces of *heche pakpakee* into the river. On the last of the four signals, the men splashed noisily into the water. They dove down to the bottom, and each of them retrieved four small stones. With these stones they made the shape of a cross across their breasts and uttered the death cry, and then they threw the stones into the water.

The women repeated this ritual, and then so did the children. Teresa, in her Spanish dress, was happily in the midst of them. As they splashed about, they took pains to wash all of the ashes and white clay off their bodies.

When I later asked Teresa what all of this meant, she said that they had washed all traces of the past year from their bodies forever in the hope that the coming year would be better than the last.

When all had completed their bathing, the Raven picked up his cane pole and led the people, in the same order, back to the plaza, where he planted the cane pole in the center beside the ball pole. Dancing began again, but the people were dancing now for their own enjoyment, more relaxed than before. They would continue to dance in this way until dawn.

Teresa never did rejoin me. When I was ready to return to my quaters for the night, she was nowhere to be found. Finally, I walked back alone.

The *posketa* was over, but for several days afterward, the people of Coosa were festive. It must have been a great relief to them to simply expunge many of the worrying problems that had troubled people in the previous year. After the *posketa,* the people might remember these problems—and surely they did—but they were supposed to act as if they had never occurred. The exception was that they never forgave the killing of one of their own, this being an act that always required revenge or some kind of compensation.

I should not have allowed Teresa to participate in the green corn feast on the last day of the *posketa*. It drew her too far back into the Coosa world. I searched for her but could not find her during the dancing that night because she had slipped away to a storehouse with Chola Háácho. I did not have to ask her if they had sinned. Her demeanor gave her away. She was unrepentant, and I endeavored to refrain from condemnation, for I did not want to drive her further toward the Coosa world, where such behavior would not be condemned at all. Her mind was very much on the fellow. She said that Chola Háácho remembered her as a young girl in Coosa, and he claimed to have admired her even then. He also remembered her mother and her younger sister, and he told her how they had grieved deeply for Teresa after she had been taken away by Soto. He was saddened, he said, when both the mother and the sister died some years later of the "coughing disease," an epidemic that had afflicted many Coosas at the same time and for which their curers could do very little. Perhaps to assuage my fears about Chola Háácho, she explained that his name, "Mad Fox," did not mean that he was crazy, but rather that he was heedlessly courageous in battle. He fought madly, as if he had no regard for his person, and the word *háácho,* mad, was something of a title among Coosa warriors. But when he was with a woman, she said, Chola Háácho was surprisingly gentle and endearing.

I did not know what to say. If I spoke against him, she would cease to trust me and would no longer speak freely to me. But if I pretended to be in favor of him, it would encourage her on this dangerous path away from Christ. So I said very little at all. In time, when she was open to me, I would try to help her see things more clearly.

More pressing matters intervened. The "new year" that followed the *posketa* was hardly under way before we found ourselves involved in warfare, Coosas and Christians together. The trouble had been brewing for some time. It seems that Sun Chief had come on several occasions to our leader, Mateo del Sauz, complaining bitterly about Coosa's problem with the Napochín. For a long time the Napochín had been tributaries of the Coosas. But after Soto humiliated Sun Chief, the Napochín saw weakness and opportunity, and they had broken away from the peace of the Sun Chief of Coosa. They refused to pay their annual tribute, and lately they had killed some Coosas who were out hunting in the wilderness. They had even killed a Coosa woman and her son who were working in their cornfield, almost within sight of town. The Napochín had made it dangerous to travel the trail from Coosa north to Tali, Coste, and Chiaha. Something was going to have to be done to bring these renegade tributaries back into line. Finally, the leading men and warriors of Coosa came to Sauz in a delegation and echoed the complaints of their chief, adding that they would be able to serve the Christians better if they would help them subdue the Napochín.

Sauz called a meeting of his captains to consider whether we should join with the Coosas on a raid against the Napochín. Some were concerned that this could be a Coosa trick to cause us to split our force, leaving us vulnerable to attack. Sauz argued that even at half strength we had overwhelming military superiority over the Coosas, and that we would be on full alert as we traveled to Napochín country, as would the force that remained in the town. All of us appreciated the value of any food we might be able to take from the Napochín, for the Coosas were growing increasingly resentful of our drain on their food supply. So it was decided that we would take 25 footmen and 25 horsemen to accompany Sun Chief's 300 Coosa warriors. Sauz commanded me to go along as a priest, and Teresa was to serve as translator between the Coosas and the Christians.

I was interested to see that Coosas take the same steps in preparing for war as they do for the ball game. The war captain builds a new fire using a drill. The warriors fast for four days, drinking medicines, and they don freshly washed clothing and pass their weapons back and forth through the heat of the newly built fire. Of course, the warriors must strictly avoid touching women. The war chief places some of the new fire in a clay pot and takes this along on the raid. Any fire they use along the way must come from this special fire. I was told that if the fire happens to go out, they return home immediately.

Teresa learned from Chola Háacho that warriors are attentive to what they regard as omens. For example, if a screech owl comes at night and cries on either side of them, right or left, they take it to be a sign that they will be victorious. But if the owl goes out in front of them, or comes in behind them, they are apt to turn around and return home, this being a particularly bad omen. Chola Háácho, however, has never been one to turn back. That is why they call him "mad."

On the day we were to set out, the warriors assembled, armed with war clubs and with bows as long as the men were tall. They made a great show of examining their bows and arrows, which were fitted with very sharp triangular flint points. They were so skillful with these bows that I had several times seen them hit a bird on the wing, and they could launch their arrows in astoundingly rapid succession.

The Coosa warriors organized themselves into eight companies, with two companies positioned in each of the four directions, forming an equal-armed cross—that familiar pattern encountered so often in the Coosa world. This formation as much as said that the Coosas were lords of the four quarters of their realm. Each of the eight companies was led by a captain who held up a cane pole about twelve feet long with white feathers attached to its end. With Teresa translating, I asked one of the captains why they were traveling under the white color of peace and not the red color of war. He explained that the Coosas did not want to wage war on the Napochín; they only wanted to make them come back into the white peace of Coosa, resume their tributary status, and pay the Coosas all the tribute that was owed since the Napochín became disobedient.

Our combined forces set out in high spirits. Near the end of our first day of travel, some of the Coosa warriors suddenly ran toward Sun Chief, howling like so many wolves, and picked him up bodily and carried him forward, taking him to the foot of an abandoned mound that we had come upon. Our Christian soldiers were at first startled by this act, and not understanding the symbolic meaning of wolves to the Indians, they laughed uproariously at the mad music the Coosa warriors used to honor their chief.

The mound told me that we were in an abandoned Coosa town. The Indians at first circled around the mound and then deposited Sun Chief at the foot of some crude steps. Sun Chief climbed up the rotted wooden steps to the top of the mound and walked around it as if he were an emperor, looking out with great severity. His men handed him a kind of fan made of beautiful feathers, which he flourished, occasionally pointing it toward the land of the Napochín. His men gave him some little seeds from a fern-like plant, which he chewed up and spat out in the direction of the Napochín, as if it were so much venom. Teresa was of the opinion that these were the poisonous seeds of the water hemlock plant, whose leaves have a vaguely fern-like appearance. If so, this was a dangerous act for Sun Chief to have performed, for these seeds are reputed to be quite poisonous. After spitting out the chewed-up pieces, he turned to his war leaders with a triumphant expression, telling them that the Napochín would be crushed like the seeds he had just crushed in his teeth.

The following day, we drew near the first Napochín town, and we bivouacked in order to rest so that we would be fresh for a raid early the next morning. Chola Háácho and several of the warriors went out to scout the countryside. The Coosas warned me that the Napochín always had spies in the woods, so I agreed this night to leave off the trumpet call which was the signal for the men to recite the Ave María. Instead, I went around myself to each of the companies and told the men when it was time to pray.

Later that night some of the Coosa scouts came back with the news that the Napochín were asleep, unaware that we were approaching. The scouts had with them two scalps from Napochín guards they had killed, as well as a few ears of green corn and some beans and squashes from Napochín gardens to prove to us how close they had gotten. Chola Háácho was not one of the ones who returned. He and some others were still out near the Napochín town, keeping a watchful eye.

In the faint light of early morning we silently surrounded the Napochín town, where all was quiet. But some of the Coosas were uneasy. The Napochín were too quiet, they said. They were right, for when we rushed into the town, we found it abandoned. From the state of their smoldering fires, it was clear that the Napochín had fled abruptly not long before our arrival. Clearly, one of their spies had chanced upon our Coosa scouts and had gone back to warn the people.

Soon after we entered the town, a commotion arose in the plaza. When I went to investigate, I found our Coosa warriors gathered around a pole, perhaps twenty feet tall, to which a number of scalps were attached. In a fury they took a Spanish hatchet and cut it down. I did not have to be told that these were Coosa scalps. Weeping for the dead, the warriors stamped their feet on the ground and shook their fists in anger. Then, examining the scalps more closely, they discovered that one of them was still bloody. Who else could it have come from but a Coosa scout? I looked for Teresa, but she was already ahead of me, pressing in to see. She pushed forward to examine the scalp. Later I learned that what she saw was a multicolored glass bead braided into some of the hairs—a bead she had given to Chola Háácho. At the sight of it, she wailed and began to tear at her hair. The Napochín must have killed Chola Háácho just before dawn and quickly put his scalp on the pole as a special affront to the invading Coosas. I felt sorry for Teresa, but alas, I must say I was somewhat relieved that the powerful temptation that this young man posed for her had been removed.

In anger and vengeance, the Coosas began setting fire to the Napochín houses, heedlessly burning up the very supplies of food we so desperately needed. We were at last able to contain the fires they had started, and indeed we found even more stores of food than we had expected. Though saddened by the loss of Chola Háácho, the Coosas had won the town. They celebrated their victory by dancing and playing music on some rather discordant cane flutes.

We went from that place to a second Napochín town, which was also found to have been abandoned. All of the Napochín had fled to an island at a ford across a very wide and shallow river. The Coosas called this river Oquechiton, "the great water." We assumed that it was the headwaters of the great river to the west, the Río de Espíritu Santo. When the Napochín realized how great was our military superiority, and that we were marching under white color, they surrendered and came to declare their obedience to Sun Chief. They were grateful for having been spared greater retribution, and they apologized and promised to resume paying tribute. We rested for a few days and then returned to Coosa, taking with us as much plundered food as we were able to carry.

Upon returning to Coosa, those warriors who had shed the blood of Napochín were sequestered outside the town for four days to purify themselves. They sat by the war fire drinking emetics and medicines. Again their clothing had to be washed, and they passed their weapons and the scalps they had taken through the heat of the fire to cleanse them. This done, the war captains carried the war fire and accompanied the warriors to the temple for a reception by Sun Chief and the principal men. The war chief put the war fire that had been carried on the raid into the sacred fire that burned in the temple. The warriors presented the Napochín scalps to Sun Chief, saying that these were proof of valor in war. Sun Chief and all the principal men cried out their thanks. Then Sun Chief took dressed skins, beads, and other tokens from his storehouse and presented them to the warriors.

These were my last observations of the ways of the Coosa people, for in our absence word had arrived that Luna had abandoned Nanipacana and had fallen back to the port of Ochuse. He had instructed Sauz that if the country at Coosa did not appear to be a rich land that would support a colony, we should abandon it and rejoin the others at Ochuse. This was an easy decision. There weren't enough Indians in Coosa to support a colony, and the mountainous country seemed unsuitable for extensive settlement. We began packing up our gear, making ready for the long journey to the coast.

I had time for one more conversation with the Raven. When I went to fetch Teresa, I found her with her hair disheveled, very downcast in spirit. She was mourning for Chola Háácho, and I think she was saddened as well at having to leave Coosa for a second time. Surely she had thoughts and feelings that I could not even imagine. But as distraught as she was, I was surprised at how willing she was to go with me for one more conversation with the Raven.

We approached the Raven's house in midafternoon. He was sitting in the shade of his storehouse. His bird Pruk was striding about, picking up small bits of food. The old man motioned for us to sit down, and I was pleased to see him offer some kind and reassuring words to Teresa. She told me later that she was moved when he addressed her as the Climber, her childhood name.

As a memento, I gave the Raven a copper escutcheon that had come loose from the cover of my bible from Mexico. On the escutcheon an Aztec artisan had incised images of the Lady of Guadalupe de Tepeyac, a pagan beast, and the angel Gabriel clad in Aztec clothing. I knew that it would never be more than a curiosity to the old rogue, but it could do no harm to leave with him a tangible image of Christianity in the New World.

He acknowledged my gift and then handed me an object wrapped in a piece of white deerskin. I unwrapped it and saw that it was a small transparent crystal.

"It is a *sapéya,*" he said, "from a small horned serpent. When you return to your home you must find a safe place where you can bury it in the earth. On each full moon, you must rub it with the blood of a

Lady of Guadalupe

freshly killed animal. When you learn to use this *sapéya*," he smiled at his challenge, "it will help you to discover the hidden causes of things and to see into the future."

He put his hand on my shoulder and said, "It is true that this *sapéya* grew on the forehead of a horned serpent, but do not worry, horned serpents are not of the lineage of the serpent who tempted Eve." He cackled that mocking laugh of his, but it quickly died away, and he grew serious and thoughtful.

"I have something to say to you," he said.

"I have done as I promised. I have told you about the land of Coosa and about the beings that inhabit it. I have told you stories about the everyday beings of Coosa—the four-footeds and the flyers—and also about the great beings—the Master of Breath, Thunder, Lucky Hunter, Corn Woman, Rabbit, Horned Serpent, and Wild Thing. And I have told you about persons of ancient renown—first Sun Chief, first Sun Woman, and Tastanáke.

"And so I ask you this, as one priest to another: Knowing all that I have told you, do you continue to think that we Coosas are stupid? Do you think that we are less than you are? How could you think that we would ever turn our backs on our great beings of the upper world? How could you think that we would ever be willing to extinguish the pure fire of the Sun that burns in the Sun Chief's house? How could you think that we could ever embrace Christ, who seems to us to be a well-meaning but naive and unfortunate young man who loves every-

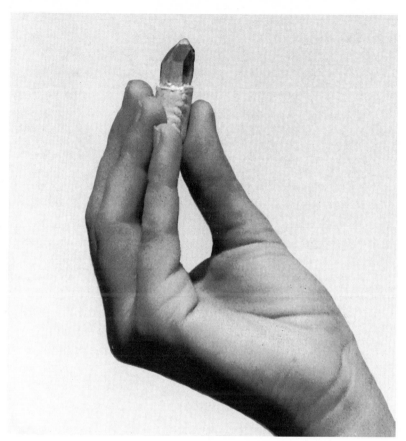

Sapeya *crystal*

one and, therefore, like a bear, turns away from vengeance? That you would follow such a man as that is a path even stranger than that taken by bears.

"And yet you are a people like none that we have ever known. Your men lack the valor and skill of our best young warriors, and yet your weapons are such that we are not equal to you on a field of battle. We greatly fear your warriors who ride upon *cholthákko*—the great deer. Your cutting tools are so superior to ours that Coosas would do anything to own them.

"You have caused disorder in Coosa and in the four directions. Soto came and did as he wished. He took food from us, forcing us into the woods to subsist on bear food—acorns, roots, and berries—and we had a very hard winter. He enslaved some of our people. He humiliated our Sun Chief by taking him away as a hostage, and he heedlessly stole Sun Chief's principal sister, Sun Woman, who was to mother his heir and successor. Sun Chief returned to Coosa a sad and diminished man, exhorting our young warriors to seek revenge against Soto in the attack planned by Tascaluza at Mabila. Our heavy losses there were another blow to this great man, who was as fine and wise a Sun Chief as ever ruled Coosa.

"Because of Soto, the greater peace of Sun Chief began to falter and shrink. The Napochín broke away. The Talisi, who were being courted away by Tascaluza even before Soto came, began to act more independently. Even the people of Tali, Coste, and Chiaha began complaining about the dangerous travel between their towns and the Sun Chief's town. They asked whether Sun Chief could be counted on to help them in their ancient struggle against the mountain people—the *Chelookhookâlke*.

"To add to our problems, some years after Soto was here, the coughing disease came to Coosa. It was new to us. It did not seem to have been caused by the Sun, or by our ancestors, and surely not by vengeful flyers or four-footeds. Many people died.

"Beset by problems on all sides, Sun Chief died while he was still in his prime. He was succeeded by our present Sun Chief, who is the son of a younger sister of the former Sun Chief. Our present chief is a wise and capable man, but some wish for our former Sun Chief, as he was in the days before Soto.

"What troubles me most about you *Nokfilaki* is that I do not understand what you want. Soto asked for yellow metal, and when we showed him Thunder's metal, he spurned it and became angry. Did Soto wish to be paramount over Coosa? Then why did he not remain in Coosa? Do you come here to sprinkle water on our heads and have us honor Christ? You say you want this, and yet you do not work very hard at it. In all the time you have been here, you have only sprinkled water on the head of one sick old woman, who promptly died.

"What worries me most about you *Nokfilaki* is that you are so persistent. Soto came and did not find what he wanted; he suffered great losses at Mabila and went away. Now you come saying you want to build a trail all the way from Ochuse to Coosa to the great eastern ocean. But now you are walking away. Where can you be going? How is it that you keep coming to our land but we cannot go to yours?"

With this, the Raven brought our conversations to a close. He had said all that he intended to say. I knew he did not expect an answer to his final questions. I thought there was nothing left for us but pleasantries when, to my surprise, Teresa indicated to both of us that she had something to say. She informed us that she would first tell me what was on her mind, and then she would say the same to the Raven.

Turning to me, she looked boldly into my eyes, but then, as she began to speak, she looked down in the usual manner of a Coosa woman.

"I am but a woman. I have been listening to the two of you speak, and I have been speaking to each of you on behalf of the other. Now I have something to say to both of you.

"As a young girl, I did not want to leave Coosa when Soto put an iron collar around my neck and took me away in chains to be a camp slave. But I had no choice. I became like an orphan, like Dogwood Flower, the mother of Tastanáke, who was at the beck and call of everyone. Teresa do this; Teresa do that. I did it so well that Soto's men threw scraps of food to me, and I stayed alive. I survived three winters. When Soto's men fled down the Río de Espíritu Santo I found a place on one of the boats, actually feeling fortunate as hundreds of abandoned Indian slaves stood weeping on the river's bank, hopelessly far from their homes. Most of them were doomed to a horrible death. Oh, how I missed my mother, and my sister, and my clansmen as that boat took me all the way to Mexico. Would I live out my life without ever feeling the warmth of my kinsmen again?

"But when Don Tristán de Luna began recruiting for his colony, I did not want to return to Coosa. I had lived as a slave in Mexico for seventeen years. I was not sure that I could still speak the language of Coosa. I did not know what I would say to my clansmen. Was I still one of them? Or was I Christian now? Could I even remember how I should behave as a Coosa woman? I did not think I could face coming back. But I have done as I was bidden. I am but a woman, and a slave as well.

"When I came to Coosa, was I embraced by my kinsmen? No. I was treated as if I were one who had committed incest or some other unspeakable crime. And when the Raven began interrogating me about my menses, I felt it was an offense for me to be a woman. Then some malicious person began working sorcery on me. Being in Coosa was like being in hell. There was no love here at all. I would gladly have traded places with a galley slave in Mexico. I thought of eating some water hemlock and killing myself.

"Things began to change when my mothers and sisters began coming to me. They did not come to me for love, but for favors, and more often than not, they asked for favors I could not give them or get for them. They did not embrace me back into my clan, but at least I was no longer an outcast. I no longer envied the galley slaves of Mexico, and I surely did not want to die.

"Then, miracle of miracles, Chola Háácho turned his heart to me. He was a pagan, it is true, but his heart was kind and strong. He was one of the handsomest men I ever knew and certainly the bravest. We had played together as children, and he had grieved when I was kidnapped and taken away.

"Chola Háácho and I began to talk of running away and hiding in the wilderness until after the Christians departed. I might actually have done that and stayed with him here in Coosa, but then came the raid on the Napochín. Chola Háácho had an old score to settle with the Napochín, and nothing could have kept him from going on that raid, even if he had known the outcome. But why did it have to be he who died, of all the warriors in Coosa? Why did it have to be my Chola Háácho?

"And now what shall I do—go or stay? My clan has finally taken me back in. I could stay here now and be the Coosa woman I was born to be. But do I want to? The company of Coosa women is something that any Christian woman would envy. Coosa women stick together for life; marriage does not dislocate them. They do not own property in the Christian sense, but they surely do manage it. They are the farmers—the producers of vegetable food—and they are the managers of the households. For all of that, I would like to stay. But Coosa women work very hard. At birth a Coosa girl is given a pack basket, not as a mere toy but as a token of what she will do all her life. Until Coosas possess horses, their women will do this work.

"And it is hard to bear lightly the rules of Coosa life. Having to sequester myself from men during my menses will not make me happy, not unless it is a respite from the thousand rules of Coosa behavior. And the fearful scrutiny of everyday village life in Coosa is hard even for one who has lived her life as a slave in Mexico.

"And on top of this, as my own Chola Háácho has shown me, the peace of Coosa is not very wide, and it is not that secure a peace. You don't have to go out on a raid to be knocked on the head and killed. Anyone can be cut down by an enemy marauding quite close to the villages and farms of Coosa.

"So, what am I to do? Go back into exile as a slave in Mexico, where I can at least live in safety and where I have come to be treated with a measure of Christian kindness? Or stay here as a free woman with all the hardships that accompany this Coosa life? This is what it has come to for me. This is what I have to decide."

Teresa fell silent. She sat looking at her hands, retreating back into herself. By rights, after this confession, I should have had her put under restraint, or at least under close surveillance. But how could I do that to a woman who had served me so faithfully and had suffered so much? If she wanted to stay here in Coosa, I knew I would not try to stop her. In the end, God wants us only if we choose Him. Teresa herself had to make the choice.

The Raven reminded us that he had not yet heard what she had to say, and so Teresa had to say it all over again. I watched his confident demeanor dissolve as she spoke to him. When she fell silent, the Raven was silent too. I am sure he had never heard a Coosa woman speak in this way.

I did not make a parting speech. It seemed disrespectful of the Raven's gift of such patient teaching to counter him with words that would only be empty unless I could stay here and back them up with an example of a Christian life being lived out before him. The copper Lady of Guadalupe de Tepeyac I gave him would have to suffice as answer enough for now.

After we took our leave from the Raven, I returned to my quarters and reflected on all that had passed between us. In some ways the Coosas are to be admired. They respect and care for their chiefs and priests. Within their clans they love and protect each other. They hold their food in common, and none goes hungry. They seldom quarrel. If, added to this, they were to come into the Christian fold, they would have a richness in their lives that many Christians might envy.

I think, in the end, it must be said that either the Coosas have no religion, or else everything they think and do is religion. For Christians, religion requires an act of faith, and it sometimes happens that one's faith weakens or slips away. Such is not the case with Coosas. It is not that they are incapable of skepticism. The Raven told me that Coosas are often skeptical about the claims of some of their rainmakers and healers. But they do not doubt the existence of the Sun, Moon, or Thunder. They do not doubt the existence of rivers or of the animals they see before them every day. And they do not doubt the existence of Spearfinger, whose evil progeny they gossip about endlessly.

How is some future missionary to break through such beliefs, connected as they are to the very fabric of Coosa life? Clearly it will require long and patient work. The best approach may be to sternly prohibit the Coosas from practicing some of the customs that take place in the open for all to see. By this I mean such customs as feeding to the fire a bit of liver or tongue from a freshly killed deer. Or divining on riverbanks. Or their custom of greeting the full moon each time it appears. Or their custom of marrying their wives' sisters. Any future Christian missionary to Coosa will have to be patient. For a very long time, the most we can hope for will be to drive the old Coosa religion underground.

Above all, any future missionary to Coosa will have to keep a close watch on the Raven and his kind. It will not do to simply drive such men from Coosa. The people of Coosa respect the Raven, and I have to admit that I myself have come to have grudging admiration for him. He lives in error, without benefit of the Christian faith, but he is not a stupid man. Far from it. His knowledge of the totality of Coosa life is remarkably comprehensive. Knowing what I know now, I have to say that he is truly a priest of a kind. If only I understood Christians as thoroughly as he seems to understand Coosa people.

In thinking back over my conversations with the Raven, seeking the crux of their import, I see that it is a conundrum. As a Christian, I know that the Coosas live in error, and yet as a reasonable man, I have to say that the Raven is neither a fool nor stupid. On the contrary, Coosa people constantly seek his advice, counsel, and wisdom. If this is so, can the Coosa people be said to be totally devoid of truth? It comes down to this: Can truth, in any degree or quantity, be said to exist within the larger, embracing error of those who are ignorant of the gospel of our Lord Jesus Christ? I have the wit to ask this question, but not the wit to answer it, and thus my labors here are at an end.

A Note on the Spelling of Creek Words

I am most grateful to the linguist Karen Booker for drawing on her extensive knowledge of the Muskogean languages to devise a way of spelling Creek words that is user-friendly for English-speakers. Readers who want to know the more precise phonemic representations of these words should consult the technical works of Karen Booker and other Muskogean linguists.

1. Most Creek consonants are similar to their English equivalents. When *p, t, k,* and *ch* occur between vowels, they sound more like English *b, d, g,* and *j.*

2. The Creek sound *ch* is pronounced approximately as the final sound in "itch."

3. The Creek sound *lth*—troublesome to English-speakers— sounds approximately like the final sound in "wealth."

4. The diphthong *ey* is pronounced as in English "hey".

5. Pitch is important in the spelling of Creek words. The acute accent (á) indicates that the vowel is pronounced with high pitch. The circumflex (â) over a vowel indicates that the vowel is pronounced with a falling pitch. If a word contains no accent marks, it is pronounced with level pitch.

6. The doubling of consonants and vowels indicates that they are pronounced long. A long *lth* sound is indicated by *lth:* and a long *ch* is indicated by *ch:.*

Sources

ABBREVIATIONS

ITLM   Swanton, John R. *Indian Tribes of the Lower Mississippi Valley and Adjacent Coast of the Gulf of Mexico.* Bureau of American Ethnology, Bulletin 43. Washington, D.C.: GPO, 1911.

KS   Hudson, Charles. *Knights of Spain, Warriors of the Sun: Hernando de Soto and the South's Ancient Chiefdoms.* Athens: University of Georgia Press, 1997.

MC   Mooney, James. *Myths of the Cherokee.* 19th Annual Report of the Bureau of American Ethnology. Part I. Washington, D.C.: GPO, 1900.

MTSE   Swanton, John R. *Myths and Tales of the Southeastern Indians.* Bureau of American Ethnology, Bulletin 88. Washington, D.C.: GPO, 1929.

NAL   Lankford, George E. *Native American Legends: Southeastern Legends: Tales from the Natchez, Caddo, Biloxi, Chickasaw, and Other Nations.* Little Rock, Ark.: August House, 1987.

NNS   Kilpatrick, Alan. *The Night Has a Naked Soul: Witchcraft and Sorcery among the Western Cherokee.* Syracuse, N.Y.: Syracuse University Press, 1997.

OS   Howard, James H. *Oklahoma Seminoles: Medicines, Magic, and Religion.* Norman: University of Oklahoma Press, 1984.

RBMP   Swanton, John R. *Religious Beliefs and Medical Practices of the Creek Indians.* 42nd Annual Report of the Bureau of American Ethnology. Washington, D.C.: GPO, 1928.

SECC   Galloway, Patricia, ed. *The Southeastern Ceremonial Complex: Artifacts and Analysis.* Lincoln: University of Nebraska Press, 1989.

SEI   Hudson, Charles. *The Southeastern Indians.* Knoxville: University of Tennessee Press, 1976.

SFC   Mooney, James. *Sacred Formulas of the Cherokees.* 7th Annual Report of the Bureau of American Ethnology. Washington, D.C.: GPO, 1891.

SG   Brain, Jeffrey P., and Philip Phillips. *Shell Gorgets: Styles of the Late
       Prehistoric and Protohistoric Southeast.* Cambridge, Mass.: Peabody
       Museum Press, 1996.

SOC   Swanton, John R. *Social Organization and Social Usages of the Indians of
       the Creek Confederacy.* 42nd Annual Report of the Bureau of
       American Ethnology. Washington, D.C.: GPO, 1928.

SP   Longe, Alexander. "A Small Postscript on the Ways and Manners of
       the Indians Called Cherokees." *Southern Indian Studies* 21 (1969): 1–49.

TT   Haas, Mary R. *Tunica Texts.* University of California Publications in
       Linguistics, No. 6. Berkeley, Calif., 1950.

W   Witthoft, John. *Green Corn Ceremonialism in the Eastern Woodlands.*
       Occasional Contributions from the Museum of Anthropology of
       the University of Michigan, No. 13. Ann Arbor: University of
       Michigan Press, 1949.

YT   Wagner, Günter. *Yuchi Tales.* Publications of the American
       Ethnological Society, volume 12. New York: G. E. Stechart, 1931.

INTRODUCTION

a once powerful polity: Charles Hudson, Marvin Smith, David Hally, Richard Polhemus, and Chester DePratter, "Coosa: A Chiefdom in the Sixteenth-Century Southeastern United States," *American Antiquity* 50 (1985): 723–37.

In 1540 the Hernando de Soto expedition: Hernando de Soto first heard of Coosa in April 1540, when he was in the territory of the chiefdom of Ocute, located along the floodplains of the Oconee River in the vicinity of present-day Milledgeville, Sparta, and Greensboro, Georgia. The people of Ocute told him that Coosa was a large, wealthy polity that lay to the northwest. Had Soto not fashioned a plan the previous winter to travel toward the northeast in search of the chiefdom of Cofitachequi, where he expected to find silver and gold, it is likely that his next stop after Ocute would have been Coosa. Had he taken a northwesterly direction from Ocute, he would have followed the old Hightower Trail, which lay on or near the current Georgia Railroad. He would have gone to Etowah, at present-day Cartersville, and from there he would have gone north to the main town of Coosa near present-day Carters, Georgia.

But following his plan, Soto set off toward the northeast. From Ocute, he led his expedition to Cofitachequi, near present-day Camden, South Carolina, where he was disappointed to learn that the silver and gold he expected to find were actually slabs of mica and pieces of copper. He also learned that the people of Cofitachequi had been struck by an epidemic two years earlier and that many had died. Perhaps because of this, native supplies of food in

Cofitachequi were not ample. From Cofitachequi, he led his expedition north-ward across the mountains and into the Tennessee Valley. Here, on an island in the French Broad River, he came to the central town of the chiefdom of Chiaha, affiliated with the paramount chiefdom of Coosa. Soto and his men had a pleasant stay in Chiaha. It was a beautiful land that perhaps reminded the Spaniards of their homeland. They found plenty of food, and the men amused themselves by swimming and fishing in the French Broad River.

The Spaniards' demands for food must surely have taxed the people of Chiaha. Nonetheless, they complied, seemingly meekly. But when the Span-iards demanded women, the people of Chiaha began to run away and hide. However, there is no evidence that they resisted militarily, and the Spaniards forcibly took some people of Chiaha to serve as burden bearers and as concu-bines.

Soto led his expedition southward from Chiaha to Coste, another island town, this one in the mouth of the Little Tennessee River, near present-day Lenoir City, Tennessee. There the Indians began to show signs of resisting, particularly when Soto's men took food from their storehouses. The Indians of Coste took up arms and made ready to fight, but Soto used a clever strata-gem to avoid actual bloodshed. At Coste, Soto again impressed some Indians into service as burden bearers and as concubines.

They continued southward to the main town of Coosa in northwestern Georgia. Here they met a chief—a chief of chiefs—who was treated with more pomp than any they had met on their travels from their landing at Tampa Bay up to this point. The paramount chief of Coosa came out to meet them seated on a litter carried upon the shoulders of his subjects. He was surrounded by principal men who sang and played upon flutes as the litter was carried along. Soto and his men remained in Coosa for about a month. Again, the Spaniards enjoyed ample stores of food, and again the Indians tried to run away and hide to escape being impressed into service.

When Soto departed from Coosa, he took the paramount chief and some of his relatives and principal men as hostages. He also rounded up and took away some of the people in chains. They traveled southward to Etowah and then westward to Ulibahali, at present-day Rome, Georgia. The people of Uli-bahali were tributaries of the chief of Coosa, and they proved their loyalty by taking up arms and threatening the Spaniards in an attempt to gain their chief's release. But the chief of Coosa told them to lay down their arms, and they did.

When the Soto expedition departed from Coosa, they left behind a black man named Robles, who had become ill and could not walk. He is described as "a very fine Christian and a good slave." After Soto had traveled downriver from Ulibahali for two days and had come to a small village—probably at a notable archaeological locality, the King site—he discovered that another of his men was missing. This was Feryada, a Levantine. According to Garcilaso de la Vega, one of the chroniclers of the expedition, this man told the Indians of Coosa that rather than having to cast his eyes every day on Soto, who had reprimanded and verbally insulted him, he would prefer to defect and live out his life among the Indians. Soto made an effort to coerce the Indians to return Feryada so that Soto could punish or kill him, but the Indians refused to do so. One wonders whether Feryada would have been emboldened to remain behind at Coosa had not Robles been forced to stay there.

Soto continued on to Talisi, near present-day Childersburg, Alabama. This was the southern limit of the power or influence of the chief of Coosa. Here Soto released the chief and his principal men, but he refused to release enslaved Coosas, and this included the chief's sister. Because of this, the chief of Coosa wept as he took his leave of the expedition. Soto next went to the territory of Tascaluza, an aggressive chief in central Alabama who was much respected and feared by neighboring Indians. Soto took Chief Tascaluza and some of his principal men hostage, just as he had done with Chief Coosa, but Tascaluza and his people reacted differently. They struck the Spaniards a serious blow in a surprise attack at Mabila, a tributary town of Tascaluza. Several of the Spaniards were killed, and almost all of them were wounded, some more than once. Tascaluza's people, on the other hand, suffered a devastating loss. Perhaps 3,000 of their best fighting men were killed.

After the battle ended, the Spaniards learned that people other than those who were subject to Tascaluza had taken part in this battle. The people of Coosa are not specifically mentioned in the Soto documents, but there is other documentary evidence suggesting that they probably were participants in the battle. For example, in 1567, Indians told the Spanish explorer Juan Pardo (see Charles Hudson, *The Juan Pardo Expeditions: Exploration of the Carolinas and Tennessee* [Washington, D.C.: Smithsonian Institution Press, 1990]) that several of Coosa's allies in towns along the Little Tennessee River had killed some of Soto's men. Soto had gotten a uniformly peaceful reception as he traveled through the chiefdom of Coosa. But the chief of Coosa either changed his mind after Soto had enslaved some of his people, including his sister, or the chief of Coosa may have been plotting with Tascaluza from the very beginning. That is, they may have agreed that the chief of Coosa would give Soto a peaceful reception and lull the Spaniards into carelessness, and then when Soto entered Tascaluza's territory, the combined forces of the two paramount chiefdoms would deliver a coup de grâce at Mabila.

For a full narrative of the Soto expedition, see my book *Knights of Spain, Warriors of the Sun: Hernando de Soto and the South's Ancient Chiefdoms* (Athens: University of Georgia Press, 1997).

a detachment of men from the Tristán de Luna expedition: For Spain, the Soto expedition was a failure in that it did not succeed in finding a state-level society with gold and silver and a large and willing laboring class. But the expedition did learn that a large continent existed to the north of the Gulf of Mexico. As time went on, Spaniards grew afraid that their European rivals—particularly the French—would found a colony on that continent to the north. If this were to occur, it could make it difficult or impossible for Spaniards to establish a colony there. Such a colony might also make it possible for the French to find a road to the fabulously rich silver mines in Zacatecas, in northern Mexico, and in so doing they could pose a military threat to this important source of Spanish wealth. To defend against such a possibility, Don Tristán de Luna y Arellano was selected to found a Spanish colony in North America, or La Florida, as it was called. On August 14, 1559, Luna's fleet of thirteen ships approached Ochuse at Pensacola Bay, a harbor that he expected would provide safety in any storm. But a short time later a hurricane struck, sinking and damaging all but three of his ships. Most of his food was lost. As his colonists began starving, Luna moved most of them north to the town of Nanipacana on the Alabama River, but they found very little food there. Nanipacana had been seriously impacted either directly or indirectly by the Soto expedition, and remembering this bitter experience, the inhabitants ran away from Luna and his colonists, taking what food they could and destroying some of the rest.

Luna eventually decided to send a party of men northward to Coosa, where Soto had found such ample supplies. He sent Mateo del Sauz with 40 cavalry and 100 infantry to go in search of Coosa. This party also included the friars Domingo de la Anunciación and Domingo de Salazar and an Indian woman who could translate Spanish into the language of Coosa. They departed from Nanipacana on April 15, 1560, and they reached Onachiqui, the first town of Coosa, in early June and the capital town in August.

This contingent remained in the capital town of Coosa from August until October. Two veterans of the Soto expedition were among this contingent, and they were at first surprised at how much the place had declined in the twenty years since they were last there. Some of those who had spoken of the country in such grand terms said they must have been bewitched for it to have seemed so rich and populous. The power of the chief of Coosa appears to have eroded in the wake of the Soto expedition. In fact, one of the reasons the Coosas were willing to feed their uninvited visitors is that the Spaniards agreed to go with the Coosas on a raid against the Napochín, a tributary people who lived in the vicinity of present-day Chattanooga, Tennessee. The Napochín had rebelled. Not only were they not paying tribute to the paramount chief of Coosa but also they were waging war on him. Anunciación departed from Coosa when Sauz ordered his men to return to Nanipacana and Ochuse. Within a few months, as the colony ended in failure, Luna's people abandoned Ochuse.

From the documents of the Soto and Luna expeditions, it is possible to learn quite a bit about the chiefdom of Coosa. Much of this is contained in letters that Fray Anunciación wrote while he was in Coosa and in an interview he gave to the historian Dávila Padilla many years later. Anunciación appears to have been more interested in the ways of the Indians than were his Dominican brothers. In addition to these documentary sources, much detailed information on the material and economic life of the people of Coosa has been developed by archaeologists who have worked for over a century in north Georgia and the Tennessee Valley.

The story of the Luna expedition is briefly recounted in Charles Hudson, Marvin T. Smith, Chester B. DePratter, and Emilia Kelley, "The Tristán de Luna Expedition, 1559–1561," *Southeastern Archaeology* 8 (1989): 31–45. An account of the raid on the Napochín may be seen in Charles Hudson, "A Spanish-Coosa Alliance in Sixteenth-Century North Georgia," *Georgia Historical Quarterly* 62 (1988): 599–626. I am grateful to John Worth for unearthing documents correcting the spelling of Napochie to Napochín.

The third expedition to Coosa was led by Captain Juan Pardo: Hudson, *The Juan Pardo Expeditions.*

Griaule recounted this experience: Marcel Griaule, *Conversations with Ogotemmêli: An Introduction to Dogon Religious Ideas* (London: Oxford University Press, 1965).

many of the stories he collected were shared by seemingly disparate people: *MTSE,* 267–75.

the Southeastern Ceremonial Complex, first identified by: Patricia Galloway, ed., *The Southeastern Ceremonial Complex: Artifacts and Analysis* (Lincoln: University of Nebraska Press, 1989).

Antonio Waring and Preston Holder: "A Prehistoric Ceremonial Complex in the Southeastern United States," *American Anthropologist* 41 (1945): 1–34.

a dance pattern that endured into the twentieth century: W. L. Ballard, *The Yuchi Green Corn Ceremonial: Form and Meaning* (Los Angeles: University of California, American Indian Studies Center, 1978), 10.

John Gregory Keyes: "Change in the Mythology of the Southeastern Indians" (M.A. thesis, University of Georgia, 1993).

But when there are gaps in Muskogean materials: As John R. Swanton noted, most of the information on the world view of Muskogean-speakers was collected late, after much of it had been forgotten, and some of what remained had been influenced by European cultural beliefs and practices (see *RBMP,* 477). An even greater problem is that because this information is culturally eroded, it contains evident inconsistencies.

Muskogean color symbolism: *RBMP,* 624.

A LETTER

We knew when we first reached the capital town of Coosa: Charles Hudson, Marvin T. Smith, Chester B. DePratter, and Emilia Kelley, "The Tristán de Luna Expedition, 1559–1561," *Southeastern Archaeology* 8 (1989): 41. This description of the domestic structures owes much to Richard R. Polhemus, "Mississippian Architecture: Temporal, Technological, and Spatial Patterning of Structures at the Toqua Site (40MR6)" (M.A. thesis, University of Tennessee, Knoxville, 1985), 20–79.

Coosa is densely wooded: Charles Hudson, "A Spanish-Coosa Alliance in Sixteenth-Century North Georgia," *Georgia Historical Quarterly* 62 (1988): 606–8. The principal town of Coosa has been identified as the Little Egypt site, now beneath the waters of Carters Lake. The two streams are the Coosawattee River and Talking Rock Creek. It has not been established that the Little Egypt site was surrounded by a palisade, but such palisades were built around many late prehistoric towns in the Tennessee Valley.

barbacoa: Spaniards adopted this Taino word referring to a wooden framework raised up on poles, whether as the floor of a storehouse or for roasting meat over coals. It is the source of the English word "barbecue."

arquebus: An arquebus was a heavy musket that was fired by pulling a trigger that caused a slow-burning fuse to ignite the powder in the flashpan.

the Napochin: I am grateful to John Worth for unearthing documentary evidence of the correct spelling of this word.

I wrote letters comparing the people: Anunciación's letters from Coosa are dated August 1, 1560. Herbert I. Priestly, ed., *The Luna Papers,* vol. 1 (Deland: Florida State Historical Society, 1928), 228–48.

the Raven: *RBMP,* 622.

a tattered white deerskin mantle: *RBMP,* 621.

He was a grave, solemn old man: *RBMP,* 621.

Teresa de Coosa: Hudson, "A Spanish-Coosa Alliance," 602.

put out one of her eyes: That Luna took with him as translators one or more Coosa women, presumably enslaved by Soto, is well documented. The blinding of the Sun Woman is fiction. Teresa and Sun Woman are loosely based on a letter from Don Luís Velasco to Luna, dated May 7, 1560. Velasco told Luna that a woman owned by his niece, Doña Beatrice, would be useful as an interpreter, but she was badly crippled. Velasco also wrote that a "woman of Tlaxcala" owned by his sister-in-law could likewise serve as an interpreter, but she had hidden herself (Priestly, *The Luna Papers,* vol. 1, 121).

a black slave named Robles: *KS,* 220.

Robles and Feryada themselves died: Hudson, "A Spanish-Coosa Alliance," 610.

CHAPTER 1. *The Coming of the* Nokfilaki

As we stooped and entered the low doorway: See house descriptions in Richard R. Polhemus, "Mississippian Architecture: Temporal, Technological, and Spatial Patterning of Structures at the Toqua Site (40MR6)" (M.A. thesis, University of Tennessee, Knoxville, 1985); Patricia Kelly, "The Architecture of the King Site" (M.A. thesis, University of Georgia, 1988).

a raven the old man had tamed: *RBMP,* 496.

a man of Ocute: *KS,* 164–65.

fat-lighter pine: The resinous, highly combustible center of large pine trees that have died. When split, fat lighter forms very sharp splinters.

Nokfilaki: SOC, 68; *NAL,* 136–37; *YT,* 157–58. Karen Booker could not confirm this as a Creek word. It may no longer be used.

they had taken hostage a woman: *KS,* 185–86.

They were enslaving people: *KS,* 202–3.

hang them in trees: *KS,* 111.

Tascaluza: *KS,* 229–30.

large dogs: *KS,* 74–76.

the people of Coosa began to flee: *KS,* 218.

yellow metal band: *KS,* 130. Sixteenth-century Southeastern Indians knew about and worked freely occurring copper, but there is no evidence that they knew of the existence of gold, or if they did, whether they distinguished between copper and gold.

He was as greedy as a cougar: James Adair, *The History of the American Indians* (London, 1775), 431. This cat, once widespread in the Southeast, today barely survives in Florida, where it is known as the Florida panther. Elsewhere in the United States it is known as the mountain lion or puma.

One was Robles: *KS,* 220. We do not, in fact, know what was the nature of Robles's illness or infirmity.

Nanipacana: Charles Hudson, Marvin T. Smith, Chester B. DePratter, and

Emilia Kelley, "The Tristán de Luna Expedition, 1559–1561," *Southeastern Archaeology* 8 (1989): 34–37.

CHAPTER 2. *The Contest between the Four-footeds and the Flyers*
Ancient Days: *SEI,* 156.

A Contest between the Four-footeds and the Flyers (50% paraphrase, 50% original): This entire myth, substantially rewritten, is drawn from *MTSE,* 22–23, and from *MC* 286–87.

flying war club: *SEI,* 248.

Mockingbird: *MC,* 285. Cherokee mothers sometimes fed their children the still warm heart of a mockingbird so that they would be quick to learn.

Turkey wears to this day a scalplock: *NAL,* 125. This explains the long black feather that hangs from the breast of a mature male turkey as well as the ridges just above his feet.

Both of them had four feet: *MTSE,* 23.

maypop fruit: Passion flower (*Passiflora incarnata* L.). Produces a green, egg-shaped fruit that is hollow and pops when one steps on it. *OS,* 27.

CHAPTER 3. *More Animal Stories*
Raccoon and Possum (10% direct quotation, 80% paraphrase, 10% original): *MTSE,* 41. This myth is fabricated from two stories collected by W. O. Tuggle.

they seem to grieve at night: *OS,* 49.

The Terrapin's Back (60% direct quotation, 30% paraphrase, 10% original): This myth is drawn with little change from *MC,* 278.

went out together to hunt persimmons: Persimmons were perhaps the most important wild fruit collected by the Southeastern Indians. They come ripe in late fall and early winter, when no other wild fruit is available. The Indians squeezed out the pulp, removed the many seeds, and dried it into loaves or into a leather, and this was an important dietary source of vitamin C through the winter months. Opossums are inordinately fond of persimmons.

sááfke: SEI, 304–5. This was the basic food of the native Southeast. It was made from cracked hominy, and hence it was quite similar to modern grits.

Groundhog's Tail (65% direct quotation, 25% paraphrase, 10% original): This myth was drawn with few changes from *MC,* 279.

at the green-corn dance of the *posketa:* See chapter 13.

How Bobwhite Quail Got His Whistle (65% direct quotation, 30% paraphrase, 5% original): This myth is drawn with little change from *MC,* 289.

The Race between Hummingbird and Great Blue Heron (65% direct quotation, 30% paraphrase, 5% original): This myth is drawn with some changes from *MC*, 290–91. Mooney has this as "crane," and he may have referred to the sandhill crane (*Grus canadensis*), but this bird is not widespread in the South. In contrast, the great blue heron (*Ardea herodias*) is widespread, and southern country people call them cranes.

How Kingfisher Got His Beak (45% direct quotation, 35% paraphrase, 20% original): This myth is drawn with significant changes from *MC*, 288–89.

CHAPTER 4. *Rabbit*

Rabbit: Mary Haas noted (see *TT*, 7) that neither the Tunica nor the Natchez appear to have had rabbit as a trickster, nor did their oral literature include any sort of trickster. This would seem to question the generality of the rabbit trickster in the Southeast, or it could even strengthen the hypothesis that the rabbit trickster is African in origin. However, the absence of the rabbit trickster among the Tunica and Natchez could also have been a consequence of cultural loss.

How Rabbit Stole Otter's Coat (70% direct quotation, 25% paraphrase, 5% original): This myth is drawn with little change from *MC*, 267–68.

How Buck Deer Got His Horns (89% direct quotation, 10% paraphrase, 1% original): This myth is taken with little change from *MC*, 275–76.

a length of hard cane: *KS*, 334.

Rabbit and Bear (70% direct quotation, 25% paraphrase, 5% original): This myth is taken with little change from *MTSE*, 55–56.

How Rabbit Seduced His Wife's Sister (80% direct quotation, 20% paraphrase): *MTSE*, 57.

he succeeded in seducing his wife's sister: In the myth Swanton collected, Rabbit makes her his bride. In the matrilineal organization of most Southeastern Indians, sororal polygyny was a preferred form of marriage. That is, it was desirable for a man to marry two or more sisters.

putrid stew: James Mooney, "The Cherokee Ball Play," *American Anthropologist* 3 (1890): 110.

Master of Breath (*Hesaaketamesee*): John R. Swanton was dubious that the Master of Breath existed in Creek beliefs prior to the introduction of Christianity (see *RBMP*, 481–82). James Adair's discussion concerning the Chickasaw spiritual being "the great holy fire above" is probably closer to something authentically native (see *RBMP*, 482). And it is notable that in the Yuchi creation myth, the Sun is the most important spiritual being present, and the Master of Breath is absent (see *YT*, 3–13).

ásse: SEI, 226–29. Also see Charles Hudson, ed., *Black Drink: A Native American Tea* (Athens: University of Georgia Press, 1979). By 1559–61 the only caffeinated beverage Spaniards had experienced was cocoa from Mexico. Asian tea first reached Holland in 1610 and France in the 1630s. *Ásse*, brewed from the parched leaves of *Ilex vomitoria*, contains caffeine. Although Europeans often assumed that it was an emetic (and still do), it is no more an emetic than is coffee or Asian tea.

a menstruating woman: *RBMP*, 651.

How This World Began (100% original): This myth is my own construction based upon various elements of Southeastern Indian myths and culture.

a circle made of two concentric lines: Among the Choctaws, a circle represented the Choctaw people. See James H. Howard and Victoria Lindsay Levine, *Choctaw Music and Dance* (Norman: University of Oklahoma Press, 1990), 35.

Red is the blood: *SEI*, 318–19.

white is the right hand: *RBMP*, 512. When traveling on a road or path, Creeks would always encamp on the right-hand side of the road, and they assumed that ghosts encamped on the left side.

I had previously seen this curved line: Among the Choctaws, a variant of this design with reversed spirals at either end represented the Horned Serpent. See Howard and Levine, *Choctaw Music and Dance*, 35.

the creatures of the upper world began wondering: This paragraph and the one following are loosely based on *MC*, 239–40.

four ivory-billed woodpeckers: *RBMP*, 488.

Crawfish: SP, 26; *RBMP*, 488; *YT*, 3–6.

Firefly flew around: *YT*, 7.

male sphere: SP, 26–28.

a larger female sphere: The Cherokee, Yuchi, Tunica, and Biloxi believed the sun was female (*NAL*, 57–63). The Creeks also generally believed the sun to be female (*RBMP*, 480). In later times, the Creeks may have considered both the sun and sacred fire to be male (*RBMP*, 484).

a great toad: *RBMP*, 479. In the 18th century, when an eclipse occurred, the Indians would run out and shoot their guns to frighten away the toad.

Why the Sun and Moon Are Not Together in the Sky (5% direct quotation, 65% paraphrase, 30% original): This is largely based on *MC*, 256–57.

'luminary of the day': *MC*, 257.

'Grandmother' and 'Grandfather': *RBMP*, 484.

Where Thunder Came From (100% original): This myth is my creation.

the colors of the rainbow: *MC*, 257.

lightning arrows: *RBMP,* 486.

Whenever one of these strikes a tree: SP, 40.

The splinters from lightning-struck trees are powerful: *NNS,* 99.

we gaze across the surface of a river: James Mooney, "The Cherokee River Cult," *Journal of American Folklore* 13 (1900): 1–10.

Master of Breath and the Four Directions (25% paraphrase, 75% original): *MC,* 239. Swanton found much variability in Creek and Natchez color symbolism (see *RBMP,* 623–24); I have elected to use the Cherokee pattern, the one for which the most evidence exists.

the four edges of the island earth: *RBMP,* 477.

The Mountains, the Seventh Height, and the Under World (50% direct quotation, 47% paraphrase, 3% original): This is closely based on *MC,* 239–40.

seven handbreadths high: To ritually raise something to the seventh level, a Cherokee priest would hold his arm straight out in front and sight over his hand to the horizon and recite a verbal formula. Then he would raise his arm a level, sight over the width of his hand, and repeat the same until when he reached the seventh level his arm would be pointing straight up at the apex of the sky.

It is full of surprises: *RBMP,* 491.

Night Creatures and Evergreens, Rabbit and Horned Serpent (14% direct quotation, 1% paraphrase, 85% original): Aside from the first paragraph (*MC,* 240), this myth is my own fabrication out of various mythological and cultural elements.

Horned Serpent: This anomalous being is based on numerous Mississippian representations of horned and sometimes winged serpents, on the Cherokee *uktena* (*MC,* 253, 297–301), and on the Creek Horned Serpent (*RBMP,* 494–616).

Horned Serpent is so powerful he can change the course of rivers: *TT,* 147.

Horned Serpent can make blue lightning: *RBMP,* 494, 502.

the Master of Breath knew he had to do something: SP, 10–12. The contemporary Creek belief in the *Hayohkâlke,* "the four moaners" (Karen Booker, personal communication) may bear some relationship with the four winds.

CHAPTER 6. *Sun, Corn Woman, Lucky Hunter, and the Twosome*

long, drawn-out syllables: *SEI,* 226–29. This *yahóóla* cry was uttered ceremoniously by Muskogean-speaking Indians in the 18th century when they drank *ásse,* the black drink.

First Man and First Woman (2% direct quotation, 25% paraphrase, 30% original adaptation, 43% original): I fabricated much of this myth using the sources cited in notes below, drawing especially from *MC,* 242–49.

Backbone of the Earth: This phrase occurs in Creek mythology. If the Coosas in fact recognized a sacred range of mountains, it could well have been the Unaka Mountains, which lay to the north of the capital town of Coosa, the Little Egypt archaeological site. The Unakas are thought to have been the range of mountains described by Tristán de Luna's soldiers. See Charles Hudson, Marvin T. Smith, Chester B. DePratter, and Emilia Kelley, "The Tristán de Luna Expedition, 1559–1561," *Southeastern Archaeology* 8 (1989): 40–41.

drops of her menstrual blood: *NAL,* 58.

where the stones were piled: This is Fort Mountain, just north of the capital town of Coosa. Its principal feature is a long, sinuous pile of rocks, seemingly ancient and the subject of much local speculation.

Then it fell to First Woman: The inspiration for this episode is the Birger figurine. See Thomas E. Emerson, "Water, Serpents, and the Underworld: An Exploration into Cahokian Symbolism," in *SECC,* 51.

a little storehouse: I am grateful to Richard Polhemus for this reconstruction of typical Dallas storehouses.

The animals took pity: This and the following six paragraphs are taken, with changes, from *MC,* 240–42. The screech owl (*Otus asio*) is the only small owl with ear tufts. Mooney's "hoot owl" is probably the barred owl (*Strix varia*), and I have therefore made this substitution.

When a boy was born: *SEI,* 319–24. In the native Southeast, sexual segregation began at birth.

But in the course of time: This and the following two paragraphs are based, with changes, on *MC,* 242–49.

Fách:aséko: MTSE, 5; *NAL,* 165–70. *Fách:aséko* means "not correct" (Karen Booker, personal communication). The name "Wild Thing" is of my own devising.

The Twosome (85% paraphrase, 5% original adaptation, 10% original): Much of this myth is based, with changes, on *MC,* 242–49.

rubbed her navel: *MTSE,* 230–31.

'I bequeath to you this flute and headdress': *W,* 65; *MTSE,* 11.

rammed an arrow up his anus: *MTSE,* 7. In the 16th century, Southeastern Indians would sometimes defile a slain enemy by thrusting an arrow up his anus. *KS,* fig. 21.

They waited for the sky-bowl: *RBMP,* 478.

small, inferior versions of themselves: *RBMP,* 496–97. This connection between the Twosome and the little people is speculative.

the skirt of Corn Woman: *MTSE,* 13.

How Farming and Hunting Began (40% paraphrase, 10% original adaptation, 50% original): Half of this story is original, and half is drawn, with changes, from *MC,* 242–49.

the color of Corn Woman's hair: *NAL,* 156.

They taught them to skin a deer: *SEI,* 275–76. This hunting technique is well documented from 16th-century Virginia.

Whenever they do kill a deer: *RBMP,* 516–17.

CHAPTER 7. *Horned Serpent, the Clans, and the Origin of Bears*

These are the herbs on which Horned Serpent twisted his coils: Because Anunciación would have been unfamiliar with many of these plants, I have invoked poetic license in having him identify them. These are only the more important Creek and Seminole medicines. They knew the uses of many others.

páássa: OS, 29–32. Button snakeroot or rattlesnake master (*Eryngium yuccafolium* Michx.). Though reputed to be an emetic, it may not in fact be one. Vomiting after drinking it appears to have been caused by a cultural expectation. Only men drank *páássa,* and it was thought to enhance male virility. It is also purported to induce a feeling of tranquility.

meekko hoyanéécha: OS, 42–45. Red root. Several species of willow were used. In Oklahoma it was *Salix humilis* Marsh. (small pussy willow). The Houma used *Salix nigra* Marsh. or *Salix langipes.* They used the roots, beating them in a mortar and then steeping them in cold water. The active ingredient in willow root is salicin, an ingredient similar to the acetylsalicylic acid in aspirin. This too is not an emetic even though it has the reputation of being one. It was used to purify people who had had contact with the dead, to cure rheumatism, and for other illnesses.

ásse: A tea made from the parched leaves of *Ilex vomitoria.* It is not, as the name implies, an emetic. The active ingredient is caffeine in about the same concentration as in Asian tea or coffee.

heche lapóchkee: Tobacco (*Nicotiana rustica* L.). It is a much smaller plant than the *Nicotiana tabacum* L. commonly smoked today.

hummingbird-hawk moth: See Vernon James Knight and Judith A. Franke, "Identification of a Moth/Butterfly Supernatural in Mississippian Art," manuscript.

weláána: OS, 52–53. Wormseed (*Chenopodium ambrosiodes* L.). Strongly scented, the Oklahoma Seminoles use it to "kill the green wood" after square grounds are refurbished at the beginning of their green corn ceremony.

achína: Red cedar.

kofochka-lthákko: OS, 39–40. Horsemint (possibly *Collinsonia canadensis* L.). A tea made of this was used as a diuretic.

heche pakpakee: "Little tobacco" or "tobacco bloom" (almost certainly *Lobelia inflata* L.). Used to ward off ghosts. Containing lobeline, in small dosages it produces euphoria and it is an effective emetic. In large doses it causes coma, paralysis, and even death.

carved in the form of an old-fashioned war club: This pipe form was particularly used in Chiaha, in the northern reaches of the paramount chiefdom of Coosa. See Thomas M. N. Lewis and Madeline Kneberg, *Hiwassee Island: An Archaeological Account of Four Tennessee Indian Peoples* (Knoxville: University of Tennessee Press, 1946), 121.

where men and women make love: *NAL,* 143–44.

How the Clans Began (70% original adaptation, 30% original): I constructed this myth using the sources cited in the notes below.

Who could oppose Horned Serpent?: This part of the story is loosely based on *MC,* 315–16.

The old women sent up a cry: This and the following three paragraphs are loosely based on *SOC,* 107–14.

The souls of the slain: *RBMP,* 512.

The Clans and Their Rules (100% original): I wrote this using the sources cited in the notes below.

drive two wooden stakes: This was a free-hanging warp, known to have been used in the Mississippian Southeast. See Penelope Ballard Drooker, *Mississippian Village Textiles at Wickliffe* (Tuscaloosa: University of Alabama Press, 1992), 84.

In the marriage ceremony: *ITLM,* 99.

We need special words to weave us together: The basic reference on Creek kinship principles is *SOC,* 80–97.

The Clansmen Who Became Bears (70% paraphrase, 15% original adaptation, 15% original): This story, including the basic form of the song, is taken, with changes, from *MC,* 325–27.

The Bear-man (65% paraphrase, 35% original adaptation): This myth is taken from *MC,* 327–29.

satirical dances: This is an inversion of the Cherokee practice of dancing satirical dances about animals. See Frank G. Speck and Leonard Broom, *Cherokee Dance and Drama* (Berkeley: University of California Press, 1951), 25–39.

spicebush: *Lindera benzoin* L.

Because bears are scarce: John H. Hann, *Apalachee: The Land between the Rivers* (Gainesville: University Presses of Florida, 1988), 105.

CHAPTER 8. *The Vengeance of Animals, the Friendship of Plants, and the Anger of the Sun*

The Vengeance of Animals (55% paraphrase, 45% original): The myth in this discourse is primarily based on *MC,* 250–52.

the people began to increase very rapidly: This and the following thirteen or so paragraphs are drawn, with changes, from *MC,* 250–52.

Because bears do not seek vengeance: The seeking of vengeance for injury was a very important principle in Southeastern Indian life. Charles Hudson, *Elements of Southeastern Indian Religion,* Iconography of Religions, sec. 10: North America, fasc. 1 (Leiden: E. J. Brill, 1984), 12.

Next the deer met together to exact vengeance: *RBMP,* 637–38.

Little White Deer: Compare with Creek belief (*RBMP,* 498).

echo pólsee: RBMP, 639.

mucousy diseases of the stomach, liver, and lungs: *RBMP,* 638.

he wriggled off on his back: Some grubworms do, in fact, seem to travel by wriggling on their backs.

Coosas do not kill him: There is a famous passage in William Bartram's *Travels* where he tells of a very large rattlesnake that crawled into a Seminole town. The Seminoles persuaded Bartram to kill the snake for them. William Bartram, *Travels of William Bartram,* ed. Francis Harper (New Haven: Yale University Press, 1958), 164–65.

Water hemlock is often used: The identity of this plant is somewhat uncertain. See the note at the end of chapter 9.

Each person has four souls: John Witthoft, "Cherokee Beliefs Concerning Death," *Journal of Cherokee Studies* 8 (1983): 68–70. Also see John H. Hann, ed. and trans., *Missions to the Calusa* (Gainesville: University of Florida Press, 1991), 237–38.

The Anger of the Sun (1% direct quotation, 80% paraphrase, 19% original adaptation): This myth is drawn, with changes, from *MC,* 252–54.

spreading viper snake: That is, the eastern hognose snake (*Heterodon platirhinos*).

a sourwood rod a handbreadth long: The symbolic appropriateness of this use of sourwood (*Oxydendrum aboreum*) has yet to be explained. But it may be significant that the Cherokees used sourwood staffs in making eagle feather wands. See Frank G. Speck and Leonard Broom, *Cherokee Dance and Drama* (Berkeley: University of California Press, 1951), 39.

cardinal: Mooney has this as "redbird" (*MC,* 254), but the bird in question seems to be *Richmondena cardinalis.*

And we send gifts to go with their souls: SP, 26.

We encourage souls to go to the west: *RBMP*, 653.

When we go to water: James Mooney, "The Cherokee River Cult," *Journal of American Folklore* 13 (1900): 1–10.

CHAPTER 9. *Divination, Sorcery, and Witches*

Many foods are forbidden: *NNS*, 101; *RBMP*, 517–21.

purge themselves by vomiting: *NNS*, 48, 104.

The moment of daybreak: *NNS*, 50.

makes it into a switch: *NNS*, 145.

A more reliable way is the beads: *SEI*, 355–56.

Don Tristán de Luna: Tristán de Luna did begin acting strangely, and some of his colonists thought he was going mad. See Herbert I. Priestly, *Tristán de Luna: Conquistador of the Old South* (Glendale, Calif.: Arthur A. Clark, 1936), 117–18.

This is my *sapeya: RBMP*, 498–501.

Sapeya are prized by hunters: *RBMP*, 501; *OS*, 89.

My *sapeya* wants more clothing: *SFC*, 395. For their services, medicine men were often given a gift of cloth or deerskin.

he hoped she had either a husband or a lover: *RBMP*, 499.

bear's bed fern: *SFC*, 346. Christmas fern (*Aspidium acrostichoides*).

crow's shin fern: *SFC*, 346. Maidenhair fern (*Adiantum pedatum* L.).

este poskálke: NNS, 27.

Listen! Ha! In the Sun Land (85% direct quotation, 15% paraphrase): This and the following four paragraphs are quoted, with changes, from *SFC*, 346.

A *kéélth:a* fasts and goes: SP, 34.

A famous old *kéélth:a: SEI*, 337–38; *RBMP*, 629–31.

Listen! O now you want to make love (85% direct quotation, 15% paraphrase): *SFC*, 387–88.

stacks of firewood: SP, 36.

Listen! O, now you have drawn near (100% direct quotation): *SFC*, 380–81.

I empowered some tobacco: *NNS*, 73.

Your pathways are black (80% direct quotation, 20% paraphrase): The formula is quoted, with some changes, from Jack F. Kilpatrick and Anna G. Kilpatrick, *Run toward the Nightland: Magic of the Oklahoma Cherokees* (Dallas: Southern Methodist University Press, 1967), 127.

Witches are inherently vicious: Raymond D. Fogelson, "An Analysis of Cherokee Sorcery and Witchcraft," in *Four Centuries of Southern Indians*, ed. Charles M. Hudson (Athens: University of Georgia Press, 1975), 127–28.

Sorcerers are human; witches are not: *NNS*, 18.

When witches attack one's liver: John Witthoft, "Cherokee Beliefs Concerning Death," *Journal of Cherokee Studies* 8 (1983): 69.

injecting objects undetected into the bodies: *RBMP*, 634, 654.

The corpse of a person killed by a witch: *NNS*, 4.

Coosas gossip and speculate endlessly: *RBMP*, 632.

Spearfinger (89% direct quotation, 10% paraphrase, 1% original): This story is taken with little change from *MC*, 316–19. The Tunica stone witch is similar to Spearfinger (see *TT*, 27, 47, 167).

The chickadee is a messenger bird: SP, 44. The song of the chickadee (*Parus carolinensis*) so closely resembles that of the tufted titmouse (*Parus bicolor*) that it can confuse experienced bird-watchers.

they transform themselves into owls in the dark of night: *NNS*, 9; *RBMP*, 618. Scholars differ over which species of owl was the offender. Jack and Anna Kilpatrick report that the Western Cherokees identify it as the long-eared owl (*Asio otus wilsonianus*) as well as the screech owl (*Otus asio* L.). Arlene Fradkin has identified it as the great horned owl (*Bubo virginianus*). My personal favorite is the latter. It is a large bird, nearly two feet in length, and it makes a five-note sound like *hoo, hoo hoo, hoo, hoo* in a voice with almost human timbre. It is very shy and is utterly silent when it flies.

The fire in a hearth is an old woman: Witthoft, "Cherokee Beliefs," 71–72.

If the unmasked witch does not soon die: *NNS*, 10; *RBMP*, 631–32; *OS*, 97.

this is a piece of water hemlock stalk: The identity of this plant is uncertain. Mooney identifies it as "wild parsnip" (*Peucedanum*) but with a question mark (see *MC*, 424–25; *SFC*, 392). But he makes it clear that the plant in question was poisonous, and Cherokees used it both to commit suicide and to poison others to death. Alan Kilpatrick identifies it as *Pastinaca sativa* L. or perhaps *Pratensis pers* (see *NNS*, 93). My own suspicion is that it was water hemlock (*Cicuta maculata*), whose stem exudes a yellow sap with a parsnip-like odor. Its root also has the sweetish taste of parsnip. It is extraordinarily toxic, the most poisonous plant in North America.

He peeled the hollow stalk open: *NNS*, 92–93.

As a precaution: *OS*, 83–84.

CHAPTER 10. *Sun Chief and Sun Woman*

the Climber: SP, 32.

Sun Chief and Sun Woman (15% original adaptation, 85% original): I have fabricated this myth out of various mythological, archaeological, and cultural elements.

so dazzling to the eyes: *ITLM*, 169–70.

kept this purest of fires always burning: *ITLM,* 159–60; *RBMP,* 484.

It was never to be doused with water: *RBMP,* 484.

The elders of the clans asked the young man: John Reid, *A Law of Blood: Primitive Law of the Cherokee Nation* (New York: New York University Press, 1970), 11–122.

The first feast of the year: This calendar of festivals is based on *ITLM,* 109–10. No precise correlation can be achieved between a lunar calendar and the Old Style Julian calendar or the calendar we use today. But a rough correlation between the two is as follows: Deer Moon (late March), Strawberry Moon (April), Pokeweed Moon (May), Squash Moon (June), Plum Moon (July), Mulberry Moon (late July–early August), Great Corn Moon or *Posketa* (late August–early September), Turkey Moon (October), Rabbit Moon (November), Bear Moon (December), Cold Meal Moon (January), Chestnut Moon (February), Hickory Nut Moon (late February–early March).

They called out the people of Coosa to build an earthen mound: Cameron B. Wesson, "Mississippian Sacred Landscapes: The View from Alabama," in *Mississippian Towns and Sacred Spaces: Searching for an Architectural Grammar,* ed. R. Barry Lewis and Charles Stout (Tuscaloosa: University of Alabama Press, 1998), 94–95, 100.

'the high place': SP, 14.

they built a porch: SP, 22.

converse with the Sun: *ITLM,* 102.

Sun Chief liked his new house atop the mound: Their directions were, of course, not arbitrary points on a compass aligned with magnetic north. Rather, it seems that east was at the sun's rising, and the other directions were aligned accordingly. Cf. Charles Stout and R. Barry Lewis, "Mississippian Towns in Kentucky," in Lewis and Stout, *Mississippian Towns and Sacred Spaces,* 165–67.

The ashes are cleaned out: SP, 36.

He must achieve it: *ITLM,* 103.

When a young man finishes this instruction: *RBMP,* 617–18.

hou: ITLM, 93.

Sun Chief has an ally in the Master of Breath: SP, 14.

he was communing with Horned Serpent: *RBMP,* 616.

Sun Chief could charm Horned Serpent: *OS,* 25, 90–94. Also see Vernon J. Knight Jr., "Some Speculations on Mississippian Monsters," in *SECC,* 209.

The Negligent Fire-Keeper (100% original): This is a story I fabricated out of archaeological and historical information on Coosa and the comparative ethnography of chiefdoms.

the fire had gone out: *ITLM,* 171–72.

The sickness ended: For a handy précis of archaeological evidence for events such as these, see *SG*, 162–64. However, Jeffrey Brain and Philip Phillips envision a different scenario of how the temple contents ended up in the pit. They suggest they were cast into the pit by "fanatical [European] invaders," presumably Soto and his men (see *SG*, 174–75).

They razed the temple: *ITLM*, 103.

CHAPTER 11. *Tastanáke and the Ball Game*

Tastanáke (75% original adaptation, 25% original): I fabricated this story out of cultural, archaeological, historical, and mythical elements.

Panther, Bear, and Blue Jay: John H. Hann, *Apalachee: The Land between the Rivers* (Gainesville: University Presses of Florida, 1988), 331.

As the boy grew up: Much of the remainder of this conversation about Tastanáke is based on the Apalachee ball game myth. See Hann, *Apalachee*, 331–50.

a remarkable power over water: *RBMP*, 631.

The Contest between Tastanáke and Lightning Bolt (85% original adaptation, 15% original): Elements of this story are found in Hahn, *Apalachee*, 331–50, and *MC*, 311–15.

some mud from a yellow jacket nest: *OS*, 189. The Yuchi tale "Thunder's Son and Red Copper" appears to be similar to the one told here (see *YT*, 71–77).

CHAPTER 12. *Everyday Life Is Their Book*

You may have noticed that after telling a story: *RBMP*, 521.

One can stand atop the mound: Richard Polhemus, ed., *The Toqua Site: A Late Mississippian Dallas Phase Town*, vol. 2 of *Report of Investigations 41* (Knoxville: University of Tennessee, Department of Anthropology, 1987), 1240–41.

The floor of this house is as square as is the island earth: David J. Hally and Hypatia Kelly, "The Nature of Mississippian Towns in Georgia: The King Site Example," in *Mississippian Towns and Sacred Spaces: Searching for an Architectural Grammar*, ed. R. Barry Lewis and Charles Stout (Tuscaloosa: University of Alabama Press, 1998), 51–54.

In the town, the plaza represents the earth: R. Barry Lewis, Charles Stout, and Cameron B. Wesson, "The Design of Mississippian Towns," in Lewis and Stout, *Mississippian Towns and Social Spaces*, 11–12.

Each household compound has its rectangular storehouse: Hally and Kelly, "Towns in Georgia," 54–55.

Men who are to embark on a raid or a ball game: *RBMP*, 625.

Like water, fire purifies: Hally and Kelly, "Towns in Georgia," 60–63.

CHAPTER 13. Posketa

Posketa: This reconstruction of the *posketa,* or green corn ceremony, is based primarily on John R. Swanton's compilation of ceremonies described in historical documents and in his own firsthand field researches (see *RBMP,* 546–614). Secondarily, it is based on John Witthoft's *Green Corn Ceremonialism in the Eastern Woodlands* (*W*).

My reconstruction does not precisely match any of the versions recorded by Swanton. Instead, I draw on dominant themes in all of the variants, and into this I have inserted fictional episodes consistent with Mississippian culture and social organization. My aim has been to reconstruct a ceremony that possesses both symbolic and dramatic integrity.

The several *posketa* described by Swanton took place over the course of four to eight days. Swanton believed that he eight-day celebration in fact consisted of two four-day rituals (see *RBMP,* 577). In order to meet the constraints of a fictional work, I have elected to stage my *posketa* in four days.

The *posketa* was performed when the large flour corn came ripe (*RBMP,* 550). In most places this was July or August. Luna's contingent arrived in Coosa around July 26, 1560. Their raid on Napochín departed from Coosa on August 21. Hence, our fictional *posketa* fell in about the third week of August. Spain was still on the old Julian calendar in 1560, and hence those who wish to modernize these dates should add ten days to each of them.

Readers should be put on notice that it is conceivable that the *posketa* had far more importance in the 18th century and later times than it had in late prehistoric to early historic times. That is, the ceremonial devices of the *posketa* may have better served the organizational interests of 18th-century coalescent native southeastern societies than they did the interests of Mississippian chiefdoms in precontact and early contact times.

They were feasting prodigiously: *RBMP,* 590.

They even swept the plaza clean: Charles Stout and R. Barry Lewis, "Mississippian Towns in Kentucky," in *Mississippian Towns and Sacred Spaces: Searching for an Architectural Grammar,* ed. R. Barry Lewis and Charles Stout (Tuscaloosa: University of Alabama Press, 1998), 158.

nettaa hátkee: RBMP, 547.

chew on a leaf: SP, 14.

honey locust: *Gleditsia triacanthas* L.

seemed lascivious to me: This dance memorializing Sun-Moon incest is my creation. But note the Cherokee friendship dance discussed in Frank G. Speck and Leonard Broom, *Cherokee Dance and Drama* (Berkeley: University of California Press, 1951), 65–67.

If any violated: SP, 14.

They painted it inside and out with white clay: Speck and Broom, *Cherokee Dance and Drama*, 9.

half-circle fan of eagle feathers: SP, 22.

the attendant . . . uttered the word *choh!*: RBMP, 539.

I asked Teresa what the *yah-hóó-la* cry meant: RBMP, 485.

the Raven first spat in each of the four directions: RBMP, 610.

a pot full of *páássa*: RBMP, 623.

a two-foot length of hollowed river cane: OS, 23.

and sprinkled inside the temple: RBMP, 552.

icha opánka: OS, 126–27.

Its feathers are a brilliant red color: In fact, though, the brilliant red one is the male of the species.

"Girls! I want girls!": Speck and Broom, *Cherokee Dance and Drama*, 29, 31.

seized Sun Chief bodily: *ITLM*, 111–12.

youh, youh: RBMP, 570–71.

several scalps from slain enemies: RBMP, 544–45.

a length of split hickory that had been heated: This would seem to have been similar or identical to the implements used in the stickball game from the 18th century onward. This game is not known to have been in evidence among males in the Southeast until the 18th century.

he might as well talk to the posts in the temple: SP, 16.

so openly show his true feelings: *NNS*, 139.

he especially admonished the women: RBMP, 582.

still dressed in the white deerskin clothing: RBMP, 594.

sassafras stick: RBMP, 609. Scott Jones (personal communication) has verified that this combination of sassafras and poplar will produce fire.

The Raven stood before the fire: SP, 20.

In came four young men: RBMP, 583.

called out the name of a direction: RBMP, 588.

the Raven's earthenware bowl: SP, 20.

white war club: SP, 22.

They formed up single file: James H. Howard and Victoria Lindsay Levine, *Choctaw Music and Dance* (Norman: University of Oklahoma Press, 1990), 59–61. Horned Serpent's head is my own invention, inspired, no doubt, by the Chinese version of this monster in the Chinese New Year's festival. It should be noted, however, that the Cherokees made and wore masks in some of their dances into the 20th century, including one type of mask that had a rattlesnake carved onto it. See Speck and Broom, *Cherokee Dance and Drama*, 25–28.

the men played ball games against the women: The Yuchi played a similar game as recently as 1975. See W. L. Ballard, *The Yuchi Green Corn Ceremonial: Form and Meaning* (Los Angeles: University of California, American Indian Studies Center, 1978), 6.

Bets were placed: *RBMP,* 555.

We were ready now for the closing: *RBMP,* 578.

CHAPTER 14. *The Last Conversation*

He fought madly: This sense of "mad" is perhaps comparable to the ancient Viking berserker, that is, one who attacks with such frenzied abandon that he has no regard for his own welfare.

the Napochín saw weakness: This interpretation of the cause of the trouble between Coosa and the Napochín is no more than plausible.

Coosas take the same steps: SP, 44, 46.

On the day we were to set out: Charles Hudson, "A Spanish-Coosa Alliance in Sixteenth-Century North Georgia," *Georgia Historical Quarterly* 62 (1988): 599–626.

to the foot of an abandoned mound: Hudson, "A Spanish-Coosa Alliance," 614–16.

some little seeds from a fern-like plant: In an earlier publication I took this "fern" identification literally (see Hudson, "A Spanish-Coosa Alliance," 615), suggesting that it might have been cinnamon fern. I am now of the opinion that poisonous seeds of the water hemlock (*Cicuta maculata*) is a more likely identification. Only people with a death wish should put these seeds in their mouths.

Río de Espíritu Santo: This was the Spanish name for the Mississippi River. They had come to the Tennessee River at or near present-day Chattanooga. They had no way of knowing, of course, that the Tennessee River empties into the Ohio River, and the Ohio River in turn empties into the Mississippi River.

Upon returning to Coosa: SP, 46.

a copper escutcheon: I take the liberty of stating baldly as fact what James B. Langford Jr. has persuasively hypothesized. James B. Langford Jr., "The Coosawattee Plate: A Sixteenth-Century Catholic/Aztec Artifact from Northeast Georgia," in *Columbian Consequences: Archaeological and Historical Perspectives on the Spanish Borderland East,* vol. 2, ed. David Hurst Thomas (Washington, D.C.: Smithsonian Institution Press, 1990), 139–51.

who ride upon *cholthákko:* Several Southeastern Indian languages derived their word for horse from their word for deer. For example, Choctaw has *issi,* deer, and *issúba,* horse. Betty Jacob, Dale Nicklas, and Lou Spencer, *Introduction to Choctaw* (Durant: Southeastern Oklahoma State University, 1977), 214.

Chelookhookâlke: "People speaking a different language." This referred to Cherokee-speakers, among others. As a matter of fact, the name "Cherokee" may be derived from this Creek word.

Coosas are to be admired: SP, 24.

sternly prohibit the Coosas: See, for example, the confessional set forth by Francisco Pareja in Jerald T. Milanich and William C. Sturtevant, *Francisco Pareja's 1613 Confessionario: A Documentary Source for Timucuan Ethnography* (Tallahassee: Florida Department of State, Division of Archives, History, and Records Management, 1972), 23–39.

Illustration Credits

Route of the Luna Expedition to Coosa (Courtesy Julie Smith)

Raven (From Jim Harter, *Animals: 1419 Copyright-Free Illustrations of Mammals, Birds, Fish, Insects, Etc.* [New York: Dover, 1979], 150)

Turkey (From Alexander Wilson, *American Bird Engravings* [New York: Dover, 1975], 39)

Peregrine falcon (From Alexander Wilson, *American Bird Engravings* [New York: Dover, 1975], 76)

Terrapin (From Jim Harter, *Animals: 1419 Copyright-Free Illustrations of Mammals, Birds, Fish, Insects, Etc.* [New York: Dover, 1979], 194)

Wolf (From A. A. Gould, ed., *The Naturalist's Library* [New York: C. Wells, n.d.], 145)

Hummingbird (From Alexander Wilson, *American Bird Engravings* [New York: Dover, 1975], 10)

Great blue heron (From Alexander Wilson, *American Bird Engravings* [New York: Dover, 1975], 65)

Kingfisher (From A. A. Gould, *The Naturalist's Library* [New York: C. Wells, n.d.], 566)

Rabbit (From Jim Harter, *Animals: 1419 Copyright-Free Illustrations of Mammals, Birds, Fish, Insects, Etc.* [New York: Dover, 1979], 88)

Otter (From Jim Harter, *Animals: 1419 Copyright-Free Illustrations of Mammals, Birds, Fish, Insects, Etc.* [New York: Dover, 1979], 10)

Bear (From Jim Harter, *Animals: 1419 Copyright-Free Illustrations of Mammals, Birds, Fish, Insects, Etc.* [New York: Dover, 1979], 41)

Ásse (From Nathaniel Lord Britton and Addison Brown, *An Illustrated Flora of the Northern United States, Canada and the British Possessions,* vol. 2 [New York: Charles Scribner's Sons, 1913], 487)

Shell cup (Courtesy University of Georgia Laboratory of Archaeology)

Rim-incised pot (Courtesy University of Georgia Laboratory of Archaeology)

Ivory-billed woodpeckers (From Philip Henry Gosse, *Letters from Alabama* [London: Morgan and Chase, 1859], 92)

Water spider: shell gorget (Courtesy Frank H. McClung Museum, University of Tennessee)

Wild Thing and his brother: "spaghetti" gorget (Courtesy Frank H. McClung Museum, University of Tennessee)

Deer (From A. A. Gould, *The Naturalist's Library* [New York: C. Wells, n.d.], 344)

Blue jay (From Alexander Wilson, *American Bird Engravings* [New York: Dover, 1975], 1)

Carolina parakeet (From Alexander Wilson, *American Bird Engravings* [New York: Dover, 1975], 26)

Chunkey stone (Courtesy University of Georgia Laboratory of Archaeology)

Cougar (From A. A. Gould, *The Naturalist's Library* [New York: C. Wells, n.d.], 176)

Hornworm and hummingbird-hawk moths (From Philip Henry Gosse, *Letters from Alabama* [London: Morgan and Chase, 1859], 246)

Páássa (button snakeroot) (From Nathaniel Lord Britton and Addison Brown, *An Illustrated Flora of the Northern United States, Canada and the British Possessions,* vol. 2 [New York: Charles Scribner's Sons, 1913], 622)

Meekko hoyanéécha (willow) (From Nathaniel Lord Britton and Addison Brown, *An Illustrated Flora of the Northern United States, Canada and the British Possessions,* vol. 1 [New York: Charles Scribner's Sons, 1913], 592)

Heche lopóchkee (tobacco) (From Nathaniel Lord Britton and Addison Brown, *An Illustrated Flora of the Northern United States, Canada and the British Possessions,* vol. 3 [New York: Charles Scribner's Sons, 1913], 170)

Heche pakpakee (lobelia) (From Nathaniel Lord Britton and Addison Brown, *An Illustrated Flora of the Northern United States, Canada and the British Possessions,* vol. 3 [New York: Charles Scribner's Sons, 1913], 303)

War club pipe (Courtesy Frank H. McClung Museum, University of Tennessee)

Chipmunks (From Jim Harter, *Animals: 1419 Copyright-Free Illustrations of Mammals, Birds, Fish, Insects, Etc.* [New York: Dover, 1979], 91)

Cardinal (From Alexander Wilson, *American Bird Engravings* [New York: Dover, 1975], 11)

Divining with beads (From Jack F. Kilpatrick and Anna G. Kilpatrick, "Eastern Cherokee Folk Tales Reconstructed from the Notes of Frans M. Olbrechts," in *Anthropological Papers,* no. 80, and *Bureau of American Ethnology Bulletin,* no. 196 [Washington, D.C.: GPO, 1966], 433)

Red sumac (From Nathaniel Lord Britton and Addison Brown, *An Illustrated*

Flora of the Northern United States, Canada and the British Possessions, vol. 2 [New York: Charles Scribner's Sons, 1913], 482)

Tufted titmouse (From Alexander Wilson, *American Bird Engravings* [New York: Dover, 1975], 8)

Chickadee (From Alexander Wilson, *American Bird Engravings* [New York: Dover, 1975], 8)

Great horned owl (From Alexander Wilson, *American Bird Engravings* [New York: Dover, 1975], 50)

Water hemlock (From Nathaniel Lord Britton and Addison Brown, *An Illustrated Flora of the Northern United States, Canada and the British Possessions,* vol. 2 [New York: Charles Scribner's Sons, 1913], 658)

Etowah site (From C. C. Jones, *Antiquities of the Southern Indians, Particularly of the Georgia Tribes* [New York: D. Appleton, 1873], plate 1)

Horned serpent (Citico gorget) (From William H. Holmes, "Art in Shell of the Ancient Americans," in *Second Annual Report of the Bureau of American Ethnology* [Washington, D.C.: GPO, 1883], plate 63)

Looped square gorget (From William H. Holmes, "Art in Shell of the Ancient Americans," in *Second Annual Report of the Bureau of American Ethnology* [Washington, D.C.: GPO, 1883], 282)

Tastanáke warrior dressed as a falcon: embossed copper plate from Mound C, Etowah site (From Warren King Moorehead, *Etowah Papers,* Department of Archaeology, Phillips Academy, Andover, Mass. [New Haven: Yale University Press, 1932], 36)

The Etowah statues (Photograph by the author)

Lady of Guadalupe (Courtesy Julie Smith)

Sapeya crystal (Photograph by the author)

Index

Able, 70
Achína, 72, 204
Adam, 50, 68, 70
Alabama Indians, xvii
Allah, 12, 50
Alligator, 15
Ancient Days, 14, 19, 44, 87, 97, 120, 139, 145
Anunciación, Domingo de la, xiii, xv, xviii
Apalachee Indians, xvii
Ásse, 39, 44, 52, 72, 73, 87, 90, 91, 97, 103, 140, 150, 154, 163, 168, 201, 204

Backbone of the Earth, 53, 203
Ball games, 15–18, 139, 143–44, 172, 212
Ball pole, 139, 162
Barbacoa, 2, 197
Barred Owl, 55
Bat, 18, 47
Bear, 15–17, 34, 40, 81, 83–84, 87–88, 139, 160; and grease, 34–35; song, 81; town house of, 87. *See also* White Bear
Bear-man, 82–84
Beast of diverse parts, 135, 142
Beautiful Bird, 26–28
Blackberry, 64
Blood, 146; Law of, 122
Blue jay, 62
Bobwhite, 25, 89
"Broken days," 152
Brother Moon. *See* Moon

Burnt-by-the-Sun. *See* Robles
Button snakeroot. See *Páássa*

Cain, 70
Canebrake, 137
Cardinal, 95, 157
Carolina parakeet, 62
Cedar, 48, 91, 96. See also *Achína*
Chelookhookâlke, 184
Chenopodium. See *Weláána*
Cherokee Indians: color and directional symbolism of, xvii
Chiaha, xiii, 177
Chickadee, 33, 114–15
Chickasaw Indians, xvii
Chief of the Waters. *See* Tastanáke
Chipmunk, 89
Choctaw Indians, xvii
Chola Háácho, 151, 176, 180, 186
Cholthákko, 183
Christ, 134, 150, 162, 164
Chunkey, 65, 136, 141, 145
Clans, 74–77; naming of, 76; rules of, 77–79
Cofitachequi, 9
Coosa Indians: archaeological research on, xiii–xiv; belief system of, xii, xv–xvi; capitol town of, 1, 127; chiefdom of, xi; and Coosawattee River, xii; descendants of, xii, xv; houses of, 1, 7; paramount chief of, xii; polity of, xii, 85
Copper, 198
Corn, 68–69; origin of, 62–63
Corn Woman, 54–68, 74, 121, 148, 158

Coste, 177
Cougar, 47, 66, 135, 136, 158
Crawfish, 42, 46, 146
Crazy Fox. *See* Chola Háácho
Creek Indians, xii, xvii
Crow, 54, 66

Dance, 96, 157
Darkening Land, 94, 95, 110
Dark Swamp, 136–38
Death cry, 174
Deer, 33, 39, 59, 88, 103; song, 70; tongue, 168. *See also* Little White Deer
De Soto, Hernando, xii, 10, 192–95
Divination: bead, 99; crystal, 101; fire, 116; water, 98
Dogon, xiv–xv
Dogwood Flower, 135, 136, 185
Dry-scratching, 165

Eagle, 15, 39, 137, 162
East, 45
Eepóóska. See Menstruation
Enslavement, 9
Etowah, 121–28; Sun Chief and Sun Woman statues in, 130
Eve, 19, 50, 68

Fasting, 97, 153
Feasts, 124–25
Feather dance, 163
Feryada, 4, 11, 150
Fictionalized ethnography, xi
Fire: everyday, 56; sacred, 121–22, 127, 150
Firefly, 43
Fire-keeper, 131–32
First Man, 50, 53
First Woman, 50, 53
Flint, 136–37
Flyers, 15, 20, 39
Flying squirrel, 18, 47
Fog, 75
Fort Mountain (Ga.), 203

Four directions, 45, 147, 178
Four-footeds, 15–18, 19, 39
Four winds, 45, 49, 128

Garfish, 165
God (Judeo-Christian), 14, 50–51, 79, 99–101, 111
Great ball game, 15–18
Great Black Snake, 55, 97
Great Blue Heron, 26–28
"Great medicine," 166
Griaule, Marcel, xiv
Groundhog, 23
Grubworm, 89–90
Guadalupe de Tepeyac, Lady of, 181, 182

Hawk, 75–76
Heche lopóchkee, 72, 73, 90
Heche pakpakee, 72, 155, 157, 159, 162, 168, 173, 174, 204
Heneha, 158, 165
Hesaaketamesee. See Master of Breath
High Priest, 127
Holly, 48
Hominy, 153
Horned Serpent, xvi, 47, 48, 53, 73, 75–76, 90, 93–94, 101, 106, 121, 129, 142, 157, 171; horns of, 48–49
Horsemint. See *Kofochka-lthákko*
Hou, 126, 128, 163
Hummingbird, 26
Hummingbird-hawk moth, 72

Incest, 45

Jesus, 134, 150, 162, 164

Kéélth:a, 106–8
Keyes, John Gregory, xvi
Kingfisher, 28–29, 136
Kinship terms, 77–79
Koasati Indians, xii, xvii
Kofochka-lthákko, 72, 204

Lady of Guadalupe de Tepeyac, 181, 182
Laurel, 48
Lightning, 69; blue, 48; yellow, 48
Lightning Bolt, 135–42
Little Black Racer, 55, 90, 97
Little Screech Owl, 55
Little White Deer, 88
Lobelia. See *Heche pakpakee*
Locust trees: black, 53; honey, 64, 120, 155
Lucky Hunter, 53–68, 74, 121, 148, 158
"Luminary of the day." *See* Sun
"Luminary of the night." *See* Moon
Luna y Arellano, Tristán de, xii, 195–96, 207

Mabila, 11, 109
Master of Breath, 37, 39, 48, 49, 50, 78, 128, 157, 200
Meekko hoyanéécha, 72, 90, 157, 159, 168, 169, 204
Menstruation, 38, 53, 57, 59, 72, 123, 150
Mississippian social world, xi, xv–xvi
Mistletoe, 21
Moon, 44, 77, 97, 153, 157
Moses, 134
Mounds, 1, 125, 152, 178
Muskogean language family, xvii

Nanipacana, xii, xiii, 181
Napochín, 2, 84, 177–80
Natchez Indians, xvii
Nettaa hátkee, 152–53
Nettles, 64
Nokfilaki, 9, 10, 11, 12, 112, 119, 127, 184
North, 45

Ochuse, 181
Ogotemmêli, xiv, xv
Opposites, 145–50

Oquechiton river, 180
Otter, 30–36, 155
Owl, 47, 116, 119, 208; great horned, 49; screech, 177. *See also* Barred Owl; Little Screech Owl

Paaskóófa, 125. *See also* Plaza
Páássa, 72, 90, 157, 169, 204
Palisade, 1, 197
Pardo, Juan, xiii
Pensacola Bay (Fla.), xii
Peregrine Falcon, 18, 39, 101, 158, 160
Persimmons, 21, 199
Pine, 48
Plaza, 1, 125, 152, 168
Porch, 158
Portico, 155
Posketa, 23, 45, 69, 124, 152–75, 176, 211
Possum, 20–21, 39, 140
Purple Martin, 18

Quail, 25, 89

Rabbit, 31–39, 48, 52, 79, 157
Raccoon, 20, 21
Rattlesnake, 90, 93–94, 158
Raven-mocker, 116
Ravens, 7–8
Red, 40, 122, 142
Red ocher, 101
Red sumac, 106, 129–30, 140
Río de Espíritu Santo, 180
River, 98
Robles, 4, 11, 150

Sááfke, 22, 103, 139, 199
Salazar, Domingo de, 2
Saliva, 146
Salt, 153
Santa Elena colony, xiii
Sapeya, 101–2, 133, 181–82, 183
Satan, 50, 99
Sauz, Mateo del, 14, 84, 177
Scalps, 162, 179

Seminole Indians, xii, xvii
Seven, 64
Shell cup, 38
Sister Sun. *See* Sun
Smilax brier, 64
Snakes: copperhead, 93; spreading viper, 93. *See also* Great Black Snake; Horned Serpent; Little Black Racer; Rattlesnake
Sorcery, 103–11
Soto, Hernando de, xii, 10, 192–95
Souls, 91–92
South, 45
Southeastern Ceremonial Complex, xvi
Spearfinger, 111–19
Spider, 108; fire-carrier, 77–78. *See also* Water Spider
Spruce, 48
Square, 147; looped, xvi, 45, 164
Squash, 53
Storehouse, 53, 149–51; of Sun Chief, 123–24, 154
Sumac, red, 106, 129–30, 140
Sun, 43–44, 46, 52, 73, 75, 92–96, 97, 121, 157; daughter of, 93–94
Sun Chief, 9–10, 121–33, 135, 141, 150, 153, 159, 167, 169, 176, 181, 184
Sun Woman, 3, 121–33, 163, 184
Swanton, John, xv

Tali, 177
Talking Rock Creek, 112
Tascaluza, 10–11
Tastanáke, 134–43, 158, 160
Terrapin, 17, 21, 22, 25, 39, 103, 105, 170
Thunder, 45, 48, 54, 97–98, 142, 157
Thunder's metal, 10, 128, 132. *See also* Copper

Thunder's tree, 153
Toad, 43
Tobacco, 73, 109–10, 140. See also *Heche lopóchkee*
Tortoise. *See* Terrapin
Tribute, 177
Tufted titmouse, 114–15
Tunica Indians, xvii
Turkey, 16, 159
Turkey Buzzard, 35, 46
Twosome, 58–71, 92–94, 97, 159, 171

Under world, 41, 47, 97, 148; language of, 42
Upper world, 40, 148

Vomiting, 97, 155

War captain, 177
War club, 160, 170, 178
Water hemlock, 91, 118, 179, 208, 213
Water Spider, 55–56, 167
Weláána, 72, 154, 204
West, 45
White, 40
White Bear, 87
White clay, 154, 74
White day, 153
White refuge house, 122
Wild Thing, 58–66
Willow. See *Meekko hoyanéécha*
Witchcraft, 165
Witches, 111, 119
Wolf, 23, 63–65, 139
Woodpecker, ivory-billed, 15, 42
Wormseed. See *Weláána*

Yahóóla, 52, 113, 155, 202
Yatéka, 157–58